Renato

DARK MAFIA BILLIONAIRE ROMANCE

CALABRESI MAFIA
BOOK THREE

L.K. RYAN

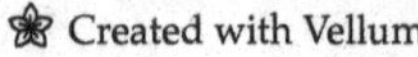 Created with Vellum

Disclaimer

Warning: There are a few scenes that may trigger. Be aware. Contains strong language and explicit sexual content and is only intended for mature readers. A Dark Mafia Billionaire romance with an asshole alpha male, possessive, and aggressive. This story may contain unconventional situations, language, and sexual encounters that may offend some readers. This book is for mature readers (18+).

Calabresi Family

Elio Calabresi - Father, Retired Don
Adelina Calabresi - Mother
Savio Calabresi - Boss
Sante Calabresi - Underboss
Renato Calabresi - Enforcer
Elio III - Consigliere
Vincenzo - CEO of Calabresi Holdings

Are you signed up for my newsletter?

Join today and find out all the latest in new releases, contests, giveaways, sneak peeks and more.

www.authorlkryan.com

Acknowledgments

This book wouldn't happen without the support of my amazing readers. I can't thank you enough.

Synopsis

Renato

The night started as usual with me finding someone to take care of my needs, and the only problem was that I didn't expect any complications or feelings to get involved. As the enforcer of the Calabresi family, my heart held no love for anyone outside my parents and brothers. So tell me why the devil in a blue dress that left in the middle of the night while I slept held a secret that I wasn't sure I could forgive, let alone live with. They say flings aren't for everyone, and they may be correct, but this one brought something I couldn't keep at bay for long.

A fling, hate to love, marriage of convenience Dark Mafia romance, Book 3 in an interconnecting, stand-alone series, and guaranteed to have an HEA.

CHAPTER 1
Renato

MY BROTHER WAS part owner of a gentleman's club before he got married, which I visited to let off some steam after completing a job. A few staff members greeted me as I passed through the VIP area. A few bottle girls smiled when they saw me but stayed away. In the past, I'd opted for a warm body to relieve some stress after a long night, but a drink would do for now.

"Boss, did you hear me?" Ian nudged me and passed the bottle of scotch.

"No, what did you say?"

"You want to get some private dancers up here?"

I watched the crowd move in sync with the music from the DJ.

"Not tonight." I exhaled a groan rivaling a rusty hinge.

"Come on, you always leave with somebody."

"Too tired," I retorted.

"That was a huge score we landed."

Tonight was Ian's chance to handle an enemy of the family that popped up and made noise. He'd been skimming off the top for a few months, and we never caught him after he was told we were looking for him. Tonight, he came back into town.

"Shit!" I heard him curse.

"What?"

"That dancer over there."

The dark lights covered the left side of the cage she was dancing in. Her breasts were plump, her backside curvy, and her legs long. I squinted my eyes to get a good look; she reminded me of someone.

"Who is that?" I questioned.

"She must be new."

Ian had suggested we come here almost weekly, if we weren't out working for my family.

She flipped her hair back and wheeled around, and I finally saw her face, and my eyes bucked wide in surprise. I jumped up, ran out of the VIP booth and down the steps, and pushed through the crowd.

"Boss!" I heard Ian call my name as I reached the cage, but he was not important.

"Argh! Let me go!"

I reached out, grabbed the cage door, yanked it open, and pulled her out.

"Shut the fuck up!" My voice was laced with frustration.

"Help! He's trying to kill me!" she choked out.

Some of the guards tried to walk up on me, and I pulled my gun from my side and aimed it at them.

"If you don't follow me, then see what happens." A twinge of anger laced my voice.

"Help! He's crazy!" she hollered, trying to peel my hand off.

"Shut up!" I shot back.

"Come on, Renato. Do we need to call Savio or Sante?" a guard groaned.

To make a statement, I lifted the gun, aimed at his foot, and shot him.

"You're crazy!" she screamed and dropped to the ground. I pulled her to the back exit, shoved her to the wall, and removed my jacket to cover her body. She was only wearing panties and tassels on her breasts.

"Please let me go," she pleaded, her eyes squeezed into thin slits.

"Where's my money?" My jaw clenched.

"Renato, I'll get it for you." Her fists drew up like angry stones.

"I want it now." I jerked a thumb in her direction.

"I can get it out of the bank tomorrow," she lied.

I pressed the gun to the side of her head.

"Either you give it to me right now, or I will kill you."

"Please, no! I… I'll… get your money, just don't hurt me." She pleaded with a distraught look.

"Tell me why I should spare you." I caught her in a dark gaze.

"Because I—"

Pop! Pop!

Gunshots not from my gun went off, and I slid to the side of the wall. My back was to the wall, and I gazed out into the crowd from there. Gunmen were robbing the club. I glanced behind me; Sonya pushed the door open and ran out through the back alley.

Pop! Popppp!!!

"Renato!" I heard Ian yell out my name. I didn't have time to chase after Sonya. I'd need to pay to have my guys look into her more.

Rattatat

I returned fire, ducked down, and eased over to the back of the bar to catch up with Ian.

"Where the fuck did you go?" Ian checked his chamber.

"Doesn't matter. Who the fuck is shooting at us?"

Ian stood and caught one of the guys on the shoulder. He dropped the gun and grabbed his arm.

"I don't know, but we need to get out of here."

Boiling with fury, I ground my teeth and clenched my jaw so tightly it hurt.

"My car's in the back." I mentally prepared myself for the fact that I might get shot trying to get out of here, but I wouldn't go down by myself. I glanced toward the ceiling at the strobe lights and figured I could get them taken out first and run out the back alley.

Pop! Pop!

"Follow my lead."

"What the fuck are you doing?" Ian shouted. I rose, pulled the second pistol from behind me, and delivered three shots toward the lights. I sent the other gun to the two men that stood by the stage. They bent down. I ran out of bullets, abandoned the revolver, and motioned for Ian to get up.

"Let's go!" I yelled, ran out the back exit to my car, and hopped inside. Ian leaped into the passenger side. I slipped my keys in the ignition and pulled out.

Pop! Pop!

Bullets shattered my back window. As I sped up, Ian leaned out the side window and sent shots back. Turning out of the back alley to the main street, I looked out the side window to make sure no one was following me.

"Shit! That was close." Ian sat back in his seat and put his seat belt on.

"We need to get the video footage."

Ian removed cigarettes from his pocket and lit one, holding it out for me, but I shook my head.

"I'll have our guys speak with the manager."

"I know I wounded one of them. Keep an eye on the hospitals."

We'd just gotten done with the takeover of the Colombo territory, and I hoped this wasn't another war we'd have to handle. More than anything, I was pissed that my opportunity to get my money from Sonya had been interrupted. That bitch thought she could steal from me and get away. I had been drunk that night, but not fucked up enough to forget her waiting until I went to sleep to take a hundred grand off me. I arrived at Ian's apartment and left the car running as he talked on the phone.

"Do you want to call a meeting tomorrow?" Ian held the phone close to his ear and peered at me.

"Yeah." I rubbed a hand down my face.

"Boss wants a meeting with all our men—somebody's gunning for us," Ian said, and I felt my phone vibrate in my pants. I slid it up to check the name scrolled across—my father.

Pops: Come to the house.

Me: It's two in the morning.

Pops: I got a call. You were involved in a shoot-out.

I slammed my hand on the steering wheel.

"Shit!" A grimace wrinkled my face.

"All right, tomorrow." Ian ended the call.

Me: No reason for me to ask who told you.

Pops: Glad you know.

I closed out of my message thread.

"Has to be your father since you're pissed."

I nodded with a scowl.

"He wants me to come to the house."

"Someone told him." Hearing the words, he frowned with sudden concern.

"Nothing gets by him," I replied, putting the phone back in my pocket.

"Keep me updated, Boss." He pulled himself to his feet, and we shook hands. The door snapped shut before he jogged into his building. I pulled off and headed to my parents' home. Once there, I punched in the gate's code and pulled up the driveway toward the house and parked my car. I tore the front door open, not waiting for the butler to let me inside.

"Renato, come to my office." Father spoke with his hand around the rustic knob from his office, clearly awaiting my arrival.

I marched up to him just as it was about to latch closed. He stood near his bar in his robe. Picking up a glass, he poured a small amount of scotch. He motioned with the bottle toward me.

"I'm good."

"What happened?" He stared at me.

"Shoot-out at the club."

"Do you know who it is?"

"Not sure." I strolled into the room and sat on the couch.

"I got a call about it tonight, and I didn't want to worry your mother."

"She shouldn't worry."

"Maybe you should take some time away from the clubs."

"I disagree."

"That's not a request, Renato. You've had a lot of run-ins lately."

I grunted and mumbled under my breath in my native tongue.

"Nothing's going to happen to me."

"Old expression, you should never underestimate advice from your parents, no matter how old you get."

"Do Savio and Sante listen to your advice?"

He smirked at my statement.

"Maybe this was a wake-up call you need to hand over being the enforcer to someone else."

"I'm the best and the only one who can find our enemies."

"Any of us can be replaced."

"Old man, you're drinking too much scotch." I rose from the couch, and he held his hand up to stop me.

"Tomorrow, we'll send the video footage to Sante and me."

"I don't need you checking up on me."

"Silence!"

My jaw twitched, and I balled up my fists.

"Sit this out until we can get information on who tried to kill you tonight."

"I can't do that."

"Renato, that is not a request." His left brow rose.

"I'll think about it." I turned my back to him, walked out of his office, and headed out of the house. Unlocking on my phone, I sent a message to my tech guy.

Me: I need you to find information on someone named Sonya.

Semion: What's her last name?

Me: Not sure, but she works at the club Sante co-owns.

Semion: I'll look into her.

Hopping in my car, I drove out of the gates and headed to my home a few blocks from my parents'. I pulled up to the gate, entered my code, and watched them open before I swerved into my circular driveway and parked. I walked up to my door and turned the alarm off before the cops showed up. Even though we had a few people on our payroll, I hated the police because of the corruption. They wanted to put us down when they were just as bad as any mafia. They'd take a payoff to get to the next level in a heartbeat.

My father knew I wouldn't stop trying to find out who was behind the shooting. Unlike Savio and Sante, I could move in silence as the enforcer because people didn't expect me to have to answer to anyone besides Save, and I rarely did that unless I needed approval for a killing.

After I checked the temperature of the shower, I

removed my shirt, pants, and boxers and stepped inside, leaning under the water to let it roll down my back. Showers brought me peace. Thirty minutes later, I climbed into bed, placed my hands behind my head, closed my eyes, and remembered why I'd gone to the club in the first place. I felt my dick stir.

"Shit." I groaned, slid my hand under the sheets, squeezed my dick, and pictured the full plump lips of the bitch who'd stolen my money wrapped around my dick. The speed of my strokes increased, and I felt the release in the palm of my hand.

"Fuck!" I needed to shower again. I flung the covers back and hopped out of bed to forget about her other than as an enemy.

CHAPTER 2

Sonya

I SNUGGLED FARTHER in the bed and pretended last night hadn't happened. It was like a scene out of a movie with shoot-outs and people screaming, running for safety. I felt like it was my fault. I shouldn't have gone back to where he could find me so easily. My life had been going okay for the most part, besides working two jobs to support myself and my son.

Knock!

"I'm sleeping."

"Then why answer?"

"What time is it?"

"Eight, and I have to work in an hour." Brilynn passed a cup of coffee toward me. I eased out of the covers, slid up against the headboard, and took the cup out of her hands.

"You have work tonight?" Brilynn sat on the edge of the bed.

"Yeah, but I don't—"

Boom! Boom!

We both jumped at the thudding noise from the door.

"What the hell!" Brilynn hopped up, and I followed

behind her to the living room and gasped in shock. The door is kicked open.

"I'm here to collect." Renato smirked and held a gun toward us.

"Renato, please put the gun down," I pleaded, raising my hand in surrender.

Brilynn tried to jerk away from the guard holding her captive.

Renato motioned with his hand for the guard to let her go.

"Get away from me," Brilynn hissed.

When the sudden cry came from the bedroom, I froze.

"What's that noise?" Renato asked.

I moved to the bedroom.

He motioned for his guard to go with me.

"No, no." I panicked and tried to beat him to the bedroom.

"I'll get you your money. Please leave," I yelled.

Renato stalked forward and closed the space between us.

"Who's back there?" Renato asked.

I looked back at Brilynn for help.

I closed my eyes, trying to control my breathing.

"My son," Brilynn called out.

Renato inclined his head toward Brilynn, and I prayed he believed her.

"Go grab it."

His guard strolled into the room and came out with my son.

"No, wait." I tried to fight, but Renato grabbed my arm.

"It's a baby boy," the guard said.

"Give him to me." Renato picked him up.

"Don't touch him."

"I may be a monster, but I'm not heartless."

He rubbed his back soothingly and narrowed his eyes in confusion.

"Where's my money?" Renato insisted.

The lump in my throat caused me to freeze up as he watched my son, then me.

"It's in a safe place," I replied, trying to reach for my child.

"You have something of mine. So now I have something of yours." Renato pointed at Brilynn, then me.

"You don't want to do this, Mr. Calabresi." I felt my hands get sweaty.

"Put on some clothes and let's go." Renato turned to leave, and I planted my hand on his shoulder. He shook me off and kept walking.

I ran behind him, screaming and yelling. "He's innocent. Let them go."

Renato stood with his back to us.

"If you want to see your son, do as I say."

"Wait." Brilynn tried to intervene.

"Put on some clothes. And come downstairs with my money." His tone was even, deadly.

I ran back into the bedroom and paced in front of the dresser. The entire situation was complicated, and I'd thought I had more time to fix things.

His guard followed Brilynn, then closed the door.

"What are you going to do?" Brilynn whispered.

"This wasn't how this was supposed to go."

"Sonya, you have to tell them. That entire family is dangerous."

I tossed my head back and blew out a breath in frustration.

"Listen to me. Stop pacing."

"We need to think," I said.

"If we want to get out of this alive, we have to play by his rules. And right now, he has the upper hand."

"I know. I thought I had more time to get out. Get us out of here." I motioned between the two of us.

"Once he figures out that's his son, and you've kept him from him…" Brilynn reminded me.

"I know, Brilynn."

"How's your mom doing, anyway?"

"Better. I still have some of the money, but not all of it." I reached down for my pants on the floor.

"Maybe we can negotiate," Brilynn suggested. I reached for shoes, my phone, and keys.

"I'm supposed to work tonight."

A knock interrupted us.

"Boss said to come on," his guard stated.

"Give us a moment," Brilynn fussed.

She ran toward her bedroom and grabbed her coat and shoes.

The guard gripped my arm and escorted us to the elevator. I stood in corner when the doors opened, my eyes closed in deep thought.

A few seconds later, we stepped off the elevator and left the building. A black stretch limo was out front.

I went to reach for my son, and Renato stopped me.

"Get in the car," he demanded, and I nodded, climbing in after Brilynn and seeing my baby in his car seat.

He started crying.

"He's been dealing with a cold," I lied.

"I'll give him to his mother." Renato motioned Brilynn to change seats, and I froze.

"Where are we going?" I asked to distract him.

"Where's the money, Sonya?"

"You have to understand. I didn't mean to steal from you."

"Do you often sleep with strangers and steal $100,000 from them? Maybe that was your setup."

"It wasn't like that." I ran a hand through my hair out of habit when I lied.

"I remember bringing a bag, and it was near the door in the hotel's living room. When I woke up, it wasn't there," Renato explained.

"She didn't mean to do it," Brilynn said, soothing my baby to sleep.

"What's his name?" Renato wondered, and my eyes widened in shock.

Brilynn and I looked at each other.

I felt a lump in my throat.

"I promise you I'll get you the rest of the money."

"What's his name?"

I ignored his question.

"I'll get you the rest. Let us go."

He had some of his features, but I tried my best to ignore the same bushy brows or the black eyes that seemed like he could see through my soul.

"What's his name?" Renato asked again.

"That's not important."

Renato reached into his pocket and pulled out a gun.

"His name is Renato Jr.!" Brilynn yelled, and my chest tightened.

His eyes grew wide in shock.

"Stop the car!" he shouted. The driver pulled over to the side of the road, and Renato hopped out. Then he reached in and grabbed me by the arm.

I screamed as he yanked me by the hair and put a gun to my neck

"Repeat that name," he snarled.

My chest heaved up and down, and tears rolled down my cheeks.

"R-Renato Jr. Calabresi," I stuttered.

He screamed, cursed, and released the hold on my hair.

After that, I fell to the ground and considered my options.

I pulled my hands up in prayer and begged for my life.

"Please let us go. I didn't mean for this to happen."

He rubbed his forehead and glared at me.

"You didn't mean for this to happen."

"It was a mistake. I promise to get you your money."

"How do I know you're not lying about him?"

I ignored his question.

"I'm dealing with my mom being sick, and I saw the money and thought it could help her with the medical bills."

"You'll get me the money but tell me about the boy who looks a year old and has my name."

"I forgot to take the Plan B pill. I was distracted. After we had sex, the condom must have broken."

"You know who we are, Sonya."

"I didn't plan to get pregnant. I would have told you," I shouted.

"When?" he screamed back, eyes darkening in terror.

"It was too late. When I found out, I was four months. I'd been focused on my son and taking care of my mom. She'd been diagnosed with cancer."

Renato's phone started to ring; then RJ started to cry, causing us both to glance in the direction of the limo. The look of disgust on his face directed at me sent a chill down my spine. He gripped me by the arm, marched me back over to the limo, and forced me back inside before he answered the phone.

RJ cried out, and I went to pick him up. Renato blocked me.

"Hold on," Renato said into the phone, then covered the receiver.

I bit my bottom lip.

"She can handle him." Renato motioned at Brilynn, and we made eye contact as she mouthed *sorry*.

"It's okay, little guy," Brilynn whispered to him, placing the blanket on top of him.

"Let's go," Renato yelled through the partition.

The car pulled back into traffic, and I slid the seat belt on and listened to him discuss business next to me. It was like the noise of the baby didn't faze him at all. Maybe he was the type of guy to pay me off to go away to avoid a scandal. Most men like him at his age weren't ready for children, so I needed to play nice and not upset him any further.

He ran a hand down his jaw and rubbed his chin. The low beard was neatly shaved, and I hated how his attractiveness still caused arousal in me, even when he was angry. If I recalled that night, he had been pissed and needed to let off some steam; I was the lucky girl to get him when all the other girls were declined. That was the first time I'd slept with a client of the club. Maybe it had to do with me not wanting to see my mom in pain any more or the stack of bills that were piled up with "past due" on top. But he made it all disappear when his lips touched mine and he held me close while we had sex the entire night.

"I need to stop at the compound first, but I'll check it out."

Brilynn and I made eye contact.

"Set it up. We can clean up later," Renato said. I knew that was code for killing somebody.

Was he talking about me?

"Call Savio and let him know." Renato hung up as the car turned down a winding street. Miles of land spread out with trees and massive homes.

"I made a mistake that night."

"I'll have a DNA test set up ASAP," Renato replied.

"She had a good reason, Mr. Calabresi," Brilynn backed me up.

"If you just let us go, I'll never do it again. We can disappear," I told him. "I promise we don't want anything from you."

He stared at me as the car slowed.

The gates opened. RJ was asleep when the car pulled into the driveway. Another car door slammed shut, and I glanced over my shoulder at two black SUVs.

"Bring them with you. Now. Watch her," Renato growled, motioning at Brilynn and RJ.

I tried to yank out of his grip, but he tightened his hold on my arm.

He pushed me into the arms of another bodyguard and marched toward the front of the house.

The solid wood door opened to an older woman. I didn't know if this was this mom.

Maybe I could plead for my child's safety at least.

"Renato, what's going on?" she said, lifting her hand at the baby.

He leaned down and kissed her cheek.

"Tell my parents to meet me in the living room," Renato answered, the angry expression disappearing from his face when he saw her.

His guard nudged us forward. Brilynn and I clasped hands while scanning the spacious front entrance. Spiral staircase, large paintings on the wall, vases taller than me, gold chandeliers.

We entered the living room, and it was just as captivating and expansive with a large fireplace, an entrance leading to the dining room, and a table full of expensive dishes.

Brilynn started to sit next to me, but Renato forced her to the couch on the opposite side.

He paced in front of us, cursing in his native Italian.

"Renato. What's going on, dear? We hear you brought some guests," a soft, warm, elegant voice spoke. We looked up at an older couple who were the spitting image of Renato.

"You had a son?" she asked, holding a hand to her chest.

His nostrils flared, and I put my head down, afraid of what would happen.

"Tell them," he demanded.

My leg bounced from nervousness.

"Tell her," he yelled.

"I'm sorry." I held both hands up.

I hesitated.

"This is Renato Jr."

Renato stopped, planting both hands on top of his head.

"When did this happen? He looks about a year old," his mom said, proceeding closer to Brilynn.

Tears fell down my cheek.

"I was going to find him and explain, but it happened so fast, and things got away from me."

His mom reached out both her hands to pick him up.

"I didn't plan to keep him away for so long. I promise, ma'am."

"Stop giving that bullshit line," Renato spat.

"Watch your mouth in front of this baby, Renato," his father, I assumed, fussed.

CHAPTER 3

Renato

AS THEY GOT OLDER, my parents got soft, and I hated how they were falling for Sonya's excuses. I gave her a cold stare.

"She stole $100,000 from me. We fucked one night. I woke up, and she was gone. The money was gone."

"I didn't plan it that way," Sonya blurted out; I could tell she felt horrible with how it sounded.

My parents were old school. To meet them under these circumstances was considered disrespectful.

Mom looked at me, and her eyes showed disappointment.

"Is this true?" she asked me.

I nodded.

"What's your name?" she questioned. Sonya held her son in her arms. I couldn't say for certain he wasn't mine, but too many women in the past had claimed I'd fathered a child, and it came out as a lie. Once my mother got attached, I'd never get them out of my life, so I needed to get tests done soon as possible.

"Sonya, and this is my best friend Brilynn."

"He's beautiful." She rubbed the baby's back.

Sonya nibbled on her finger and murmured low, "Thank you."

"I have another grandson. Is that what you're telling me?" Mom wondered.

"Uhmmm." Sonya held him close to her chest.

"Why do you look so afraid? Renato, what did you do to her?" Father demanded.

"Nothing yet." I slid my hands into my pockets.

"Mr. and Mrs. Calabresi—" Brilynn started to speak.

"Renato won't hurt you; I promise." Mom went to sit down next to Sonya on the couch, and my eyes widened in shock. I started toward them, but my father stopped me.

"Renato," he called and shook his head to stop.

"She can't be trusted. How do we know she's not working for someone?" I growled.

"You can say what you want about me. But leave my child out of some mafia business," Sonya argued. Her statement caught me off guard. As the enforcer, I killed a lot of people, but children never crossed my mind.

"Your child. You mean the one you kept hidden from me for a year," I answered.

"Renato, go clear your head," Mom hissed, crossing her arms.

"I want my money back from this bitch."

Mom raised her brow at me. "We do not behave like that."

I waved her off.

"Have you lost your sense, boy?" Father shouted, and I dropped my shoulders in remorse.

"Brilynn, is it?" Mom reached a hand out to shake.

"Yes, ma'am."

"He's a big boy." Mom stood and rubbed the top of his black, curly hair.

Sonya followed her roommate and my mom out of the room. I trailed behind them.

"Are you two hungry?" Mom questioned, and we shared a look.

"Start from the beginning." Father turned and inclined his head to follow him.

"We were at home when our entryway was kicked in and forcefully removed from our apartment, so we didn't get a chance to eat," Sonya explained, and my father released a hard sigh.

"They're not fucking eating!" I shouted.

"You will respect them in my house, Renato, and they are guests for now," Mom said. Father smacked me on the shoulders, pushed me forward into his office, and slammed the door behind me.

"He's beautiful."

I couldn't believe what was happening right in front of my eyes. A baby. Someone who could possibly belong to me with slight features of my face and hair.

Someone I've never met before.

He had Sonya's nose in my opinion, but if he was mine, I could see it in his eyes.

And what had kept him from me? Sonya Eden.

Do I even want kids?

"I had a one-night stand over a year ago. She works at Sante's club."

"Are you telling me she's a stripper?"

I stared out of the window into the garden my mother had built.

"Yeah, more or less."

"Do you think she set you up, honestly?"

I shrugged.

If this were true, and I did have a son, I hadn't seen his first smile or first cry. Hell, even changing a diaper.

He had been kept from me.

I was ready to kill, and she'd stolen from me.

"It's the principle of stealing from me. She waited until I

was asleep. Fuck that, I should go in and blow her head off," I seethed, leaning my head on the back of the couch.

"Are you calm now?" Father asked.

"How can you be so calm about everything?"

"Your mom should not get too caught up in this kid until we know for sure."

"I agree."

He chuckled.

"What's so funny?" I said.

"You and I both know that's your son. He looks exactly like you, Renato."

"I'm supposed to be okay with how she lied all this time. What if I hadn't found her the other night? We'd probably still be clueless."

"What you should do is be mature. Sit down and have a conversation. Your mother and I didn't raise you to act this way."

"You raised me to be a killer, and I do that pretty well."

"She has to stay here under my authority."

My head whipped around in surprise.

"What are you saying?"

He picked up the phone.

"She is not to be touched, her or the boy."

"Did you forget you retired, Father?"

"And did you forget I'm your father? I created you, and I can destroy you. She is not to be touched."

"That will make me look weak. She needs to be punished." I lunged up and got in his face.

"We will have this test done. We all know if that is your child. My grandchild. And as the mother of your child, she must have respect."

"Savio and Sante are fine with you running their life, not me."

"We want a relationship with our grandchild; that

means having a relationship with the mother." He ignored my statement.

"You need to sit and talk to her after you've calmed down."

"Do as you say or what?"

"Well, you won't like the outcome," he replied, the veins in his neck sticking out.

I respected and loved my father, but sometimes he was too forgiving.

"We got word that Tulio Costa tried to hit our area, and I want you to look into that."

"What property?"

"Over on Lancaster and Third."

"Calabresi owns the entire block."

"Obviously, Tulio is getting cocky. We don't need rumblings of people hitting our territory."

"I did get a call about someone hitting our club. It could be connected."

"He's the brother of Emers Costa. We can't do more than talk. Not without permission, and we've done enough killing that our reputation is very questionable," he explained.

"Once I leave here, I'll take a few men to check it out."

"Don't do anything beyond talking, Renato."

The cherry door swung open, and I looked back over my shoulder. My mom was holding the baby, and for just a minute, I forgot why I was here in the first place.

"What are you doing?" I asked.

"They were hungry. So, I fed them." Mom stepped around my father's desk, and he took the boy out her arms.

"You need to take the baby back to his mother."

"Renato, be nice," Father said.

"You want to hold him?" Mom asked.

"No," I answered.

"He has your entire appetite. Eats just as much as you did when you were a baby," Mom recalled.

"I told you don't get comfortable with him. He might not be mine." I swallowed the lump in my throat.

"You worry too much. He's your son."

"Looks exactly like your grandfather." Father grinned.

"Got to be kidding me," I groaned. Trudging out of the office down to the kitchen, I heard my brothers laughing.

"What are y'all doing here?" I headed to the fridge and grabbed a bottle of water.

"We got a call about a hit on his club." Savio texted on his phone.

"Plus, Mom said you had an emergency." Vincenzo cut into his burger.

I cracked my knuckles.

"We need to ride over to that area," I said, addressing the first point.

"What's the issue?"

"Tulio Costa." All of my brothers knew when I spoke that name, it meant a problem.

"What's the emergency with you?" Sante asked.

I hesitated.

"I might have a child."

The entire room went quiet.

"I just need to grab some milk. Oh, sorry." Sonya tried to back out of the room.

"Who are you?" Elio pointed at her.

I hadn't noticed what she was wearing when we'd snatched them from the apartment, but something about her ass and breasts looked bigger than last time.

I cleared my throat. "This is Sonya."

"I didn't mean to interrupt."

"No interruption. We're Renato's brothers." Sante then stated all of their names.

"Your mom said I could make him a bottle." Sonya lifted her eyes at me.

I gnawed at my lip. One minute, I was ready to kill her, and the next, I wanted a repeat of our night together. The moans and cries of the electrifying sex we'd had couldn't be forgotten if I tried. I hated myself at this moment for it.

"A kid? You're kidding, right?" Savio said.

"No, I'm not kidding. This woman lied for a year, and I happened to see her at the club the other night and went to get my money back that she stole."

Brilynn roamed into the kitchen, holding two plates in her hands. If my mom had Marilyn fix them food, I knew they were serious about keeping them here until the test was done.

"We have to take a test." I tossed the bottle in the trash.

"A girl or boy?" Elio asked.

"That's not important." I smacked the back of his head.

"A boy," she answered.

"If we want to catch Tulio, we need to leave now," I said, changing the subject again.

Out of the side of my eye, I saw Sonya freeze up at Tulio's name.

I hope she hadn't fucked him too. This was a small world, and people talked.

"So we're uncles," Elio joked.

"Not a laughing matter, Elio. Get the fuck out."

I tried to charge at him, but Sante held me back.

"Elio, stop acting like a child and check into the Costa family with Sante. Vincenzo, go look into this baby situation. I'll go with Renato because I know his temper will put us in a worse position before we start," Savio announced.

Everyone nodded their heads and roamed out of the room.

I grabbed the keys to my Ferrari that I kept in my parents' place off the hook and headed out of the house.

"Do you want us to ride shotgun?" Remo, my guard, had been with me the longest, and I trusted him like a brother.

"Tulio won't be a problem," Savio replied.

"He's not stupid. We will be fine." Savio and I hopped in the car.

I could see it out of the corner of my eye. He was watching me, waiting to question me about the baby. Besides my father, Savio was the one we all went to for advice or told our secrets to.

"Go ahead." I slid my seat belt on and pulled out of our family's home.

"What the fuck were you thinking?"

"Shit, I needed to fuck. I didn't think anything."

"Now you see what your fucks do? You end up with a child. Who knows how many more you got out there?"

"Fuck you, Savio. Let's not act like you don't do shit."

"The difference is that I grew up and matured as a husband and father now."

"I'll never get married. Praying this ain't my child, and we can get rid of her."

"What about this alleged money?"

"She's got to pay it back. Supposedly, she took it to take care of her mom. I don't care. I just want her out of my life."

"And if this is your child?"

My grip on the steering wheel tightened, while his breathing heightened.

"If it's my child, I'll take care of them, but I'm not looking to be a husband."

"If it's a Calabresi, we take care of our own, and as always, you take care of your son."

The thought of being a father scared me because of the life I lived. Some nights I didn't even come home from a job or at short notice, I flew out of town. *How would I juggle that with a child?*

"Get out of your head."

We arrived a few minutes later at Viva La Italian Restaurant. This neighborhood was under our protection in the west side of Chicago. Clubs and a few mom-and-pop stores were under Calabresi territory.

I got out of the car, slammed the brass doorway, and fixed my suit.

Savio followed next to me.

The Costas were known to hang out in this area. Even though we'd agreed to a truce, they still tried to push our buttons. Savio normally stayed out of the area and these situations because of his high profile as the boss of the family. The way people wanted hugs and approached him for a picture, you'd think he was a celebrity.

CHAPTER 4
Renato

AND RIGHT ON CUE, they were laughing and drinking.

I couldn't stand Tulio Costa. Always wanted power but was terrible whenever he was given control of any deal. His brother Emers, the boss of the Costa Mafia, let him oversee a restaurant they'd taken over in downtown Chicago. Only enough to make him think he was in charge. Now he was trying to encroach on our area, and that was something he couldn't do.

We neared the table as the waiter placed their food on it. I clamped a hand on one of his guard's shoulders and smiled.

"Tulio, what's so funny? I love to laugh." I slid my jacket to the side and showed off my holster.

"Renato Calabresi. To what do I owe the pleasure?"

"You tell me. I hear you trying to claim something that doesn't belong to you," I said. The guard to his right clenched his fists.

Tulio and I both knew it would be stupid to charge at me.

"We had this area first. Your family stole it from us." He grimaced.

"Costas never lost something that didn't belong to them."

"Coming from a two-bit enforcer, I heard you've had a few mishaps."

I chuckled at his statement. "Hey, does your brother still own that little nightclub?"

"What club?"

"I was thinking of, you know, opening my own gentleman's club. A place with beautiful women that dance." He kissed his hands.

"I doubt your brother would let you run another business, Tulio. Remember you barely opened the restaurant on schedule."

He stopped laughing, and the entire room went quiet.

"I'm only gonna say this once. Stay out of our area."

"Savio, you allow this peon to speak for you? The boss of Calabresi Mafia?" Tulio forced out.

"If I have to come in for something you started, that's going to be a problem," Savio replied.

"So enjoy your meal, fellas. On the house."

I started to turn and walk off, then heard a clear voice.

"I wouldn't be too quick to dismiss me."

"He's a bitch, Boss," his guard said.

"The other night at the club, you were seen with a woman."

My jaw twitched.

"Were you behind the shoot-out?"

He crossed his arms over his chest. "Maybe, maybe not. But there is something I want."

"Tulio, I owe you nothing."

"Do you know what she does? Her family?"

"Who is she, Tulio?" I knew it was about Sonya, but I needed to remain calm and not show any impression he'd hit a nerve.

"Oh, the redhead. Sonya Eden is a sexy thing. I looked into her."

My eyes darkened. I could feel my body heat up before marching back to the table.

Savio held me back.

"I want to collect, but my man went a little rogue when we saw you and unfortunately, that situation got out of hand."

"Collect what?"

"If you bring her to me, we can forget it and think about leaving your territory alone."

"Do you know who you're fucking with, Tulio?"

He grinned.

"You don't threaten me. I can have you killed within a split second. Walk out of here with a smile on my face. Call your woman to fuck and watch her plan your funeral."

The smile disappeared from his face. Tulio climbed out of the booth, his men covering his back. "She must mean something to you to threaten me," he replied.

"You heard what I said."

"Don't be a foolish boy. You know who my family is. We can wipe you out."

"It doesn't matter who you are and who your family is. She means nothing to me, but when you threaten me, then you're asking for trouble."

"Tulio, you heard what my brother said. Stop trying to take over our territory. Otherwise, there will be consequences," Savio said.

His eyes darted from Savio to me, then he gave a mischievous grin.

"Okay, that's fine. I will withdraw my men, but you have to give up the territory to replace the money she stole."

My stomach dropped at his statement.

"I don't even know who you're speaking about. I've never met Sonya," I said.

"Funny because we saw you with her that night, saved her life. So she must mean something to you. Give her up, and we can call it even."

We left the restaurant. When I got to the car, I slammed my hand on top of the hood.

He knows.

"Calm down, Renato. We have to be smart. It's all about intimidation. As long as she's on our property, she's safe, but I wouldn't put anything past Costas."

"He's a sadistic son of a bitch."

I started the car and flew Savio back home.

"I'll get with my man and put some extra protection in the neighborhood."

"I can't be seen making another appearance out here," Savio asserted, holding a photo of his son and wife in his hand.

"I understand."

A few minutes later, we arrived at home.

"Don't make any moves until you confirm with me." Savio held the car door open, and I pulled a cigar out of my pocket.

"Understood."

He trekked into his house. I reversed out and headed to the hotel; I had a prior engagement.

I wanted to avoid my parents and Sonya altogether. I didn't care what they said; I refused to get close to the boy, especially if he wasn't mine.

A year ago, I'd finished doing a deal with a client for guns. I put the money in the car and headed to the club for a little cele-bration. The whole week was crazy busy protecting our family from all different sides. The police were hounding Savio. Sante had to step in and take a few meetings. Plus, McKayla, being a journalist, didn't look good in the eyes of our partners. I saw

Sonya dance on the pole. Something about her called to me, and she saw me staring at her. When our eyes connected, she came over. We ended up at the hotel. I remember Remo held the bag out for me, and I set it on the floor near the couch of my usual room — women never came to my house or condo. Hours later, I heard a knock on my door. I had a hangover and felt the bed was empty on the right side. Only then, when Remo asked me about the money, did I suspect she had robbed me.

Shaking the memory of that night out of my mind, I pulled up to the hotel, held my keys out to the valet, and went up to the room I had reserved.

"Finally, you came." Natalia, a girl I'd met a few weeks ago at a party, draped her arms around my neck and tried to kiss me. I turned my head, removing her hands.

"You know I don't kiss." I trekked to the bar and grabbed a bottle of Jack Daniels. Natalia wanted more from me, and I'd told her the first time we met, I liked to fuck when I wanted and nothing else. I avoided intimacy because I had no time to feel for anyone.

She sauntered toward me and removed her robe to reveal her naked body.

I downed my drink and poured another glass when my phone rang. Remo's name scrolled across.

"Yeah," I answered.

Natalia placed her hand on my chest.

"We might have a problem," Remo murmured.

I looked at the time; it wasn't too late.

"Send me your location."

"Are you leaving?" Natalia asked.

"Business."

I removed money from my pocket and left it on the table.

Thirty minutes later, I arrived near the Costas' restaurant and saw Remo parked a few blocks away. I pulled up next to him, and he piled in my car.

"What do you have for me?"

"Tulio had a guest tonight."

"Who?"

"Mayor Kenneth Sanchez."

I rubbed my chin at his reveal.

"Is he still there?"

"For the last twenty minutes."

Mayor Sanchez held basically a truce for all the families. We couldn't interfere with his business, and he kept the police and higher-ups away from ours. Now to hear that Tulio was meeting with Sanchez this evening was interesting.

"You want us to stay on him?"

"Keep an eye on them both. Get a background on Sanchez. I need to know his entire bloodline."

Remo cracked the door wide and stepped out of the car.

"If he's betrayed the family…"

"We'll be in the business of finding someone new to vote for mayor."

———

The next morning, I heard loud banging on my front door, then it opened before being shoved closed. After I left Remo, I came here to drink and relax away from everyone. I had too much on my mind from Tulio, the mayor, and Sonya and what she could possibly have done to Tulio. Plus, I needed to schedule the test and figure out my next move.

"Here you are. We were worried about you," Mom said.

I grunted and turned over in my bed. My left eye popped open.

"What are you doing here?"

"You never came back to see if Sonya or the baby needed anything." Mom stood with the baby on her hip. I lay in bed with a sheet covering my lower half and all the lights out, with bottles on the nightstand and floor. Natalia tried to invite herself over, but I declined. No reason to start anything until I knew what my future would look like if I was a father.

"You do realize you have a child, right?"

He squirmed in her arms.

"Why are you here with him?"

"You didn't answer your phone. They're not our responsibility, but you will not treat them in any type of disrespectful way, Renato."

I pulled the covers over my head to fall back asleep.

"Renato Calabresi."

"Look, will it make you feel better if you adopt him? Or adopt another kid? I'm not having any children. It's not my kid."

Mom ignored me and ambled out of the room.

I blew out a breath. I got out of bed, went to the bathroom, and hopped in the shower.

Thirty minutes later, I came out, slogged into the living room, and smelled coffee brewing. Sonya was sitting with her son.

"Here, drink this," Mom said. I took the coffee out of her hand.

"Why are you here?" I pointed at Sonya.

"We're gonna do the DNA test now," Mom answered.

Sonya avoided eye contact with me.

"What do you know about Tulio Costa?" I glanced at her son as he sat in her lap.

"Renato, that can wait. We need to get the test done." Mom came out of the kitchen with a plate of food.

I finally noticed a woman in scrubs with a bag on the table.

"Let's get this over with, then you need to tell me about Tulio Costa."

"How long will it take to get the results?" Mom wondered.

"I'll get the results pushed through fast, Mrs. Calabresi."

"Thank you. This is a sensitive subject. I hope I can trust you to keep this under wraps." Mom watched the nurse as she swabbed Sonya, then the baby.

"You can, ma'am."

"Gabriella, can you wait outside for us please," Mom said after she finished swabbing my mouth.

"Of course, Mrs. Calabresi," Gabriella answered.

"I need you to get dressed and spend time with Sonya. I'm taking the baby, and you two need to figure out some type of co-parenting. No matter what you lied to him about, you need to get on the same page because I refuse to let my grandchild be in a hostile situation. Are we clear?" Mom demanded.

Sonya and I nodded in agreement.

"Talk and figure it out. Another thing, Renato. Your father informed me about the territory situation, and he explained that Sonya had a past with Tulio."

Sonya gasped in shock and peered down at the ground.

"I... I... promise I don't know Tulio personally."

Mom pulled out a folder from her purse and placed it on the table. It had photos of Sonya and Tulio at a hotel.

"You stole from Tulio, didn't you?" Mom tilted her head, looking at Sonya for an answer.

Sonya nodded.

"That's what he was talking about," I whispered.

"You met with Tulio?" Sonya blurted out.

"Doesn't matter. We have a bigger situation. To keep you under protection, you'll need to marry Renato," Mom said. I felt my chest ache at the thought of becoming someone's husband.

"Wait a minute!" I yelled, and the baby started to cry.

"I'm not marrying him," Sonya responded.

"I don't think you have a choice, Sonya. You not only did this to my son, but you also did this to someone else who's just as powerful with a dangerous family. Only way to protect you is to put you under our family's name. You will become Sonya Calabresi and have access to everything, but I want to make it clear. You will not steal from anyone else and put my grandchild in harm's way—if the results come back true, of course."

"If he turns out to be mine, I'll take the child. We don't need to get married."

"Over my dead body!" Sonya hopped from her seat and got in my face.

"Sonya, I raised five boys. I know you're young and this would be overwhelming, but you stepped over the line, even though the reasons were for your family. The mafia families will not care," Mom explained.

"I'll take the baby and leave the country," Sonya pleaded.

"I'm not marrying her. We don't need to get married. Tulio's not a problem," I said.

"Renato, don't talk like that in front of a child."

"Until it comes back that he's mine, let's keep this to ourselves."

CHAPTER 5

Sonya

"GET AWAY FROM ME!" I smacked him, and he smiled as he pushed me against the entryway with his hands around my neck.

"I own you. The minute you stole from me and lied. You screwed over me and the Costa Mafia, possibly putting us at war." Renato looked demented, and I wanted to scream for help, but no one would care. I slapped him across the face to release the tight grip around my neck.

"Arghh! You bitch!"

I felt my chest heave up and down, turning my head away.

He glanced at me and chuckled as I peered over his shoulder.

"Would you like to leave?"

"What are you going to do?"

He smirked. "Try to run and find out."

Once I started to move in that direction, he spun around and looked at me.

"Oh, I forgot to mention... If you leave this property, my men will shoot you dead."

I stared at him with my mouth hanging open.

"You're lying."

"Try me." His brows rose.

He went to walk out of the room, and I reached for his hand, but he snatched it away.

"Don't fucking touch me."

"Renato, listen to me. I promise, I'll get you your money."

"You have bigger problems than my money."

I hated to admit it, but he was right, and I had no one else I could turn to for help. It was hard to imagine how a one-night stand could devastate my life so completely. I'd ignored Brilynn's warning not to go with him to the hotel that night. As soon as I saw the bag of money lying on the floor, all my problems disappeared. However, things turned out to be worse now with his mother's words.

"Neither one of us is on board with the idea of marriage, so you need to tell me exactly what happened between you and Tulio."

"Nothing happened."

Renato could be working for Tulio and sell me out. *I refuse to tell on myself.*

"How much did you steal?"

"Not a lot, a few thousand."

"Do you think this is a game?" He lifted his phone off the table.

"No, but I can protect myself."

"If Tulio finds you?"

"He won't hurt me. I'll just call the police."

A wild look appeared in his eyes at my statement.

He closed the distance between us.

"Police won't do anything. You need to worry about what I'll do."

"You heard your mother."

"Sonya, how old are you?"

"Why?"

"Because your stupidity is pissing me off."

"Fuck you, Renato! I can protect my son from Tulio and you." I stuck my hand in his face.

"What about your mother and Brilynn?"

I froze at his words. "Leave them out of this."

"You made them a part of this when you made your choices."

Tears pooled in my eyes.

"Guards are surrounding my condo. Do you think you're going to get far?" he taunted, backing me against the couch.

"If he's not your child?" I lifted my eyes.

"Then you're on your own."

"My mom and Brilynn have nothing to do with my decisions. I want them to be left alone."

"I can't promise that. Tulio already made threats about you, but I didn't know for sure until now."

"Threats like what?"

"He saw us at the club that night when I confronted you about my money."

"Shit," I mumbled, nudging him away.

With a quick knock on the door, Mrs. Calabresi stuck her head in with no baby in her arms.

"Where's my baby?" My heart raced.

"He's fine, Sonya. He's with the guards."

I started to leave, and she blocked me with a hand on my shoulder.

"They're not going to do anything. Besides, the baby is tired," she said.

"Thank you, Mrs. Calabresi."

"Please call me Adelina. One thing I can guarantee. If this is my grandchild, like I know and feel when I look at him, you'll need our protection, Sonya. Don't fight us."

"Brilynn and my mom?"

"They will be safe. Right, Renato?" I glanced from Adelina to Renato.

He was tough and bossy, but in the presence of his mother, all you saw was a little boy who wanted to please his mother.

"Right," he responded, and I stared at him. Adelina turned to leave. I looked back down the hall as Renato walked away and wondered if this would only get more complicated for me or easier as a Calabresi.

———

An hour later, Brilynn and I were sitting on a bed at the Calabresi home with the baby between us. I held my phone up, ready to call my mother to see how she was doing.

"What are you waiting on?" Brilynn played with a toy bunny in RJ's face.

"They want us to get married."

Brilynn's face scrunched up in confusion.

"Is this some traditional Italian thing?"

"I don't know, but I messed up badly."

"Renato can't hold this against you forever."

"We should be getting the results in a few days, but there's something else I didn't tell you."

"Okay, you're scaring me, Sonya."

"I stole from another person."

"Sonya, what the hell!" she shouted, and I held my finger up to my lips.

"Shushhh… Brilynn."

"Who did you rob?"

"A guy named Tulio Costa."

"For how much?"

"About ten thousand, but that's not all."

"Oh, jeez."

"It's safer if you're unaware."

"From whom?"

"Everyone."

Brilynn was like a sister to me, and I hated that she was caught up in my mess.

"They won't hurt you, Brilynn, so you'll be able to leave."

"But you have to stay here?"

I nodded. "Until we get the results."

"Then I'll stay with you."

"You don't need to do that."

"Sonya, we're best friends. If you're in trouble, then I'm here to help."

Knock! Knock!

"Come in," I said, and the older woman from when we arrived the first time stepped in the room.

"Sonya, the family is sitting down for dinner, and they'd love for you to join."

"Uhmmm… I'm not hungry."

"Mrs. Calabresi insists. Don't worry, Renato isn't here."

"He's probably out with another stripper," I mumbled under my breath.

"Not sure about a date, but you and Brilynn should come down. By the way, I'm Marilyn, the family's cook, house manager, and babysitter for cute babies." She smiled at RJ.

Brilynn picked RJ up and followed Marilyn out of the room. I slid my phone back in my pocket and reminded myself to call my mom later, so she wouldn't worry. Her doctor's appointment would be coming up soon, and I needed to be there.

Laughter came from the hallway, and I was surprised by how open and honest the family was about their work.

"Come have a seat," Adelina instructed. Brilynn sat across from the guy Renato introduced as their younger brother Vincenzo. I sat next to her, and I pulled RJ into my lap to feed him.

"He looks exactly so much like Renato, it's scary," Vincenzo said.

"Well, he's sweeter than your Renato," I blurted out, and all eyes focused on me. Brilynn pinched my thigh.

"Sorry."

"No need to be sorry. We know Renato can be a handful," Mr. Calabresi said, lifting his napkin.

"We hope you like Italian food." Marilyn held out two plates in front of Brilynn and me. Brilynn lifted her fork, ready to dive into the osso buco, which I was familiar with from some Italian meals the girls at the club told me about their dates.

"Looks delicious," Brilynn complimented.

"Sonya, tell us about yourself and your family," Mr. Calabresi asked.

"Not much to tell. It's me and Mom. Plus, Brilynn helps watch RJ when I need to work."

"Did you know who Renato was when you slept with him?" The room went silent.

"I knew he had money, but I didn't know he was into dangerous things."

"We're a protective family. When he found out, you have to understand… he's never wanted to settle down. None of my boys really, until Savio and Sante met their wives."

"The two I met yesterday," I said.

"Yes. Savio is the oldest, and Sante is the second oldest." Adelina lifted her wine glass to her lips.

I released a ragged breath.

"If it comes back that he's not your grandchild, will you let us go?"

Adelina and her husband glanced at each other.

He smirked, and I felt no matter what, I would never be

at peace from this family.

"He's our grandchild; we know it in our hearts. If he's not, you're free to live your life."

"And the money?"

"Renato will get over it," Adelina said.

"I don't believe that."

"He can be a hothead at times, but we'll make him understand to leave you alone about the money."

"Thank you."

"But the other situation is Tulio Costa," Mr. Calabresi interjected, dropping his fork on the table.

"Tulio will get his money." If I needed to take out another loan to pay him off, I'd do that to erase any trace of me from his mind. We hadn't had sex, but I'd stolen from him and knew that men like him wanted to make an example of people that wronged them.

"So you have the three hundred thousand to pay back?" Mr. Calabresi questioned me, and my mouth dropped in shock.

"I didn't take three hundred thousand. You have to believe me. It was only around ten thousand," I begged, even though they didn't have a reason to trust me.

Tulio was scum and disgusting to women. I'd flirted with him that night in his office and saw when he put some money in a safe. Then his men interrupted, and he wanted me to leave, but I'd only pretended to leave the room when I heard them talk.

Ring!

When my phone went off, I passed my son to Brilynn and took it out of my pocket. Mom's name scrolled across.

"Hey, Mom. I was going to call you."

"Sonya sweetie, I have someone…" I heard rustling over the phone.

"Hello! Mom?" Right as I panicked at her shouts.

"Sonya, you're a hard girl to find."

"Who is this? Where is my mom?" I stood from the chair.

He chuckled. "Come find out." He hung up.

"Hello! Hello! They have my mom." I looked from Brilynn, to Mr. and Mrs. Calabresi.

"Who?" Mr. Calabresi rose from his chair.

"I don't know. They just said, 'Come find out.' I need to go." I stomped out of the room, and Brilynn followed.

"Wait. Sonya, you can't go over there by yourself," Brilynn stated.

Guards stood at the front lobby.

"Move out of my way," I demanded. They didn't blink. I spun around and faced Renato's father.

"Mr. Calabresi, tell them to move."

"I can't do that, Sonya. If you leave, it brings back uninvited guests."

I ran a hand down my face.

"I need to get to my mom. You don't understand; she's dealing with cancer."

"All right, I'll have Renato check on your mom," Adelina responded, and I felt a little better. My mom had no clue of anything that was going on.

"She'll probably call the police if she sees Renato. Please let me go too so she knows it's safe."

His parents looked at each other, and Renato's father nodded to the guards, and they stepped to the side.

"The guards will drive you to your mother's home, and Renato will meet you there."

"Thank you. Brilynn is staying here." I hugged her and RJ.

He wasn't the same man who'd come with Renato to my apartment the other day, and that told me I could probably slip away after I moved my mom somewhere safe. Brilynn would have to bring me the baby because I couldn't go back to the house.

CHAPTER 6
Renato

POP!

I rechecked the bullets, pushed the gun between his eyes, and waited for him to beg for his life. Today was me doing my job, the only thing I could control at the moment to get Sonya off my brain. After the explosive fight at my condo, I needed to kill something, and I couldn't get my hands around Tulio's neck or hers, so I took a job to find the guy that Savio stated was spying on one of our properties.

"Who hired you?"

"I don't know what you're talking about. I just work for the city." Snot and sweat dripped down his face. He was stocky and short with floppy, brown hair and a small mustache, wearing a too-small white shirt.

I squatted down in front of him and placed the gun under his chin.

"Do you know who I am?"

He shook his head.

"I'm the last person you see before you die." I stood when he started to tremble as my men held him up by the arms.

"Please! Don't kill me."

Ring!

"Boss! It's your father," Remo said behind me.

I dropped the gun and turned to take the phone out of his hand.

"I'm working," I growled.

"Sonya is on her way to her mother's. Tulio has made a move."

"Shit! We need to get to Sonya's mother."

"What about him?" Remo asked.

I lifted my gun and shot him between the eyes.

"Clean this up and get back to my parents' house," I directed my other guards. Remo followed me to the Hummer, and we headed to the address saved in my phone. Sonya thought I was bluffing, but I wanted to wait before I made a move. Tulio beat me, but he'd find himself dead if he tried anything with Sonya. She could potentially be the mother of my child.

"We're fifteen minutes away," Remo said, and I texted some of Savio's guards to head in that direction. All of the family had protection so we could shift around if something happened, and he was at work with Elio at the moment. My parents told me about the stupid lunch, and Vincenzo decided to stick around to get a feel for Sonya.

"I got Savio's men heading in that direction." I wanted to call and check on the baby, but I forced myself to not get attached and keep a clear head.

"Do you think Tulio will kill her?"

"Tulio can be erratic if he doesn't get his way."

Remo cut the lane, steering toward the highway and down the back end of Wilkerson Road. The good thing was that Sonya lived near her mom a few blocks away. With traffic, we made it in time to see a car pull up, and our men hopped out and stepped over to our car.

"We haven't gone in yet," one guard said.

"Scope the backyard. I see his car is still warm."

I stared up at the house when the slam of a car door sounded behind me.

"Where is she?" Sonya ran toward the house, and I grabbed her around the waist to calm her down.

"You can't go in there."

"Get away from me. Mom! Mom!" Sonya yelled, and when I covered her mouth with my hand, she tried to bite me.

"Fuck! Sonya, calm down." I wrapped her in a bear hug and pushed her against the car.

"Renato, he has my mom."

"I know."

"Please let me go."

"If you calm down, I will."

A sigh escaped, and her chest went up and down as her breathing fluctuated.

"Let me do the talking. Tulio won't hurt your mom."

"How do you know?"

"Because he wants something. This is all a game for him."

Then she nodded her head, and I let go.

I knocked on the door. A few seconds later, it inched open, and Tulio stood at the entrance.

"Well, isn't this a charming surprise," he said. I pushed past and stepped in to see his guard holding a gun to Sonya's mom's head.

"Mom!" Sonya screamed. She tried to run toward them, but I gripped her by the elbow.

"The party can start now," Tulio joked.

"No, the party is over. You made your first move, Tulio. Now you can leave."

"I don't take orders from you." Tulio glared at me.

"If you want to live, you will leave her alone and get out of here."

"She owes me."

"I'll get your ten thousand. Just let her go."

He grinned. "Actually, you owe me far more than that, sexy." He tried to reach out to touch her hair, and I slapped his hand down.

"What's the price?"

"No price. Sorry, it's more than money can fix."

"The territory will never be yours. Get over it, Costa." I gripped my gun.

His eyes left mine, trailing down to my hip, and focused on my hand.

He smirked. "The girl for the mother."

"Yes!" Sonya shouted.

"No," I answered.

"Sonya." Her mom held her hand on her chest. She wore a scarf on her head and looked pale. I knew Sonya said she needed to help her mom. I would do anything to protect her, but her situation would have an outcome neither of them would choose.

"Seems she wants to take her place." Tulio turned to his man, and he gripped her mom's arm tighter.

"Please!" Sonya shouted.

Within a split second, I punched Tulio in the jaw, draped my arm around his neck into a choke hold, and held a gun up to his neck.

"Put the gun down, or I'll shoot him," I argued.

"Fuck you, Renato!" Tulio yelled.

"Tell your man to let her go, or I'll leave you dead on this floor. You know me, Tulio." I gripped harder.

"Okay, I'm putting it down," Tulio's man said.

"Good." Angling the gun up to the side of his head, I watched him start toward the exit. Remo held his gun on him, and Sonya ran to her mother.

I shoved Tulio forward.

"Get out here," I hissed, pointing the gun at his face.

"For now, I'll leave, but you can't get rid of me."

"She's under my protection. That means you can't touch her."

"We'll see about that soon." Tulio stared at me and padded backwards to his car while he watched us.

"I'm sorry, Mom. I should have come sooner." I heard Sonya talk to her mom when I came back to the house.

"Sonya, we need to go."

Her head whipped around to me.

"I can't leave her like this."

"She can come with you and stay with my parents."

"I can't ask your parents to do that. She can stay at my apartment with Brilynn."

"Your apartment isn't safe. Grab some things and let's go now."

———

Three days later, I moved Sonya into my house and sent her to do shopping with my mom for the baby. The tests came back, and I was proven to be the father. Since then, we'd been able to coexist peacefully. By the time the results came in, my mother and father had already fallen in love with him. Her best friend decided to stay for a few days to get them comfortable, but her mom refused to stay with her after Tulio showed up at her home.

The elevator pinged, and I headed to Savio's office. Remo continued to watch Tulio and the mayor, and we had enough evidence to make our move on the mayor, but I needed Savio to agree.

"Take the reports and send them to the attorney," Savio informed.

When I twisted the doorknob to his office and entered, I saw him talking with his secretary.

"You don't wait for me to say come in? I could have been busy," Savio said.

His secretary giggled, rose out her seat, and left his office. I watched her wink as she shut the door behind her.

"You normally don't show up here."

"We have a little more information on Tulio and the mayor."

He leaned forward in his chair.

"How are you doing with the baby?"

I scratched the back of my head.

"Fine, but we need to make a move on Tulio."

"You're nervous about being a father."

"He's small."

Savio chuckled.

"They all start out like that, but they eventually grow up."

"You're comfortable in that world; this fell in my lap."

"When you watch my son, you have no problems."

"He's my nephew. It's easier, but anyway, Tulio has been meeting with the mayor." I neared the couch and took a seat.

"About?"

"Not sure, but more than likely to take over. Tulio Costa is pissed that I humiliated him. Plus, Sonya took money from him."

He paused and listened to my next words carefully.

"We need to kill him."

"Killing another mafia's family member is not good."

"I can make it look like an accident."

Savio sat back in his chair, his eyes up to the ceiling.

"Talk to the mayor first."

"If he denies anything?"

"Make sure he doesn't deny. I've heard some things about Sonya."

"Like?" I propped my feet up on the table.

"She hasn't been back to dance, so she's going to want to work."

"Did you have problems with McKayla wanting to work?"

"Every day." He smiled.

"I have an agreement with her. As long as she co-parents, I don't care what she does."

"The marriage?"

The marriage was still on the table. I hadn't informed Sonya of what we would do, and my mom hounded me about taking her to get a ring for Sonya like we were in love or something.

"I don't think we need to get married."

"For the sake of your son, I'd advise you to talk with Sonya and come to an agreement."

"Is this advice as a brother or the boss of the mafia?" My left brow arched in question.

"Both. Less distractions the better." He shuffled some papers on his desk. I got up and headed to the exit.

"Remember, Renato. Don't kill the mayor."

"As long as no one makes a move, I have no reason to kill." I winked at his secretary and removed my cell from my pocket.

"You need me to move in?" Remo answered the phone.

"No, keep an eye on them. I'm going to be at the office for the rest of the day."

"Anything else?"

"Has Sonya left the house?"

"No, I have visuals on her and the baby."

Reaching my office, I locked the door, removed my jacket, and plopped down on the chair, turning on my computer. The corporate business world belonged to Savio and Vincenzo, but sometimes I'd come here and check in on accounts. A pile of paperwork lay on my desk, but I needed to see Sonya and the baby. I logged into the security footage of my house and watched Brilynn playing with RJ outside.

"The mayor needs to have a visit from me soon. Make sure he stays in his office."

"And the family wanted to have dinner together."

"You're right. I forgot."

"I'll keep an eye on the mayor; you spend time with Sonya and the baby."

"Why does it sound like you're soft on them?" I gritted my teeth.

"You jealous, Boss?"

"Do the job I pay you for." I hung up on him while he laughed.

I ordered lunch and worked through the files for the next two hours, then decided to call it a day and head out to spend time with RJ; hopefully Sonya and I could talk. Her attitude had only gotten worse because her mom wasn't talking to her. I slid my key in the elevator and went to the parking structure and saw my driver waiting for me next to my Lincoln Town Car.

"Where to, Mr. Calabresi?" he asked.

"The house."

"Yes, sir." He started the car and waited for the guard to lift the barrier open for us to go through. I read over Sonya's file as he eased into traffic and turned the jazz music up just as I liked.

"Are you married, Alfred?"

"Yes, sir. Thirty years."

Alfred had been a driver for me for the past three years, a retired army man that wanted to do simple work after my father retired.

"You like it?"

He shook with laughter. "Marriage can be wonderful, but it's work," he explained.

The car turned at the light, headed down the street and up the winding road of my property, and parked. We all stayed close to our parents in the same part of town. But mine was farther out, secluded for privacy with large trees and guarded on all angles.

"Take the rest of the night off, Alfred."

"Sounds good, sir."

"I told you to call me Renato."

"One day I might." He chuckled. I shook hands with him and headed into my quiet house, dropping my coat on the back of the rack.

CHAPTER 7

Sonya

THREE DAYS AGO, I officially became a part of the Calabresi family, and soon I'll be married to Renato Calabresi. I stood in front of the mirror and looked at the new clothes I'd bought for the dinner his mother was throwing for our engagement. Funny to be engaged and no ring on my finger or proposal. Adelina was determined to get us comfortable here, and I appreciated how she didn't hover over me, but I wished I didn't have to marry someone that hated me.

The door to my guest room opened, and Renato stood there and watched me.

"I thought you had work to do."

I padded to the bed, laying the dress on top.

"Where's my son?"

I scoffed at his statement of "my son" now he became overbearing and wanted to know everything about RJ. I understood the part I played, but Renato wasn't the sanest person to have a conversation with.

"Brilynn is getting him dressed."

"Did you talk with your mom?"

I stared at him, poking my lip out. "You know she's not talking to me."

"Whose fault is that?"

"Renato, not tonight, please, I just want to get through this dinner and get back to bed."

He stomped toward me and gripped both sides of my face, crashing his lips on mine. Shock disguised my initial reaction and then remembrance of our time together had a moan escape. He made me feel like I was on a rollercoaster ride of feels.

"Renato, what are you doing?" I shoved him away and tugged on my bottom lip.

"Get dressed so we can go," he panted.

He started to turn, and I stopped him.

"Wait a minute. We need to talk about this marriage."

"No tonight, it's all business anyway."

"Yeah, business."

He stopped walking.

"What else do you have on Tulio? Tell me now so I can fully protect you."

"Protect me or protect your child?"

The look in his eye told me all I needed to know; he didn't care about me. Our marriage would be about keeping his son safe, and that included the mother.

"No need to answer. Tulio didn't know I overheard him talking about a deal with the mayor." I crawled on top of the bed.

"What type of deal?"

"Tulio met with Sanchez in his office at the restaurant about making his reelection bid confirmed if Tulio were to get your territory, plus put Costa in power."

Renato's expression was neutral.

"How old are you?" He changed the subject.

"Twenty-four, and you?"

"Twenty-eight. I'll get you a ring tomorrow." Renato

angled to the doorframe of my guest bedroom when Brilynn burst in with RJ in her arms.

"Hey, oh, are we interrupting something?" Brilynn wondered. Renato kissed the top of RJ's head.

"No. I'll meet you at the car in thirty minutes," Renato said, then headed to his room.

Brilynn looked out into the hall, then closed the door behind her.

"Don't ask, I need to get dressed."

———

Renato's home was just as glamorous as his parents', only his was more decorated for a bachelor. The front door opened, and Marilyn smiled, reaching for RJ to get out of his car seat.

"He's gotten so big," she teased, tickling his stomach.

"You spoil him, Marilyn." All of the family, including his brothers, had kept RJ in their arms nonstop; sometimes it warmed my heart that he had a big family compared to my side of just my mom and Brilynn.

Renato shoved the door closed, Marilyn went to the kitchen with the baby, and I wandered to the living room.

"There's my grandson." Adelina came down the spiral staircase in a long, flowy gown. I scanned her white and silver chiffon dress and felt underdressed. Adelina approached Renato and kissed him on the cheek. She shifted to me, then Brilynn and rushed to talk to RJ like he could have a full conversation.

"He's so cute. Let Grandma see that smile." Adelina rubbed his cheek.

"Where's SJ?"

"Who's that?" Brilynn asked.

"My nephew," Renato answered.

"In the playroom. Go talk to your father and brothers."

Adelina continued to the kitchen, grabbed me by the hand, and escorted us around the island. Marilyn talked to the chef, and the housekeeper started to take out large plates of food.

"What would you like to drink?" Adelina lifted two glasses.

"Adelina, SJ wants his granny and not me." A woman carrying a boy in her arms smiled at Brilynn, then me.

"Hi, you must be Sonya, and you're Brilynn?" she asked.

"Yes, I'm Sonya."

"I'm McKayla, married to Savio, and this is our son, SJ."

"McKayla's a journalist," Adelina explained.

McKayla was really beautiful and seemed sweet. She reminded me of Brilynn. Probably Savio would fight anyone that approached his wife wrong.

"Food is ready," Marilyn said.

"Thank you, Marilyn. Come on, ladies, time to eat." Adelina held both boys in her hands.

"Is she always like this with kids?"

"Yes, get used to her and Mr. Calabresi. Their house is the playground for all the kids."

McKayla and I died laughing at RJ's reaction when Adelina poked his stomach.

Renato sat next to his brother at the table, and I looked at the names and saw I was to sit next to him. Releasing a breath, I pulled the seat out and sat down.

"Renato, how are things at the house with the family?" his father said, pouring wine into his wife's glass.

He scowled, licking his lips.

"Fine." He sipped his glass of wine.

"Have you thought of where you want to get married, Sonya?" Adelina clicked glasses with her husband.

This was still new to me, and to marry someone on

short notice or end up being killed didn't give me much time to think over my feelings.

"Honestly, something at the house would be fine."

"What are your plans after you get married?"

"Is this an interrogation?" Renato and his father made eye contact.

"I'm going back to school and find a new job."

"Calabresi Holdings is hiring," Vincenzo answered.

"No," Renato answered.

I cut into the bread, spreading butter on top.

"No to what?"

"You're not working," Renato said in a husky voice.

"I'm not a child, Renato."

"Did you forget someone is trying to kill you?"

"Renato, not at the dinner table." Adelina calmly passed the bowl of salad.

"Sorry, not hungry." I pushed back from the table and grabbed RJ out his seat and went to the backyard to clear my head.

"Sonya." A sweet voice called my name; I looked over my shoulder at McKayla.

"Sorry, I needed a moment to myself." I kissed the side of RJ's cheek, and he settled against my chest.

"Calabresi men can be hard, possessive assholes." McKayla sat next to me on the gazebo bench.

"Renato will always hate me."

"No he won't; he's in enforcer mode right now."

"How do you deal with this all day?" I waved at the house.

"Did they tell you how I became Savio's wife?"

"No, but I did hear some things in the media."

"Not all of it is true."

"He kidnapped you though, right?"

She looked back at the house and saw Savio staring at us with SJ in his arms.

"He did kidnap me. It wasn't conventional how we started, but I love the life we have."

"I can't see Renato and me becoming like you two."

"You don't need to be us, but he is protective of his family, and now that he has a child, he's going to work even harder to protect you both."

"Out of convenience."

"You like him." McKayla seemed amused by her question.

"Like Renato? Hell no. He's insufferable, arrogant and asshole."

"Sounds about right, also, Renato can be funny, sweet, a good babysitter, and loves hard so that means you'll never have to worry about him."

"You mean with other women?"

"He's known to sleep around, but when he finds that one person, she'll be his focus."

"Are you telling me this for a reason?"

"You'll find out."

"I doubt Renato has a lovable bone in his body." I stood with RJ, and we headed back in for dinner, deciding to ignore Renato for the rest of the night. Laughter went around the room as people talked, and Renato, the man that snatched me from my home and who I'd slept with one night, kept his eyes on me when I started toward the chair. He pulled it out for me, and I sat down and passed RJ to him so I could eat.

"Thank you," I whispered.

He placed his hand on my leg and squeezed, and my clit throbbed in response.

Two hours later, Renato carried our son up to his bedroom, and I removed my hair from the high bun, then removed my shoes. Brilynn went up to bed, and I sauntered to the guest bedroom and saw Renato starting to head back downstairs.

"Are you leaving?" I stood in front of my room.

"Yeah, I have work."

I shook my head. "Work? Really, Renato? I guess our fake marriage comes with privileges of side pieces."

He narrowed his eyes on me.

"You think I'm going out to sleep with someone?" A muscle in his jaw flexed.

"You don't have to explain to me." I opened my door but paused when he called my name.

"I'm going to meet with Tulio."

"We're not together, so it doesn't matter." I shut the door behind me, slid down to the floor, and felt my eyes start to water. So many things I regretted, people I'd lost in my life, to turn into a wife in a loveless marriage.

CHAPTER 8

Renato

DEEP IN MY THOUGHTS, I shut the car door behind me and glanced left to right at the quiet streets of Chicago in front of the mayor's office. Remo had been able to get information about him working late tonight. Usually, he'd be at some function to try and drum up money for his reelection campaign, which we'd donated to many times over the years. The door opened to the security guard we paid to tell us when everyone was gone out of the building. I thanked him, stalked down the hallway to his office, and tapped on the doorframe, not waiting to be allowed inside.

Remo closed the door behind me. I grinned at the mayor's head back on the chair with his eyes closed and mouth open.

"Mr. Mayor, is this what we pay your salary for?" I joked, and the woman jumped up and pushed her skirt down past her knees.

"What are you doing here, Renato?"

"I think I'm the one that should be asking the questions. Honey, you probably want to go ahead and leave. More than likely, you might want to find another job."

"It's all right, Susan, you can go," he said.

He started to fix his pants. Then he ran his hand through his hair and fixed his tie, watching the woman leave.

Remo locked the entranceway behind her.

"What are you doing here?" he questioned again.

"I hear some rumblings of you meeting with Tulio Costa. Is there something you should tell me?"

"I don't know what you mean." He took a sip of water.

"Is that how you want to play this, Mr. Mayor?" I leaned over his desk, picked up the letter opener, and placed it on the tip of my thumb.

"Look, Renato. I am neutral with all parties. I have nothing to do with the Costa family or you and your family," he remarked, touching the top of the papers on his desk.

"Interesting because I got word from my men and saw photos of you meeting with Tulio Costa at his restaurant."

"I went there for the food, Renato. It's a free country, and I do have to eat sometimes," he replied.

I chortled at his lies. "Is that how we're playing this now? You take me for a joke." I lunged, slamming the letter opener on top of the brown file folder on his desk. Startled, he started to push out of his seat. I wagged my finger in his face.

"You might want to sit, Mr. Mayor. Let me tell you a little story. Do you mind if I tell my story?"

He released a breath.

"Please don't interrupt, either, because I gather Tulio Costa wants to take over not only Chicago but other areas. Even US states through political powers."

"Don't know anything about it." He looked at Remo, then me.

"Well, here's the thing. I think you do know because if they want to get into political ties and branch out, it'd be wise to go through you, probably some of your political cronies."

"Tulio is just a friend."

I retrieved the letter opener, moving it deftly between my hands.

"Now he is a friend. At first you didn't know him or just ate at his restaurant. Which lie are you going to stick to, Mr. Mayor?"

"No idea of his plans."

"Give me your hand."

His eyes looked scared.

I motioned to his hand.

Slowly he reached his left palm out to me.

"I don't like liars and, Mr. Mayor, if you want to get reelected, let alone stay alive, you'll stop whatever you have going on with Tulio immediately." I pretended to draw a cross in his palm.

"Are you threatening me? The mayor of Chicago, A political dynasty. You know how much publicity and media will be all over your family?"

I put the letter opener back in its place and expressed amusement at his statement.

"See, everyone gets like you in these moments. You're sweating, tense, not knowing when it will happen. You're scared, not knowing my next move. And that's pretty understandable. Because everyone knows when I come, they already know, it's the call of death. You can take it as a threat. You can take it as a promise, but I always deliver. Goodnight, Mr. Mayor."

I turned toward the door. Remo unlocked the way, and I ambled out of his office.

"Oh, Susan. Next time, put a little more spit into it. Men like it extra wet." I winked my left eye at her, and she blushed.

Remo cut through traffic to our next destination. I

checked my phone and saw a message from Savio. He wanted to meet soon at the warehouse. Sonya's attempt at jealousy was different for me because most women didn't care if I played around. Everyone knew I had an open policy of not staying with one woman.

After we arrived in a known Costa area, Remo pulled up in front of a bar, where a few men stood outside talking and laughing. I watched as the women came out. The men tried to get their number but were dismissed. They became enraged and started to harass the women, so I stalked up to the leader of the group, a young guy with dirty brown hair, slender build, and a thin mustache, reached out and punched him in the face. Another one tried to charge at me. Remo gripped him around the collar and pushed him up against the wall of the bar.

I kicked him in the stomach, pulled my gun out, and beat him across the face.

"Arghhh!" He covered his face, but I pushed his hand away.

He screamed and yelled for me to let him go. This would cost us, but I didn't give a fuck. Tulio would learn to not fuck with me.

Remo saw the guy on the ground was not moving and slapped me on the back to stop. I looked at the guy. He was bloody, lying on the ground, almost unconscious, groaning in pain.

"I'll be back. Next time, I'll burn this fucking place down if he tries me again."

Forty minutes later, I was home, finally opening my front door around two in the morning. I was sore from the fight and mentally exhausted from the past few days. I removed my jacket and laid it on the back of the chair. Looking at my bruised hand, I wandered into the kitchen, grabbed an ice pack out of the freezer, and ambled to the sink to try to clean my hand, when all of a sudden the light turned on.

I glanced behind me. "What are you doing up so late?" Sonya stood in her nightgown.

"I heard something, and I couldn't sleep. So I was going to try and drink some milk. What are you..." She paused, noticing my hand in the sink.

"What happened to your hand?" she pressed for information.

"It's fine." She moved toward me, and I licked my lip at her exposed thighs in the large shirt and no pants.

"It's not fine. You're bleeding. Did you get into a fight?"

"It'll be fine, Sonya. It's a little cut; I've done worse and seen worse."

I grimaced when she rubbed on the cuts.

"Come sit; let me grab the first aid kit." Sonya strode to the pantry and pulled it from the corner. She bent over to grab the trash can, and the shirt drew up, revealing white panties. My dick got hard in remembrance. I adjusted in the chair.

"You don't have to do this. I can take care of myself."

"I know, but I feel bad looking at you now. After what I said earlier."

"Have you talked to your mom?"

"No, I'm going to hopefully talk with her tomorrow to invite her to the wedding or fake wedding or whatever we're calling it now."

"Sonya, you know we're doing this for a reason, right?"

"I fucked up, screwed up both our lives. It's not the first time she stopped talking to me when I disappointed her."

We made eye contact.

"Thank you for keeping him."

"I should thank you. He saved me when I was dealing with my mom and feeling depressed. Having him really let me know and feel like I have a purpose. He brought me back to life."

"I know I've said for you not to work. But there's a reason why." She paused to stare at me.

"Going back to the club is not the answer. Tulio is reckless; he might have people watching you. I can't be there 24/7, but I do have an idea of what you could do while you're looking into school."

"What idea?"

"Work for my family's company."

"Your family's company?"

"Calabresi has multiple businesses. We didn't get to be billionaires by just being monsters."

"What would I do?"

"Whatever you want."

There was silence in the room.

The baby cried, and she hurried to finish the wrap on my hand. I caressed her cheek; we both stood at the same time.

"Are we going to talk about the kiss the other day?" she asked.

"Not right now. I'm not a good guy, Sonya." I strode away and stopped with my back to her.

"Go to sleep. I'll take care of him." She nodded in answer.

———

Sonya and I had gotten into a routine since the night of her fixing my hand up. A few days later, we brought RJ in for a routine checkup with the doctor. As my first time in the process, I wanted to ask a lot of questions, but Sonya said it wasn't necessary because Dr. Wraith was on limited time and the baby wasn't sick.

I tried to not make it awkward. We were supposed to be

going ring shopping and planning the wedding in my parents' backyard. I was just paying for everything. I held the baby in the carrier as we advanced inside the doctor's office. She checked in while I stood next to her and listened. I hadn't heard anything from Tulio or Kenneth since our visit. I was sure he would retaliate. EJ did get back to me that he wouldn't be at the meeting because of a deal out of town. Sante and I would meet with Savio ourselves.

"We're ready for you," the nurse said.

I grabbed the carrier, following behind Sonya. She had her hair down in curls, wearing a black leather skirt, a turtleneck, and a silver coat. She'd started working at the office under Vincenzo, and I hadn't seen her, as my office was on another floor. Co-parenting wasn't too hard. Some nights I stayed at my condo. Other nights I stayed at the house. I wanted to give her space so she didn't feel over-whelmed before we got married. I placed the baby on the bed, and the nurse removed his shoes. I stood back and watched as Sonya carefully pulled his shirt over his head.

"Hello, I'm Dr. Wraith. You must be the father."

"I am."

Sonya avoided eye contact with me.

"Well, you have a great son here, sir, He's been a great patient. Never cries and is always on his best behavior. So we're doing a routine check on him today. Just to make sure the weight and everything looks good. Has he been sleeping through the night?" Dr. Wraith questioned.

"He's woken up a few times, but overall he's been good."

"No symptoms of the infection come back at all?"

"When was he sick?"

They both turned to look at me.

"A while ago," Dr. Wraith answered.

"She didn't tell me," I said.

"I didn't think it was a big deal."

"You didn't think it was a big deal? Anything that goes on with him I need to know about."

"Okay. I'll remember next time," she spat harshly.

I hated to argue in front of the doctor, but Sonya was acting like the only parent in this situation. A few minutes later, after the doctor checked him over, we wrapped up and scheduled another appointment for a follow up in a few months. We exited the building to the waiting car, and I allowed her to get in first while I strapped my son in the backseat.

The drive was quiet for five minutes, and I cleared my throat to get her attention.

"I'm sorry for jumping down your throat in there. I was just surprised he was sick."

"I get it, this is new to you and I've been doing this alone. I apologize."

"Do you want to get something to eat? I can have them drive to a place."

"No, that's fine. I have to get to work now so I'm kind of doing everything and balancing it with school and the baby."

"I'll take him while you go to work. I don't have any plans. So he can stay with me."

"Are you sure?"

"Yes. I'll be working from home today."

"You don't seem like the office type of guy."

I chuckled at her words.

"I'm not, but I do have an office there and go in sometimes."

"Okay, well, you can drop me off. Then, you and baby boy can have a guys' day."

She kissed the baby's cheek.

We went to visit my mom after we dropped her off. I marched through the entrance and saw my parents sitting on the couch together. I placed RJ on the floor in front of them near the table.

"To what do we owe this visit?" My mom started to take him out of the carrier.

"Just left the baby's checkup visit with the doctor. Sonya is at work, so I thought I'd take him for the day. To give her a break."

"Honey, watch the baby. I need to talk to Renato for a second," my dad said and stood.

I knew what this was about. If I didn't hear from Savio, then my father more than likely would confront me.

"What were you thinking?" He didn't even wait for the door to close in his office.

"I needed to make a point. Show Tulio I don't play games. Sonya overheard them plan to move in on us. We have evidence; we need to get ahead of this."

"Let Savio handle it. You go into his territory, that is asking for war."

"No, but I can finish it. They won't fuck with us. Tulio's too much of a pussy."

"Too close to the situation."

"No, he started it. He's been undermining not only his own family, but also ours. It's all a ploy, Father. If he gets this and gets Kenneth on board, we're fucked. We need to handle this now."

He studied my face, rubbing his chin. He knew I was right. But he didn't like bloodshed. Not unless it was necessary.

"Look, I got Remo to scout the area and watch them both."

"Have you gotten the ring?"

"Heading over now to get it."

"Do you love her?"

"I care that she has my child. Can that be enough?"

He looked at me with sorrow in his eyes.

"Have a contract drawn up and have her sign it soon. Then you will divorce and you will give her enough to live the rest of her life comfortably."

"I can't take her from her son."

"Then she will stay married to you. She has no ties to the family, no loyalties. She can run off. I will not allow my grandson to be raised away from us."

"Understand."

"Get it done, Renato."

CHAPTER 9

Sonya

I FINISHED the last items on my desk and turned toward my computer, opening up my email. Renato and his family made me feel comfortable at the office, and I worked on a different floor than he did, so no chance of us mixing business and pleasure. I thought of my mom and decided to try and give her a call. She'd avoided me for too long, and our relationship was better than it had been.

"Mom, please call me. I haven't heard from you in a few days. I'm worried. I know what happened was scary. But I need to talk to you." The conversation with his sisters-in-law McKayla and Rena made me want to secure my finances and apartment. Because my mom was still not working due to her health, I had to take care of her insurance. Having a regular check meant providing food, paying the bills, and saving up for an apartment. There might be no resolution to the club situation or Tulio, and staying in Renato's shadow would never be good for me.

I dropped my phone in my purse, placed it in the desk drawer, and set up my calendar for the week. The accounting department had hired me as an assistant, and I'd work alongside Savio or Vincenzo sometimes. Even though my mom wouldn't take my calls, after Tulio threatened to kill her, Renato paid to put her in a new place. Guards escorted me everywhere, McKayla and I had become fast friends, and it felt like I had known Rena forever.

Ring!

I glanced down at the drawer, slid it open, and picked up my phone, seeing my mom's name scroll across. I quickly answered.

"Hello, Sonya. How are you?"

"Fine. How are you?"

"I'm good. Better now that I've heard your voice."

"I feel better now that I've heard your voice too."

The phone got quiet.

"What's been going on?" I questioned.

"Nothing. Had another doctor's visit."

"Did you see I paid the bill for that? I have a job now."

"I told you that you don't have to pay my bill, Sonya."

"Mom, please. Let's not argue about this. You're my mother. I'm gonna take care of you."

"Are you still with that guy? Those people that came here, you need to get away from them."

I hesitated before I answered. "I'm getting married."

She sighed. "To who?"

"To my child's father."

"Sonya, what are you thinking?"

"It's only business."

"Business? Are you prostituting yourself?"

"What? No. We have an arrangement," I answered.

"This doesn't sound good."

"Listen, I stole from him. I owe him, and he promised to take care of my child. I can't fault him. He could have killed me. But we talked."

"You're gonna what? Get married? Have more kids in a loveless marriage?"

"It's not like that, Mom. He's not all bad. I know he can be a little rough sometimes—"

"Rough? He's a killer. I've heard of this family. I've seen them in the newspapers. They kill people. Why would you be around that? Why would you have your son around that?"

She rambled on with question after question.

"We're protected, Mom. Just listen to me. I want you to meet them at the wedding."

"Oh, Sonya. You're making a huge mistake."

"It's for the best. Are you going to come?"

"I love you, of course I'll come. But I don't agree with your choices."

"Great, thanks, Mom. I'll have Mrs. Calabresi send you an invitation."

"What about school? Are you still planning on going?"

"No, I'm still going to work on enrolling again. But it's just mostly online with the baby and then this job. I want to make sure I'm able to balance everything."

"You scare me, Sonya."

"I promise I'm doing okay. I'm safe," I answered.

"All right, keep me updated. Call me later and come for dinner with the man."

"I love you."

"Love you more." Hanging up the phone, I heard a throat clear behind me and jumped in surprise. Holding a hand to my chest, I tried to calm my breaths.

"Sorry, I didn't mean to scare you," Vincenzo said.

"Oh no. Sorry. I didn't mean to take a personal call while working."

"No, you're fine. We do it all the time."

I snorted. He was cute and reminded me of the guys at the club that would come in for the first time and be shy.

"How's the little guy?"

"Your nephew is fine. He's with your brother right now."

"Renato with a baby." He laughed.

"Surprisingly he's good with the baby. I was shocked."

"What are you doing for your wedding?"

"We're just going to have something small in your parents' house."

"Nice. Listen, I know a lot of people have a lot to say about Renato. But he's a good guy," his brother said.

I nodded at his comment.

"Renato told me you met at the club."

"I was a dancer."

"I know it may seem like my family can be a little over-protective. But they mean well."

"Are you in the 'family business,' too?" I put up air quotes.

Vincenzo copied the air quotes and cracked up. "No, I only work in the office business as the baby boy of the family. They don't want me anywhere near that stuff. But I do have plenty of practice with a gun." He put up two fingers, pretending to shoot.

He and I roared.

"Listen, don't worry about the craziness of Renato's world. And your mom will understand in time."

"You heard that?"

"I did. And I get it; everyone has this perception of us thinking we're killers. Evil. But we're just protective. We wouldn't do anything to hurt you or my nephew. You're safe with us."

"Thanks, Mr. Calabresi."

He waved me off and shook his head. "Please call me Vincenzo. I'm too young for Mr. Calabresi. And you're welcome."

"Do I need to order your lunch, or will you leave for the day?"

He checked the time on his watch. "Heading to the local burger joint down the street, what about you?"

"Meeting McKayla for lunch and dress shopping."

"I'll pass on girl stuff," he teased me.

"You sound like Renato."

Later in the afternoon, McKayla decided to go dress shopping at a private designer that Rena recommended.

"Have you decided what you're going to do for the wedding?" McKayla picked through dresses on the rack.

"I'm not really sure; I hadn't thought about it. I invited Brilynn."

"Sonya, with that silver hair you should do something fiery, ballsy for the party," Rena said.

"I don't know. Renato doesn't seem like the type that likes over-the-top stuff."

"He doesn't like anything. Unless he's controlling it. Mom's situation I haven't come to grips with yet."

"Are you okay?" Rena asked.

"Yeah. Nothing. I'm fine."

"What do you have in mind for your dress? What are we all wearing?"

"Um, I mean, it's going to be outside in the garden. So maybe something simple, chic. I don't know."

"Yeah, that could work. Maybe like a light cream dress. Something with the shoulders out and boobs popped out. You should flaunt them. Like hey, we're here." Rena pushed her breasts up and sauntered like a model. McKayla giggled.

"Can I ask you guys something?"

They focused on me.

"Have you ever met anyone that Renato dated?"

The room went quiet.

"Why do you ask?"

"No reason, I'm just curious what type of marriage it's

going to be. The fake one, we both get to have our own side relationship behind closed doors."

"Calabresi men aren't the type that would allow you to have a man on the side. Remember that time he messed with Sante and said you two slept together," McKayla mentioned, and I felt jealousy at Renato and Rena dating.

"I see the look in your eyes. It was a joke, but listen, it doesn't matter. He doesn't bring anyone around. We've seen women, you know, flirt with him. But you don't have anything to worry about."

"He kissed me the other night."

They looked shocked.

"What happened?" Rena asked.

"Honestly, I don't remember. It was just out of the blue. We were arguing and then it happened. And I got a little jealous when I thought he was going out to sleep with someone. I don't know what made me think that. I mean, he can do whatever he wants. He's an adult. I'm an adult. We don't have any ties."

The dress coordinator returned with two gowns for me to try on. I took one out of her hands and went to change. It had embellishment pearls that ran down each of my arms and a long split in the middle.

"Oh my gosh. Have you talked to your mom?" McKayla smiled.

"Briefly. We used to so close."

"You have to trust that your mom will come around," Rena explained.

"Renato doesn't like the Costa family. If Tulio makes another move, Brilynn needs to be careful," McKayla said.

"Try the other on and let's see how it looks." Rena took a photo of me in the dress.

"I know it's gonna be beautiful and that baby's gonna be handsome in his tuxedo." McKayla grinned. I stepped down off the stool and strolled in to change gowns.

I switched into a shorter, silky, thin-strapped white dress, then came out and turned around with a jacket over my shoulders.

"Do you like him?" McKayla probed.

"I mean, he's all right. Tell you the truth, I'm not sure what we're doing. It's just weird. How we are like, where we cross each other but we don't talk about our feelings. I don't know how I feel."

"I think you like him. What is it? You're afraid to admit it?" Rena asked.

I groaned, planting my hands on my hips.

"He's an asshole. You even said you guys used to play around when you used to dance at the club. Have you been back to the club at all?" Rena reminded me that I needed to go grab my things.

"No. I mean we only had sex once."

He refused to let me drive on my own, I recalled.

Ding!

"Brilynn." I was shocked to see her at the dress shop. We hadn't spoken in a few days.

She waved, came to me, and I gave her a hug.

"Sorry I haven't gotten back to you sooner."

"Where have you been?"

"Crazy busy with work."

"You remember McKayla ,and this is Rena." I motioned between them.

Brilynn seemed off and ignored Rena's hand.

"You look beautiful," Brilynn said.

"Thanks, picking up a dress. Then we have lunch afterwards. Do you want to come?"

"I don't know. I hate to intrude with your friends."

"You're my friend too, Brilynn."

She sat and grabbed a champagne glass, and I continued to look through dresses. McKayla took another photo, and I told her to send them to me so I could text them to Renato.

Rena joked, and the tension went away as I changed for the fourth time. It was a long gown that went up to my neck, and I felt like a princess.

Buzz!

"That's your phone vibrating," Brilynn said.

"Can you check who it is?"

Brilynn grabbed my phone, and her expression seemed off.

"Who is it?"

"The club."

"I'll check it later. Can we go eat?"

"Sure. I need to return some shoes on our way to the mall," McKayla responded.

A few minutes later, I came out of the dressing room in my regular clothes and told the coordinator which one I wanted for my wedding. I went to pay, but she stated it was already covered by the Calabresi account, and I thanked her. Then all four of us got in the car and headed through traffic to lunch.

CHAPTER 10
Renato

THE CAR RIDE to the neutral warehouse was silent while I got my mind right before I stepped inside with my brothers. As the third oldest and in the middle, I often felt like my voice didn't get heard; they only needed me to go by their rules and forget that I have opinions. Today I'd make sure it was clear that neither Tulio nor anyone else would run my life. Reno got off the freeway, turned at the stop sign, and pulled into the grassy driveway, then turned the car off. I climbed out of the car and marched into the warehouse to see Sante, Savio, and EJ seated around the conference table like it was a science club.

"What is this meeting about?" I decided not to sit and stood behind the chair.

"Let's see, you've been making some moves without us."

"You haven't done enough for me. That motherfucker is fucking with me. He needs to be handled."

"You made your point, but we're not to push in on the Costa area," EJ explained.

"What do you want me to do? Just sit back while he fucks with us? You know me, you know I can't do that."

"Emers wants to meet with us. He's coming here now to our warehouse," Savio said.

"This is bullshit, what do we do? Tulio Costa isn't running shit; they're trying to take over."

"We know your wedding is about to happen. Maybe the stress is too much."

"EJ, don't talk to me like I need a therapy session."

"Emers would be stupid to make that move." Sante tried to plead their case.

"Tulio is probably not doing this under Emers's charge. Wouldn't have his permission if Emers knew, I bet."

"What do you think the mayor is up to, Savio?" Sante started to see things my way.

"Listen, I think they're all working together to make a hit. The mayor gets what he wants. In Chicago with Tulio to help, they're going to expand."

"I hear you, but we can't step in unless they directly hit us. They just hit his club," EJ said.

"Savio, what are they talking about?" Sante waited for his answer.

"After you fucked with him," Savio said.

"We're supposed to sit here doing nothing now?"

Emers and his men showed up with Tulio. Remo motioned them in.

Tulio and his man strode inside. Preparing for gunplay, my hand went straight to my hip; I was itching to shoot Tulio.

"Savio." Emers raised his hands up to show he was clear of guns.

"Have a seat." Savio pointed at both chairs at the end of the table.

"I'm not sitting next to that asshole."

"What are you doing here?" Tulio growled at me.

"Emers, we've had a truce between us for years. We need to know why you fucked with our place of business."

Tulio's left eye twitched.

"How's little Sonya? Bitch tried to steal from me, but I've missed her lately."

I tried to charge at him. Sante jumped up, grabbed me around the shoulder, and a guard stepped in between Tulio and me.

"Did you know your brother's working with the mayor?" Savio asked.

"That's a lie!" Tulio shouted.

"It's time to go." Emers patted Tulio on the back.

I dipped my right brow, slamming my hand on the table.

"You don't want war with us, Emers," Savio commanded.

"Do what you think is best," Emers replied.

"If we need to, I will make an example out of you." I pointed at Tulio.

"The mayor is too stupid to fuck with us. So I suggest you get on board," Sante called out to their backs.

Tulio paused, shifting his arms across his chest. "Take a hooker for a wife, make us think of you as an American family, maybe I'll get you a gift since I had to skip the wedding. I mean I already had her, and most of my men said she's really sweet and tight."

I responded by drawing my gun. Everyone around me froze.

"You're not stupid," Tulio taunted.

"You wouldn't even walk out of here alive if I didn't want to have my men clean up your remains when we have plans already."

"Shoot me then," Tulio egged me on.

I tightened my grip on the gun.

"Watch your mouth, Tulio."

The standoff lasted another few minutes before they finally decided to leave.

All of us looked at each other.

"What do you think? Think Emers is fucking with us?"

"He knows us and doesn't care. He's playing clueless. But he was backing his brother," Sante muttered.

"You need to make sure all the women are covered," Savio said.

"We have a charity dinner coming up soon," EJ recalled.

"Maybe the mayor will show his face." Savio removed his cell phone from his pocket.

"You have a wedding, and we need to get the rings." Sante stood. I hugged EJ and Savio, then strolled from the limo to our car and rode in the backseat with Sante.

"I need to run by and talk to Father after this," I said after I checked my phone to see a message from him.

Sante pulled out a cigar and passed me one.

Forty minutes later, we made it to the jewelry store and parked in front. Our driver, Alfred, shut the door after we climbed out. Sante wrapped his arm around my shoulder and guided me into the store. Bill, the store owner, opened his hands and clapped as we marched through the front door.

"I'm here with my brother. He needs to get a ring." Sante patted my chest.

"Well, welcome to our store, Renato. Sante bought a ring here. Your father, your brother, now you." He rubbed his hands together.

"Are you looking to get something classy, not gaudy?" Sante asked.

"Let's take a look."

"All right, wedding rings are over here."

He pulled out a tray.

Crash! Popppp!

All three of us dropped to the ground.

Buzz!

I crawled around to the side of the register, removed my

gun, and looked out to the side of the table. I saw a car with an arm out of the window.

Popppp! Popppp!

Sante and I sent shots back. Bill ran to the employee area and opened the door, calling for us to head out the back.

"Shit! Alfred," I called out.

"We can't, Renato. Need backup," Sante said, slogging me back.

"Remo should be on the way." I pulled my phone out and hit the emergency number.

"Fuck! Who's behind this bullshit?" Sante looked through the camera and saw the shooter all over the store. Bill had installed a bulletproof hatch that locked with his handprint.

"Tulio's name is all over it." I started to go back out, but Sante jumped in front of me.

"Savio is on his way."

Popppp! Rattata!

"Look, they're leaving." Bill waved at the monitors.

Remo was outside with Savio.

Leaving the security room, I headed outside and ran to the limo. Alfred was gone.

"Where's Alfred?" I looked from Savio to Remo.

"He's headed to the hospital," Remo said.

"Did you see who shot at us?" Sante meandered around the limo.

Bullet holes splayed from the windows to the tires.

"How bad is he?"

"Not sure. They wouldn't let me near him," Remo recalled.

"Need to call his wife." I watched a thick, fluffy cloud float across the sky.

"Let's go. The police will be here soon." Savio removed his business card from his pocket and slid it to Bill.

"Mr. Calabresi, you don't have to do that. I have insurance." Bill pushed the card away.

"I insist. This is on us." Savio looked him in the eye.

———

"Alfred will be fine. The bullets didn't hit a major artery," Father said.

"Glad to hear that." I stood in front of his desk, pacing back and forth. I wanted to wring Tulio's neck.

"Have you spoken with Sonya about what happened?"

"Not yet."

"The wedding is coming up soon. You need to explain to her what's to be expected."

"Expected?" I stopped pacing.

"She's expected to marry you, but she needs to understand that if she doesn't stay in the marriage after things are cleared with Tulio, she needs to sign over her rights."

"You can't take her son away."

"Then you need to make sure she understands my grandson will not be away from the family."

"Can we talk about this later?"

"No, today is a perfect example. What if my grandson was in the car with you?" he hissed.

"She's not going to sign away her rights."

"Have the attorney make her an offer. Either she'll sign or she won't."

"Did McKayla and Rena have to sign an agreement?"

He whirled his head around at me.

"This is about your fuckup and me cleaning it up. The Calabresi legacy is on the line. I like Sonya, but you didn't present her in the right way."

He was right. Sonya and I had come into this worse than McKayla and Rena.

"I need to get home."

"She's going to be a while."

"How do you know?"

"McKayla texted. They're at lunch."

"I need a drink."

"Tell me about what happened with Emers and Tulio at the warehouse."

Buzz!

Sonya: Which one do you like?

I looked down at my phone finally and saw Sonya had messaged me earlier photos of the dresses for the wedding.

CHAPTER 11

Sonya

OUR WAITER BROUGHT our menus to us, and McKayla slid her bags under the table and placed her phone in her purse. The mottled sky ranged from mid gray to dirty white.

"What did he say?" Rena asked.

"He said he likes me in or out of anything." I giggled and closed out of the thread.

"Brilynn, what are you going to get?" Rena said. At the mall, she had been standoffish, but I tried to include her in the conversation.

"I'll just have water," Brilynn answered.

"Did Adelina tell you she has the food catered for the wedding?" McKayla opened the menu.

Rena talked to the waitress and gave her order.

"Adelina is really supportive. I'm surprised both his parents haven't pushed me away. I know a baby that falls out of the sky and ends up on their doorstep isn't normal."

I glanced at Brilynn. She rolled her eyes.

"Are you okay?" Rena questioned Brilynn.

"Huh?" She took a large swig of the water.

"Last few days, Sonya has told us about her best friend. Now we meet you, and you've been quiet and standoffish. Now you roll your eyes when she just speaks," Rena explained, with her lips pressed in a thin line.

"Excuse me," Brilynn responded, clasping her hands together.

"Jealousy is all over your face." Rena slammed her water down.

"Jealous! Sonya, who is this woman?" Brilynn pointed her finger at Rena.

"Rena, we've been friends forever," I answered, pushing Brilynn's hand down.

"Watch your back with her, Sonya. I have a feeling she's not here to support you," Rena hissed, tossing her napkin on the table.

Brilynn jumped up in a huff, grabbed her bags, and ran out of the restaurant.

"Brilynn, wait! Rena, you are out of line." I jogged after Brilynn and caught her by the arm.

"Let me go," Brilynn said, stepping back.

"It's me, Brilynn. Sorry about Rena."

Brilynn calmed down.

"You're making a mistake," she said next to the car.

"Mistake? Could you please explain?"

She scanned the parking lot.

"Sonya, you shouldn't get involved with dangerous people like the Calabresi family."

"How do you know they're dangerous?"

"Why rush a wedding? Because it's all a plan to hurt you," she hissed.

"Talk to me, Brilynn," I begged.

"Tulio can help you," Brilynn said.

After hearing her admission, I stumbled back.

"Brilynn, tell me, what did you do?"

"He can't force you to marry him, especially in less than

a week." An array of emotions flitted across her face.

"I have a job, Brilynn, money to take care of my child and Mom."

"Tulio promised he will help you."

"Tulio is a liar."

She tried to reach out to me, and I jerked back.

"Come home with me." Disapproval gleamed in her eyes.

"He's lying, Brilynn."

"Your mom wasn't protected. What makes you think he'll be around once he gets you pregnant again?"

"Brilynn, please leave." I leveled a look of unmitigated disappointment toward her.

"He's the enemy, Sonya. Think about our friendship."

"How could you do it?"

"He said if we come to him and help bring Renato in, they'll protect us and won't come after our families."

"Not sure who you are, but the friend I knew wouldn't betray me like this."

I turned and strode back in the restaurant to the table and slouched down in my chair.

Buzz!

"She betrayed you, right?" Rena could tell I was upset.

"Tulio paid her off or threatened her."

"Sorry, Sonya, but she can't be trusted, and I don't want her around us," Rena replied.

Buzz!

Finally, I looked at my phone and saw that my old boss had messaged me to come by the club and pick up my things.

"I need to go to the club I used to work at and grab some stuff I left in my locker."

"Adelina's expecting us soon, so we can drop by on our way." McKayla pointed for the waitress to bring the check.

I'd never ordered, and my appetite had left after the argument with Brilynn.

———

Mentally, I wasn't prepared to handle more hurt from people I loved as our driver rushed over to the club. McKayla reached her palm out and covered my hand. The wind whined against the windows.

"She'll come around."

"Thanks." I wiped the tears off my face.

For the ride, I had gotten it in my head that I wouldn't let her bring me down. I'd focus on myself and my child. RJ would be bigger, and I'd remind him every day of the people in his life that love him. The car stopped in front of the club, and the driver started to come around and help me out, but I held my hand up to stop him.

"Do you need us to go in with you?" Rena suggested.

"I'm a big girl. Promise I'll be fine."

I jumped out, thanking my driver.

Pop! Pop!

Loud fireworks went off, and I dropped to the ground after hearing screams from the car. Large arms wrapped around me, and I was dragged inside.

"McKayla!" I yelled.

"Get her in the office!" a bouncer shouted.

"No! I need to call Renato."

"The car is out back. We're taking you to him. Please calm down," a guy said.

"I don't know you." I tried to shove him away.

"The Calabresi family is friends of ours." Finally, I looked at him, and he seemed okay, but I needed to talk to Renato before I got in the car with him.

"I need to talk to Renato."

He pulled his phone out, dialed a number, and put it on speaker.

"Dome." I heard Renato's deep voice.

"Renato! Someone shot at us," I rushed out, nervous and fidgeting around.

"Are you hurt, Sonya?" A worried tone marred his voice.

"No, I'm fine, but McKayla and Rena—"

"They're fine. Dome will bring you to me."

"Okay." My eyes rolled skyward.

"Dome."

"Yes, Boss." Concern grew in his voice.

"Protect her with your life."

"I promise," Dome answered and ended the call.

"Do you know if McKayla and Rena are hurt?" I asked after getting into the car.

"No, ma'am."

"I'm Sonya." I extended a hand.

"Dome," he responded, shaking my hand.

The rest of the car ride was silent. The car eventually stopped at the gate of the Calabresi home, and they checked Dome's car over. A few minutes later, he pulled up at the house, and I saw the car covered with bullet holes before he could stop me. I started to get out, but Renato yanked open the door first.

"Renato!" I hugged him around the waist, and he lifted my head back to see if I had any bruises.

"Are you hurt?"

"No, I promise. He saved me." I looked at Dome. Renato nodded, released his hold, and pulled money out of his pocket to pay him.

"It's cool. She's innocent." Dome tried to push the money back.

"Come to the office and see me," Renato demanded. Dome agreed.

"Sonya!" McKayla ran over to me, followed by Rena.

"Let's get you in the house." Adelina held her left arm open, with RJ on her right hip.

"RJ, I missed you." I kissed his forehead, took him out of her hands, and headed into the house.

"What happened?" Adelina asked.

"My boss from the club texted me to meet at the club." She took my phone out of my hand.

"I'll give this to Renato. Come and have a seat." Adelina and Marilyn sat next to us.

"When you screamed and the glass broke, I saw my life flash before my eyes." I held RJ against my chest.

"Renato was shot at too," Adelina said.

"Adelina, do you mind if I go put him down? I need to relax and get my head right."

"Take your time. We have dinner almost ready."

"Thank you."

I took RJ to the guest room I'd used the last time I was in their home and lay down with him in the crib to get my nerves together.

Ring!

"Hello."

"Sonya," Brilynn whispered.

I stood up and shut the door, kicking off my shoes.

"Brilynn."

"After our fight, I didn't feel right with the way we left things."

RJ started to fuss, so I shifted him to his stomach and rubbed his back to calm him down.

"Brilynn, I was just shot at. Did you have anything to do with it?" I roamed over to the bathroom so RJ wouldn't hear.

"No. Was RJ with you?" A solemn feeling seeped through the phone.

"If he was…"

"Sonya, I think you know I would never put RJ in harm's way. If someone shot at you, then it means Renato is behind you almost dying."

"At one point, I'd have never mistrusted our friendship, but it seemed strange that after we had an argument, we're almost killed."

"Stop being naïve," Brilynn sassed.

"Goodbye, Brilynn."

"Do you need to eat?"

I gasped and looked up. Renato stood in the doorway of the bathroom.

My stomach growled right at that moment.

"Food and alcohol is what I need right now."

"Marilyn will bring you a plate. Relax up here." He started to turn away.

"Renato…" My eyes clouded, and I bit my bottom lip nervously.

"Yeah?" He stood with his hands in his pockets.

"Brilynn." Worry lined my forehead.

"I know." He rubbed his chin.

"How?" My spine jerked upright.

"McKayla and Rena told me, and I had people follow her after she moved back home."

"You should have told me."

"Sonya, we both aren't in the headspace to argue."

"Maybe we shouldn't marry."

His eyes darkened at my statement.

"This is a reason why we have to get married. Look how they won't stop until we've officially secured the deal."

"Sorry, my choices contributed and made it hard, my life is crazy." I climbed on the bed next to RJ.

"That's not true."

We gazed at each other.

"So the wedding is happening."

He cleared his throat, slipped his hand in his pocket, and pulled out a small black box.

"If you don't like it, we can find a new one," he said, lifting the lid.

"It's beautiful." Renato cupped my left wrist and slid the ring onto my finger.

Knock! Knock!

"Hope I'm not interrupting anything." Adelina held a tray in her hand.

"Need to meet with the guys."

"Okay."

"Talk to you later."

"Are you coming back for me, I mean us?" My heart stuttered.

His top lip curved up in a smile.

"Only way to have a wedding is with the bride and groom." He pressed a kiss on RJ's head.

Adelina grinned as she took the tray of food over to the nightstand and then picked up my hand with the ring. The door closed behind her, and I lay back against the head-board in thought over the past few hours and days.

"Whatever you've done, keep doing it because he's less angry."

"Doubt it's because of me." I patted RJ on the back, and she looked down at him, caressing his dark, curly hair.

"You underestimate yourself. I believe it's more than RJ that makes him want to go out right now and find who caused today's shooting," Adelina expressed.

"Thank you for the food." I needed to change the subject.

"Have you spoken with your mom about the wedding?"

"She's going to come, but my best friend won't."

"Brilynn's not coming? Why?"

"Long story. Can I just eat and enjoy my little boy for the night?"

"He's going to be so handsome at the wedding. Get some rest and try to relax."

"Thank you, Adelina. Not sure what I did to get a mother-in-law like you."

"Experiences may have been different, but to be in the mafia world, you need allies," Adelina said.

CHAPTER 12

Renato

THE WARM SMILE on my son's face was the only thing that could bring me back from going on a rampage of revenge. After the incident at the jewelry store and Sonya almost being killed, it forced me to look closer at what my next steps would be. Tulio thought we would be intimidated by threats, but he hadn't seen what I could really do. Sante helped dress RJ in his tuxedo, and Savio straightened my tie before they called us down for the wedding. Sonya and RJ hadn't left my side since we came to my parents' home that night. Vincenzo had her do work from home, and if anything was needed for our son, I had my men pick it up for her. My mom planned the entire wedding with Sonya, and McKayla helped when she could.

The family home had more than enough space to have a wedding and reception. The land our home sat on was over three acres with a pool, basketball court, play area for the kids, and tennis court. They'd set the vows to happen at the gazebo, lined the chairs with white roses, and engraved our initials of R and S on the silverware. The shoot-out still had Sonya frazzled, so I'd taken a little step back from meetings to watch over her and make sure she wouldn't run away.

Sonya hadn't heard from Brilynn since her phone conversation that day. I wanted to take care of her, but I knew hurting her would only hurt Sonya in the end. The agreement my father wanted her to sign plagued my mind. I didn't know if I still wanted to go through with it; too much was going on.

I could hear Mom barking orders downstairs, getting everything organized. Marilyn's focus was the kids, and her daughter Cora had arrived to help.

"You ready?" Savio checked over my suit.

"Actually, no." My palms became damp, my mouth dry, and my stomach was in a knot.

Savio grinned. "That's good. You should always be on your toes when you marry someone."

Sonya's mom was here. She seemed to be okay when we introduced her to my mom, and she wasn't confrontational with me. I blocked everything else out of my mind for the day. My son was next to me. My brothers. Today was about Sonya and me becoming one.

"How much more time?"

Sante checked his watch.

Knock!

"Renato, they're ready," Father said, opening the door.

He and I hadn't talked since he'd confronted me about the agreement. The other families weren't on board with my plans to get rid of Tulio. At the end of the day, no one could protect my family like me.

"Is she ready?"

He nodded.

"Time to go, nephew." Sante rose with RJ in his arms.

Savio hugged me and strolled out first, then Sante and RJ.

"She looks beautiful," Father said.

"Is Mother calmed down now?"

"She loves this stuff. Doubt we'll have any peace."

The men lined up at the back hallway that led to the backyard. Violinists started to play. Both aisles were filled with friends and families, and a few other mafia members arrived with their wives. As I drew closer to the gazebo, I shook hands with the officiator. Scanning the crowd, I nodded at Sonya's mother. Courtney didn't smile, just looked forward. I knew it would take time for her to understand what was going on. But I could always guarantee her daughter would be safe with me. To relieve Sonya's stress, I'd taken over the payments for her mother's medical treatments.

"Please stand," the pastor announced. The music started, prompting Sonya's entrance on Vincenzo's arm. Sonya came out, smiled, and headed down the aisle. A veil concealed her face, with a long train behind her. The dress fit perfectly. Vincenzo took her hand as he helped her up the stairs, rubbing her palm and kissing the back of her hand.

"Please sit," the pastor requested. I removed her veil, revealing her wide eyes sparkling with the light makeup. Her light brown hair was styled straight down with a part in the middle; I pushed a strand behind her ear and lifted her chin.

"You look beautiful."

"Thank you."

RJ giggled, and everyone laughed.

The pastor went through the vows, and I never took my eyes off her. I felt my breath hitch when I saw a locket around her neck with our initials. I became someone's husband and father in a short span of time, and shockingly, I was content. Everything started to make sense in my world.

"Do you Renato Calabresi take Sonya Eden to be your lawfully wedded wife?"

"I do."

Sante passed me the ring, and I slid it onto her finger.

"Do you Sonya Eden take Renato Calabresi to be your lawfully wedded husband?"

Sonya looked at her mom, then RJ, then back at me with a hint of a smile.

"I do."

"I now pronounce you husband and wife. You may kiss the bride." He stood back, everyone clapped, then we kissed. I pulled her close to my chest, and all of a sudden, the baby started to laugh and clap.

I leaned around Savio to grab him from Sante. Sonya waved at our friends and family, then we stepped down from the gazebo and went to take pictures.

During the reception, Savio and Sante recited speeches, the food came out, and I kissed Sonya on the lips again.

"If I didn't say it already, thank you."

She rubbed the lipstick off my lips.

"Your mom did a great job, but I'm ready to sit back with RJ and watch a movie." She gripped my hand, and I lifted it to my lips.

"I have a surprise."

"Surprise for me?"

"Honeymoon."

"Where are we going?" Panic infiltrated her eyes.

"Do you trust me?"

"Yes."

I grabbed her hand and told her to follow me. We dropped RJ off with my parents. They knew about my plans for the cabin.

"You don't seem like the honeymoon type," she teased, then hugged her mom before McKayla and Rena said goodbye.

"Well, it will help make up for what's been going on. It seems like a long time since we last been alone. We have a cabin where we can spend some time together."

At my revelation, Sonya slowed down a few feet from the limo.

"This isn't you planning to get rid of me, is it?"

I lifted my hand with the ring finger.

"It's official. You're my wife. There's no plot; it's only to protect you."

"Is it? Okay. I trust you," she said.

"Let's go."

We hopped into the limo while Remo got into another car ahead of us and drove a few hours to my private cabin I purchased when I'd made my first million. Sonya stared at the No Trespassing signs. High trees brooded over the night, and the moon clamored from the back.

"What about our clothes?" She anchored her attention on me.

"McKayla packed your things."

"Wow, Renato, this is huge." She beamed at me.

"Next time we can bring RJ."

"How many times have you come here?"

"Whenever I need to get away."

The limo drove close to the front of the cabin, the guards having scouted the area beforehand.

I helped her out of the car and lifted her train from the back so she could walk up the stairs. She scanned around, surprised at the massive layout when she opened the front door. It was around eight thousand square feet with a barn, fireplace, Jacuzzi, large TV, and a theater room in the back. Plus, I had my own shooting range for practice.

"This is beautiful." A flicker of a smile passed her lips.

"Thanks. I've had it for a while."

"Hard to believe you come here alone."

"What do you want to know, Sonya?" I fell in step with her.

"You don't bring women here?"

"No. You're the first."

She stared at me as Remo brought our bags in and dropped them by the door.

"Can I call and check on RJ?"

"Four bedrooms, pick a room."

"Oh." Sonya blinked, stunned.

A flush of embarrassment sketched her face.

"So we don't have to consummate this fake marriage." She giggled. I nudged her up against the back of the couch.

"Nothing fake about me, Sonya." I licked her bottom lip and gripped her neck. Her breath hitched. I slid my hands under her dress, pushed her panties to the side, and gripped her pussy.

"Renato." With sudden heat and sensitivity, she stood before me, baring her vulnerability.

"Yeah?" Secrets swirled around us like spirits of the dead looking in on the sins of the living.

"Take me upstairs." A grin curled around her full lips.

I bent down and gently lifted her up. She wrapped her legs around my waist as I ascended the stairs to the bedroom. Sonya gripped the back of my neck and stuck her tongue down my throat. Her body felt so good in my arms. The bulge in my pants pushed against her stomach. After shutting the door behind us, I placed her on her feet, turned her around, and unzipped the dress. She stepped out in a black thong and strapless bra. I saw a few stripes across her stomach from giving birth and dropped to my knees and kissed her scars.

"Mmmmm... Renato." Sonya held the back of my head. I ran a hand up and over to squeeze her breasts. I unhooked her bra, tossed it aside, and pulled her thong down. Pushing her to lay on the bed, I lifted her foot and massaged her ankle.

"Please," she moaned, her voice broke low on the word.

Trailing my tongue up her calf muscle, I dropped small bites up to her sex.

"Beautiful girl." My tone brooked no argument.

"Renato, stop teasing me," she said with a breathy sigh.

I grinned at her lack of patience. I stood back and removed my shirt and shoes, unbuckled my pants, hovered over her, and kissed her lips, slowly feeding her my tongue.

"I need you to understand something." I let out a breath I hadn't even realized I was holding.

"Anything." She exhaled, blinking with feigned innocence.

"What we did a year ago was just the beginning." I brushed a hand across her cheek.

"Huh." She arched a questioning eyebrow in my direction.

I flicked her nipple, and she slammed her eyes shut.

"Baby, I don't do vanilla sex." I had a mischievous look on my face.

"Okay." Her breath escaped, soft and moist, a sinless sound, almost pure.

"That's a good girl." Relief washed over me.

I slipped down to face her pussy and swiped my tongue over her lower lips; her slick opening tasted like I remembered.

"Arghhhh, God." She tossed her head back, fanning her hair.

"Pussy wet and warm, baby." I stuck my middle finger in; she spread her legs wider.

Popppp! Popp!

"What the fuck!"

"Renato! What's going on?"

Gunfire rang out, and I was pissed at the interruption.

"Stay here." My grave frown deepened into a scowl.

I fixed my pants, put my shoes back on, and grabbed a shirt.

"Where are you going?" She climbed off the bed and reached for her dress.

"To check on my men."

"Renato, did someone follow us?"

I ignored her, jogged down the stairs, and looked through the peephole. I saw Remo talking to some of my men. I unlocked the door and marched over to them, hearing loud shouts and more shots go off in the distance.

"We have company," Remo said, pointing to the back road near the lake.

"How many?"

He led me to where our men had found a breach in the security gate. Ian was standing guard. "Not sure, I heard a few shots go back and forth."

Poppp! Pop! Pop!

I raised my gun, took the flashlight from Ian, and walked through the woods. Remo whispered in the head-set, demanding an update on how many guys were surrounding us.

"Over there!" Ian shouted. I saw movement, bent down, raised my gun, and shot in that direction.

"Argh!" someone cried out; I ran to catch up.

I slowly shuffled up to him, gun raised. He was on the ground, holding his leg.

"Who sent you?" I pointed the gun at his head.

"Fuck you!" he spat.

"Wrong answer."

Pop!

CHAPTER 13
Sonya

RENATO'S SURPRISE LITTLE HONEYMOON, or lack of honeymoon, was a disaster last night. I woke up in bed wrapped in covers alone. I tried to stay up and wait for him, but he never came back, and the guards wouldn't let me leave. I tried to call and check on RJ, but it was too late, and he was asleep. I threw the covers back and stood to stretch, then headed to the bathroom and looked at myself in the mirror. All night I had nightmares. I tossed and turned, worrying Renato was in trouble or worse. I blew out a breath and picked up the toothbrush, immediately reminded of the large five-carat ring on my finger. Anyone would love being the wife of Renato Calabresi, but all I could feel was sadness.

"Don't cry," I muttered and turned to pick up the paste to brush my teeth. After rinsing out my mouth, I set the shower to the right temperature, dropped the towel, and gathered my thoughts as I cleaned the night off me. Forty minutes later, I came downstairs in shorts and a crop top that McKayla had picked out.

"Where is he?" Passing Remo, I traveled to the kitchen and started to make coffee.

"Mr. Calabresi would like for you to meet him outside."

"He can come and tell me that." I was done listening to orders.

"Mrs. Calabresi, it's important."

I whirled my head around, my stomach dropping at the sudden realization something terrible could have happened to him, and I was here cursing him in my head.

"Take me to him."

Remo opened the door, and I noticed a few bags outside.

"Tell me, Remo, is he hurt?"

"He's okay, ma'am."

"Then why can't he come to me?" I stopped and crossed my arms over my chest.

Remo smiled, and I turned around to face the back.

"Renato, what the hell?"

He stood on top of a yacht; it was massive—at least three levels from what I could tell.

"How did…" I started to walk and paused in my step.

"Nothing to worry about," Remo said.

The staff helped me to step on, and I strolled up to the deck, where Renato held his hand out for me.

"Where did you go?"

"Come inside so we can talk." He jutted his chin to the cabin.

"Renato, I want the truth." The corner of my mouth kicked up in a sneer.

"Sonya, come and talk."

He escorted me into a living room; it was set up with a table for two, food, and candles.

"Sit." He pulled the chair out for me.

"Why didn't you come back last night?"

He ran a hand down his face.

"Sonya, I apologize, but we caught some people that breached my security." His jaw twitched.

"How?"

"Not sure. Remo is investigating." He poured a glass of champagne.

"Renato, this pretending like last night didn't happen is not fair."

"I need you to understand, last night was a threat and a serious one."

"Clearly."

"One of the reasons I need to know what your expectations are in this marriage."

"Now you bring up this conversation." My brows crinkled in confusion.

His idea of making up for the night before was not going as planned. I wanted to know if we were truly moving as one.

"Father bought this when we first moved here to America."

"Changing the subject won't help."

"You look beautiful today."

"Thank you."

"I know our honeymoon got interrupted. You didn't deserve to have your life fall into such chaos."

I felt a lump in my throat.

"I wanted us to be on the same page."

"Me too."

"Tulio will be dealt with, and anyone else that tries to harm you and my son."

"I know."

He closed his eyes for a moment.

"Afterwards you have a choice." He began to stroke feather-light touches over my hand.

"Choice about what?" My hair unraveled, falling into my eyes.

"What you overheard Tulio talking with the mayor about. It is sensitive information for my family."

"I know, which is why I told you."

"With you being my wife now, there are some things you have to understand that are part of our family."

"Okay."

"You need to know that you can leave, and I'll give you a nice settlement from the agreement."

"Like a divorce agreement?" My expression turned serious.

"The second I resolve the situation, you can either stay married to me or leave and pursue your goals in school, work, and start fresh in a new home. But my son will stay with me."

I sprang out of my seat.

"Leave my son!" My blood was boiling with contempt.

"Calm down, Sonya."

"I can't have my son away from me, Renato. I don't understand."

"If you sign an agreement, you will be paid handsomely."

"Basically disappear like I never existed. He's my son. I'm not giving him up."

"Then you understand that if you stay, you're going to have around-the-clock guards. Your life will always be attached to the Calabresi name, and you will have to follow rules."

"Are you giving me an ultimatum?"

"I need you to know what you're getting into."

We glared at each other.

"I am not giving up my child, and I don't want your money. Is that what you've thought this whole time?"

"No! Last night, and the other events, should make you understand how this works."

"No, you wait. I've proven and proven my loyalty. I told you about Tulio and Brilynn. What else do you want from me? I can't give you any more of me!" I screamed, smacking him across the face.

"Do you think this is easy for me? I didn't know about him!" he shouted back.

I stormed off and found the bedroom, pushing the door open and seeing my bags.

"What are you doing?" He ran behind me.

"I'm leaving."

"You're not leaving," he said.

"Yes, I am; my son and I will be fine." I snatched the two bags up and went to step around him, but he blocked me.

"That's your problem." He grabbed the bag out of my hand.

"What?"

"Every time we talk, it's 'my son.' Your son? No, it's our son," he argued, tossing my bags across the room.

"That's not true!"

"For me to trust you fully, besides that ring on your finger, I need to know you have my son's best interests at heart, and that means him being protected at all times. Knowing that I'm his father. Do you get that, Sonya?"

I slapped him again and raised my hand to slap him once more, but he gripped my wrist and pushed me down. He grabbed me by the ankle, pulling me to the edge of the bed.

"Stop leaving me. You keep running. Taking my child away."

In that moment, I could see the fear and loss in his eyes. He looked away, and I melted at the vulnerability in his tone and felt shame for what I had done. I cupped his face, then crashed our lips together. Renato ripped off my shorts while I slid my hand down his chest and helped him take his pants off.

Our eyes stayed glued to each other. He moved down my stomach to my pussy and stuck his tongue inside, and I hissed from his long, warm tongue breaching my core. I thrust my hips forward.

"I'm sorry, baby!" I cried out.

"Prove it." He smacked my thigh, bit it gently, and clenched both my ass cheeks. Renato kissed up my stomach, then my chest, flicking his tongue over my left nipple and tweaking the right.

"You're my bitch, Sonya, you understand?"

"Mmm-hmmm… Yes, sir." A million butterflies took flight inside my belly; then he spoke, and every one of those butterflies went still.

"Good girl. Taste your sweet nectar, baby." After he removed his right hand from pussy, he fed it to me.

"Sorry, please forgive me." I tried to touch him, but he held both my hands above my head. Then I heard a click and turned to see handcuffs on both wrists.

"Renato," I cooed, my face heated.

He smirked; his dark-eyed gaze tugged at my heart.

"Light or hard?" he demanded with a curt nod.

"Huh…?" I was delirious at this point; everything in the room was spinning.

"I told you I don't do vanilla sex. Do you want it light or hard?" he growled.

"Hard!" My throat squeezed down on a scream.

He dropped his boxers and fisted his dick; I licked my lips and spread my legs in anticipation of his long, thick girth.

He used his other hand to cup my pussy lips. He rubbed his thumb across, spread them apart, spit, then smacked hard over my clit.

"Arghhhh fuck!" Our first time together, he spanked me and that experience has stayed with me forever. I'd never felt such pleasure as what he introduced me to that night.

"Keep your eyes down here." He pinched my cheek, and I watched him tap his dick against my lips.

Smack!

"You're doing good, baby." He kissed my forehead, and I slid the tip of his dick inside, pulled my legs back to my ears, and thrust forward. My mouth dropped open as he pumped in and out at a steady pace; I tried to get out of the cuffs.

"Oh, shit!" he hummed and dipped his head in the crook of my neck and down to my breasts, sucking his favorite part on my body.

"Renato, I'm coming!"

"No!" He pulled out of me, and my eyes popped open, but he flipped me over before I could protest and lifted me in a perfect arch before stroking me from behind.

Smack!

"Yes!" My eyelids fluttered like a butterfly's wing.

"Follow my rules! You understand?" He spewed his demands as thick as black smoke.

"Yes, sir!"

"You're my dirty slut, and you belong to me." His hulky mass hung over me.

"Yes! I'm yours."

He tightened his hand around my hair, biting me on the shoulder lightly as our skin slapped together, and his words of praise encouraged me.

"You're beautiful, Sonya; thank you for my son." His words came out delicate, an easy saying wrapped in a whisper.

"Ohhhh..." I cooed.

He turned my head to the side and caught my lips.

"I love you." His voice was soft.

"I love you too!" A familiar recollection filled the void in my head, spinning memories of our previous night together.

"Come for me, baby."

I shook in his arms as he picked up his pace, and I

orgasmed while my legs shook and my eyes rolled to the back of my head. After I fell on the bed and caught my breath, he fell onto me. I felt his body convulse and release itself inside of me. My eyes slowly closed, and I began to drift off to sleep.

———

Renato opened the door for me, and I climbed inside; he put RJ in his car seat and put on *Blue's Clues*, a show he watched all the time. Our time together at the cabin had been magical, and it was relaxing to see Renato shed his mafia persona. We'd cooked together, watched movies, and made love each night, morning, and sometimes in the shower. He decided to drive tonight to my mom's place; I glanced out of the side mirror and saw Remo close. When we got back to town yesterday, my mom asked if we'd come for dinner. I said sure, after we had a few days to connect and picked up RJ to go home. Now Renato and I had continued our conversation.

"Are you nervous?"

He had a way of catching me in moments where I drifted off in a daze.

"A little."

Renato extended a hand to pick up my palm, bringing it to his lips.

"Either way, I'm not going anywhere." He stopped at the light, leaned over, and kissed me on the lips.

"How many cars do you have?" The black and gold interior of his Audi looked like it cost a lot of money.

"A few."

We made it to Mom's home like we were a part of a presidential campaign, with cars following us and parked all down the block. Renato turned the car off, came around, and pulled my door open while I grabbed RJ's bag. With RJ on his hip, I took his hand as we approached the door and it swung open. I smiled and reached for a hug. She released me, and Renato tried to shake her hand, but she ignored him and took the baby out of his arms.

"Mom, this is my husband, Renato," I said.

"Yes. We officially meet, Mr. Calabresi. I'm Courtney. Come inside."

She rubbed RJ's head and pointed at a stack of toys on the ground for him.

"You can call me Renato."

Mom had cooked smothered pork chops, green beans, mac and cheese.

"I hope you eat this type of food." Mom motioned at the table.

"That's fine, Miss Eden; I eat anything," he said, winking at me. He pulled my chair out, and I sat down next to him while she continued to hold on to the baby.

"What exactly do you do, Mr. Calabresi?" she asked.

"I work at my family's company."

"So you're not a criminal."

"Mother," I hissed.

"Sonya, be quiet."

"Sonya, she's right. My family is multi-dimensional; we do many things. But I can promise you that she is in good hands."

"What about the people that tried to hurt me over Sonya?"

"That was me. I started all this."

"I don't understand. Sonya?"

"I was the one that stole from Renato."

"You did what?" she asked.

"I stole from him. He never knew, he didn't even know about the baby."

"But, Sonya, you told me that the father didn't want anything to do with the baby. But it was a lie."

"I'm not perfect. We're not perfect. You have to under-stand, but we're going to make it work."

"So you're really going to stay married?"

"Yes," he and I answered at the same time.

"I don't know what to say." She looked flabbergasted.

"I just need you to trust me and love us. Also, I need you to stay away from Brilynn."

I informed her how Brilynn had acted.

"What are you doing, Sonya? Good Lord, think it through and get an attorney. You're battling your best friend. Is he forcing you?"

"No. Brilynn betrayed me because she is working for his enemy."

Renato turned red, and his grip got tighter on my hand.

"That's not true." Mom argued.

The tension is thick.

"I can't believe any of this mess," Mom responded, shifting RJ to her lap.

"I wouldn't lie to you, Mom. We talked, she said to my face what she was up to and how she would get me away from him."

"What about RJ? How do you know something won't suddenly happen and he's without a mother?"

"He has forgiven me. I have forgiven him. And we're going to truly work on a relationship. But I need your support."

"This is too much, Sonya."

"I know. But how are you doing? Have you been going to your doctor's appointments?"

"I have, but I need you to promise me that you'll protect yourself."

"I will."

"So we will make this work together."

Renato rubbed my thigh under the table. I calmed

down, stood, and shuffled around to hug my mom. Then I told her about my position at the company.

RJ splashed the bubbles in the tub while I poured water in his hair. During dinner with my mom, she was still a spectacle, but Renato had held casual conversation with her.

"Let's see what we can do for a vacation."

"I don't know, let's try for something a little different," Renato suggested.

"What do you have in mind? Just a family vacation maybe? The three of us or include other couples?"

He wrapped the baby up in a towel and started to head to his bedroom before reading him a good night story. I showered and slid in the bed; not long after, Renato walked in on the phone. I turned the light off and started to doze off, then felt a kiss on the back of my neck and smiled.

CHAPTER 14
Renato

"COME SIT."

"Did you cook?"

"I did it to help me think, grow up in an Italian family with plenty of people to test out your meals."

"I'm surprised. You didn't seem like the type to wake up early to fix a meal." Sonya picked up a piece of pineapple and started to feed RJ.

We shared a kiss.

"What are you doing today?"

"I have work plus I have to meet with the girls. What are your plans?" She scooped up some yogurt.

"Have to meet with my brothers. We have to talk about what happened at the cabin."

"I can take the baby with me."

"I can grab him later after my meetings."

"Should we talk about dinner?"

I brought her plate to the table and sat down across from her and RJ.

"It's impossible for me to see eye to eye with your mother, as it is with you and my father."

"True, I thought he liked me." Sonya muttered.

"He does, but he's old-school Italian and doesn't like anything that will hurt his legacy." RJ tried to grab her hand with the spoon of yogurt.

"We're really married."

"Do we need to talk about anything else?"

"No, I don't so."

"Going forward we have to trust and be loyal to each other."

"I agree."

"Plus, I liked how you felt when you submitted to me."

She blushed. "Me too."

I covered her hand.

"Our bedroom is only for us, I promise."

"I trust you, and you made me feel comfortable."

"Glad you're comfortable, and we can explore more later." I winked and finished my breakfast as we talked about RJ and SJ needing to have a playdate.

———

My brothers didn't know about what happened at the cabin, so I needed to inform them. Leaving Ian to watch Sonya, I left the house and climbed into the waiting car. Sante sent me a message.

Sante: Check this out.

I opened the video and saw Sanchez doing a new conference about a reelection. I ground my teeth and patted my side to check my gun. Alfred came up to the location, pulled up, and started to get out of the car.

"I got the door, Alfred."

"They didn't take me out, Boss," he joked, and I guffawed. The shooting had left him with a shoulder wound and one to his leg.

"You rang?"

"We need to talk about some things, since you've ignored my calls." EJ scoffed.

"I was in the cabin. I didn't have time to get back here."

"But you made a move on Tulio," EJ hissed.

"He's not to be touched yet, Renato," Savio complained.

"Are you serious?"

"Yeah," EJ fussed, leaning forward.

"The motherfucker had people out at my cabin, and I'm done being nice."

"I understand. We need to think clearer and be precise," Savio replied.

"Precise about what?"

"Are we all in agreement? Take Tulio out," Sante remarked.

"I think we are, and what about his brother? If he wants to go to war, we shouldn't be quick for another war," Savio answered.

"Our names are still in the news from what happened. This video situation." EJ slammed his hand on the table.

"Fuck that. My woman and child could have been killed. I'm done being nice. Kenneth Sanchez did a conference. I want him dead."

"We can't just go get the mayor," EJ argued.

"We're not. I can make it look like an accident."

"To be clear, we are not killing the mayor," EJ said.

Sante and I made eye contact.

"The charity event is coming up. He will be at the event, perhaps we can talk to him," Sante explained.

"You can talk to him. But fuck him up. He thinks we're not going to do anything. We need to prove him wrong."

"You will be in a position that puts us on their radar." EJ threw his hands up.

"Until you get a woman you don't understand."

"What is that supposed to mean?" EJ asked.

"I mean, at my wedding, you and Cora, what's going on

there? She's like a sister to us. I hope you haven't touched her."

He tried to charge at me; I must have hit a nerve. Sante got in between us, luckily, because I was ready to hurt somebody.

"She is a friend. That's it; you just focus on your runaway bride and the son you just found," EJ said.

I started to push Sante away, extending hand to grab him and figure out a way to torture him." Sante shoved him back; Savio didn't move.

"Say that to my face," I spat.

"You two stop. We're brothers. We shouldn't be fighting like children," Sante pleaded.

"I am sitting here now watching two grown men, brothers, about to fight for childish bullshit," Savio said.

"Savio, it's not bullshit. My family was threatened. You know I don't play those games. Fuck this. I make the decisions when it comes to my child."

"Everything you do affects this entire family." Savio stood and walked around the table to get in my face.

"Get out of your head," EJ said.

"EJ is right. Like if Kenneth goes missing. They come looking at us and send a warning shot," Savio said.

"What type of warning shot did you do?" Sante asked.

"Something that goes boom."

All of their mouths dropped open.

"What did Renato do?" EJ asked.

"I knew you three would be against me killing Tulio." I jerked out of Sante's grip.

"Renato, speak," Savio demanded.

"I did the next best thing. I blew up his restaurant."

"Reckless, Renato," EJ grunted.

"I suggest you three have my back."

Savio gripped the back of my neck.

"Of course, but you didn't clear this with me or Sante," he said.

"I didn't have to clear other things."

"Those jobs didn't have to do with taking out a boss or underboss," Sante responded.

"Jobs that have to be cleared first." EJ tried to jump back in the conversation.

"Well, do your job, brother. I destroy it, and you clean it up. It's simple."

I left the warehouse and got in my car. We drove to the area of Tulio's restaurant and saw the Fire Department there, with employees of the restaurant outside crying, hugging each other. Remo had made sure that it was empty so I wouldn't hurt innocent people. But I wanted to make sure Tulio knew that when I retaliated, it was with reason. I scanned the area and saw Tulio pull up, rolling his window down to talk to the police. He happened to glance over and saw my car as I tilted my head to the right. He rolled his window back up. I rolled mine up as well and drove out of the area. *Now we'll see how he moves next.*

A few minutes later, we'd pulled up at the mayor's home to drop off a package. Remo had paid off a delivery-man, and he rang the bell. The door opened, and his wife, I assumed, signed and thanked him. She looked curiously at the envelope, flipped it open, and a hard grimace spread across her face as she dropped the contents on the ground. A second later, the mayor came up behind her and picked them up, and she started to cry and yell at him.

He looked pissed. Finally he saw my car, and I waved from my open window. He started to come outside toward my car. Remo drove off; it wasn't time. I wanted him to worry, to think we were coming—and we would. It was only a matter of time.

———

Alfred took a break after I got to work at the Calabresi building. I got off the elevator to Sonya's floor and saw her at her desk talking to another employee. Some man had her laughing. I normally didn't care, but a hint of jealousy ran up my spine. My lips formed a thin line as I moved over in between them and backed her behind me.

"Mr. Calabresi, nice to see you," he said, a wide smile on his face. The guy couldn't be more than twenty-two, a wannabe frat boy, in college a year or two with Mommy and Daddy paying his bills.

"Oh, what are you doing?" Sonya placed her hand on my lower back.

I looked at her, then at him.

"Is there a reason you're in my wife's face?"

"Oh, sorry. I didn't know you were married."

I lifted her hand to show her ring finger.

"This ring didn't make it clear."

There was no eye contact between us.

"I think I need to get back to work." His mouth gaped open.

"Yeah." I forced an exhalation through my pinched lips.

"So you didn't have to do that. It was really innocent. We were just talking."

"You don't just talk to guys. They see you, notice you smile at them, and think it's an opening."

"Are you jealous?"

"No, I'm not jealous. I don't get jealous." I took her in. Her body was a mystery, shown in moments of passion, but never completely revealed.

"Mmmmm…" She stretched her arms around my neck, and I lifted her up on top of the desk, sliding my hand under her skirt.

"We're in public."

"So?"

"Renato. You can't do that."

"Who says I can't do it? Isn't it my company?" She stood against me with one leg crossed.

"Yeah, but we're out in the open."

"Fine, come with me."

She waved at the stack of files on her desk.

"That can wait."

"Honey, we can't do anything here." She drew her shoulders in, protecting her body.

"We work in different areas." I stroked her arm.

"It will look weird, the boss's new wife getting special treatment."

I helped her down from the desk and took her to my office and locked the door behind us, pressing a kiss on her lips against the back of the door.

"Have lunch with me."

"In your office?"

"Yes, I need to talk to you."

"Please tell me you didn't kill someone." She ran a hand up my chest.

"I just need you to listen to the guards and Ian."

I grabbed her around the waist, then sucked on her ear.

"You're scared. There's nothing to be afraid of here." I captured her hands in mine.

"Tell me then." She flashed a smile.

"I blew up a restaurant." I bit her cheek gently, then licked the sting away.

"Oh my God. Are you serious?" Her eyes went wide.

"I had to make some kind of statement."

"But Renato..."

"Nothing for you to worry about besides extra security."

"Do I have a choice?" She pushed me back.

"No. Can you do that?" I drew my brows together.

"Yes." She elevated her chin, and I pinched her cheek.

"Good. Come eat. My assistant had food delivered." My

fingers danced over her flat stomach before finding her silky smooth thigh.

Sonya sauntered to the couch in my office. I had food from Savio's bar delivered and checked in on RJ from the video monitor on my phone. Sonya bit into her burger, then sipped on her Coke.

"Are cameras everywhere in this building?" she asked, her voice a bare whisper.

"Yep."

"At your house?"

"Our house, yes."

"Oh."

I rubbed up her shoulder, pulling her close to me.

"RJ and you are the most important. I wouldn't be doing my job as your husband if I didn't care."

"I understand, Renato. All of this is still new to me."

Knock! Knock!

"Let me get the door." I released her and went to unlock the door. Vincenzo stood with a wide grin on his face.

"Why is your door locked?" Vincenzo asked.

"I'm fucking my wife."

"Renato!" Sonya yelled, and I smirked.

"Don't see how she puts up with you. Here's the projection numbers for the bid on a new construction site I like."

"Thanks, I'll look them over later." I took the folder out of his hand, then shut the door in his face.

CHAPTER 15

Renato

LIGHTS FLASHED against the window of our limousine; it was time for the charity event we attended every year. A host of high-profile families and local political figures showed up, and it was all under the guise of charity work, but we did some business deals here at the same time. Everyone agreed the event was neutral ground and no gunfire should be shed, but if Tulio and Emers caused shit, I would have no choice but to engage. Sonya stepped out of the car, and I held her hand, indicating to cameras to take photos. Then I placed a hand on her lower back and strolled into the Hilton Chicago. Remo spoke into the headset, leading a team of men to surround us as we entered the building without going through security. I smiled at a few guests as I squeezed Sonya's backside.

"You look sexy tonight."

"Hopefully you can show me later," she whispered in my ear.

I groaned as Sante came into view.

"There's my brother."

The ballroom colors this year are green and white. A

banner with the name of the charity, the local food bank in the city, was hanging proudly. The director of the charity smiled at the cameras.

"Every year you come here?"

"We do."

"People can't say you're just out to kill people; your family does some good."

"We do."

I watched the crowd clap as Sanchez told a joke. Remo and Ian had both exits covered, and Sante wrapped an arm around Rena's shoulder.

"Sonya, you two look lovely tonight." Rena hugged Sonya and then me.

"Rena, you too," Sonya answered.

"Thanks, Renato, are we on our best behavior," Rena joked.

"Never." I smirked as the waiter approached; Sonya picked up a glass of champagne.

"Do you want something to drink?" she offered, and I declined.

My eyes traveled back to the mayor, and I saw his security whisper in his ear; both of them stared back at me. I pointed my finger in the shape of a gun and raised my hand, but Sante stepped in my view of him, blocking out the suggestion.

"Not here," Sante muttered.

The girls talked and ignored us.

"You scared I might do something?"

"As your brother, I know you'll do something."

"Fuck him." My nose flared.

"Calm down; we've got company."

He pointed behind me, and I looked over my shoulder to see Emers and Tulio come together. Just like them to be side by side at all times. Emers being the oldest excused his brother's mistakes and paid a hefty penny to cover his debts. I can admit I fucked up sometimes, but my brothers held me accountable.

"He better stay away from me."

"Savio just arrived with McKayla. I promised no blood tonight."

"You promised I didn't."

"Ladies and gentlemen, thank you for showing such great care for our community," the director said from the podium.

Sonya smiled at me.

"Funny we run into you here," Natalia said from Tulio's side.

Tulio kept his eyes on Sonya; I fucking hated it.

"Something is wrong with your eyes." I released Sonya's hand and pulled her behind me.

"Renato, not now," Sante muttered.

Tulio grinned.

"Who is she, Renato?" Sonya asked.

"Nobody," I answered.

"Really, Renato, I thought we were better than that." Natalia tried to imply what we had was more than it was.

"Sonya, you look different tonight. Maybe it does cost to marry a rich man," Tulio taunted, and Emers gripped his shoulder.

"Better listen to your brother, Tulio." Sante passed his glass to Rena, reading the tension.

Whenever someone tested one Calabresi brother, we all came together to let the person know if you fuck with one, you fuck with all five of us.

"Natalia, we will talk later," I answered.

"Maybe we can meet at our usual spot." Natalia smiled at me.

"I need to use the bathroom." Sonya said, and Rena grabbed her hand.

"I'll take you."

"No, I'm fine." She yanked out of my hold.

"Seems you can't keep her happy as a husband either." Tulio laughed, and Emers joined in on the joke.

"Funny, because Natalia just flirted with me in front of your face. If I wanted to take her in the bathroom and fuck her right now, she'd let me."

"Fuck you, Renato." Tulio closed the distance between us.

"How's your restaurant?"

All the light had gone out of his eyes.

"Son of a bitch! I'm not—" Emers pulled him back before he could hit me.

I expressed amusement, picked up a glass of champagne, and took a sip.

"Find someone else to play with," I taunted him.

The commotion had all eyes on us.

"Time to go." Sante shook his head in disappointment.

"Let me find my wife."

"Go straight home, Renato," Sante demanded.

I made my way to the tables and found the one decorated with our names on it. I ignored Sante's instruction and moved to kiss my mother on the cheek and talked to my father before Sonya and Rena came back from the bathroom. Sonya looked pissed.

"She's ready to go," Rena said.

We said our goodbyes and headed toward the exit.

———

"That meant nothing." I cupped both sides of Sonya's face.

Sonya closed her eyes. I licked my lips and lifted her chin as she slipped each of her heels off, placing a kiss on her lips.

"Take off your dress."

She stepped back and unzipped the side of her maroon, velvet gown.

"Slowly." I touched her hand.

She stared at me the whole time, the fabric falling from her body, then stepped out and kicked it to the side.

"Take off my clothes."

Sonya switched her hips, closed the distance between us, and one by one, unfastened the buttons on my jacket before pushing it off my shoulders. Her essence filled my nose, and I was ready to devour her, but I needed to make sure she understood that Natalia had never been a serious threat.

I ran a hand up her arm, around her collarbone, then down her back and unhooked her bra.

"Tonight you lost trust for a moment." I raked a finger through her hair.

"Renato." She hugged herself.

"Shusshh... Natalia convinced you briefly that she meant more to me."

Sonya turned her head.

Smack!

I smacked her on the ass.

"Focus on my eyes, my voice." My heart thudded louder and louder.

"Yes, sir." Her eyes brimmed with warmth.

Her pretty eyes showed lust but also confusion at her punishment.

"Turn around, bend over, grab your knees."

I walked to my closet and picked up my box of toys; she watched me remove each item: cuffs, knife, oil, bar stretcher.

"Remember you're mine, and I wouldn't do anything to hurt you."

"I know." A chill traveled down her neck.

"Safe word?" My stomach tightened.

"Red." She managed to turn the corners of her mouth upward and give a half nod.

"You know why I used to come every day to watch you dance?"

I locked her left and right ankles after I spread her legs and placed the bar in the middle. Then I kissed each ass cheek; she shuddered under my hold.

"Don't move." I skimmed my lips along the sweep of her hips.

"No." I brushed my lips across her ear, raising goose bumps across her skin.

"Something about you I couldn't explain, but your eyes told a story."

"Renato." She breathed deeply.

Smack!

"Ohhh…" She whimpered; I rubbed the sting away. I moved the small knife in front so she could see and explained what would happen next.

"Just breathe, Sonya, knife play is one of many things we will have between the two of us."

I ran the knife from her ankle up to her panties, then cut them off.

"Not tonight, but you'll experience more soon. You're doing great, baby," I encouraged her. I put the knife back in the case and retrieved a blindfold, placing it around her eyes.

I spread her ass and dipped my tongue in her asshole, and she almost stumbled over.

Smack!

"Stay put." I played with the silky tendrils of her hair.

I glided my tongue in and out, squeezing her cheeks; her cries of passion caused her juices to drip down my chin and her thighs. I started playing with her clit and stuck my thumb in her ass.

"Arghhhh… gosh." Her breath hitched a little.

"Who are you?" She needed to run, to scream, but her body had become locked at my touch.

"Yours!" she gasped.

"My what?" I let out a harsh breath.

"Your dirty girl." Her breath exploded out of her mouth.

"What else?" My chest rose and fell with rapid breaths.

I pinched her nipple.

"Your wife," she hissed.

I unbuckled my pants and slid my pole through her warm pussy and closed my eyes.

"That's right. My bitch, the only one that can be my slut in the bedroom, the number one in my world as my wife. Fuck what Natalia said to you," I demanded through gritted teeth.

Her pussy gripped my dick; she got wetter at the words I spoke.

Our combined moisture trickled down my stomach as sweat poured down my face.

"Fuck!" I ripped the blindfold off. She stumbled to the ground, and I followed, continuing to hammer her from behind. Sonya looked at me from over her shoulder, the arousal in her eyes calling for more. I engulfed an arm around the back of her head, hovered over her, and pushed her to lay flat.

"Keep going, sir," she commanded as she pounded her fist.

"You don't give me demands, sexy." I rolled us over with her sitting on top of me. Her ass bounced on my dick, and I felt her contract around it.

"Shit!" Her head flew back.

"Make this the first and last time you question where this dick belongs."

Sonya's creaminess coated my balls while I fucked her from below. Her orgasm showed in her shaking legs. I wrapped my arms around her waist as she fell back onto my stomach; I kissed the side of her face, rubbing up and down her body.

"See what you do to me?" I growled; she had me completely wrapped around her finger.

Sonya slid her hand up to my head, and I kissed the back of her palm. I continued to play in her pussy.

"Come in your wife's pussy." Her breath grew shallow as she moaned while I did just that.

On wobbly legs, I helped her off me and kissed her forehead, then carried her to the bathroom, and we showered together before falling into bed and drifting to sleep.

———

Days later, I stayed in the house with Sonya and our son. Sante checked in to make sure I hadn't done anything else to trigger Tulio, and I promised I wouldn't until the time was right. RJ had sat in my lap in the office until he fell asleep, then I passed him to our nanny while Sonya cooked lunch.

"Can you put him in his nursery, Deborah?" Deborah was a friend that Marilyn had found to help us.

"Yes, Mr. Calabresi."

"Thank you." I slipped my phone out of my pocket.

Me: Is she there?

Remo: Just walked on the elevator.

Me: On my way.

Remo: Got it.

I told Sonya that I had to run by the office for something.

Pushing through the door, Natalia pulled off her robe and stood in front of me, biting her bottom lip.

Before Sonya, she'd probably had the most access to me, and the visual of her lips around my dick got me hard.

Right now, I had bigger plans for those lips that she kissed Tulio's ass with when she'd crossed me.

"What are you doing here?"

"Put your robe back on, Natalia."

"Are you here to kill me?"

"Have you betrayed me?" I questioned and lifted my right brow at the hesitation in her eyes.

"Renato, you already turned against me." Her voice sounded like nails on someone's wall.

"My wife almost fell for your lies about me."

"Why her?" She tied the belt around her waist.

"Have I ever explained my actions to you before?"

She pouted her lips.

"Tulio and I aren't together," a snakeskin mask with a cobra-sharp tongue spoke.

"I don't care." I slipped my black gloves out.

"Renato, please, listen to me." A dark, sickening grief filled her eyes.

"You talked to my wife."

"Our friendship should mean something to you." She looked around the room for help. I had Remo outside. I shoved her against the bedroom door and wrapped my hands around her neck.

"I didn't have anything to do with Tulio's plan."

"Our friendship is over because of you."

"Did I mean nothing at all?" Natalia tried to claw at my hands.

"Just business." Her eyes widened in surprise; I cracked her neck, she went limp, and I placed her on the floor before opening the door for Remo.

"Clean this up."

"I had Dome erase her register in the computer and wipe the cameras." Remo held a plastic bag and started to wipe everything down.

I removed my gloves.

"Sonya is probably wondering when I'll get back. I need to run to the office and head home."

"What about her best friend?" Remo grabbed Natalia's bags.

"Waiting for the right time."

As I stepped out of the room, I checked down the hallway and stepped onto the elevator and put my shades back on.

Ring!

As the doors unlatched, I answered my phone, surprised by the caller.

"Mr. Mayor." My words fell dead and brittle.

"We need to talk," he demanded, thinking it would alert me to trouble.

"About?"

"The situation." His greed came with choices.

"What situation, sir?" I covered the end of the cell phone.

"Home, Boss?" Alfred asked as he turned into Main Street and bounced over the road.

"Office, then home."

"On the way," Alfred said.

"I'd like to talk in person."

"Mr. Mayor, I have already done that, and you didn't have anything to say."

He breathed heavily through the phone.

"I'm no threat." He pleaded his case like most guilty people did when I started to close in on them.

I laughed.

"Funny, because I could have told you that already." A police siren wailed nearby.

"Listen, Renato."

"Before you spill your bullshit, let me tell you what's going to happen next."

"I can have you arrested." His words grew legs.

"The answer is probably yes, but do you think it will stick? Fuck with me and find out who runs this city." I ended the call.

CHAPTER 16

Sonya

"HONESTLY SHE LOOKED LIKE HIS TYPE."

McKayla, Rena, and Adelina had come to the park with the kids to have a playdate. Other kids ran around, jumping on the swings and cutting their knees, but our kids had guards monitoring the entire area. Some of the other parents whispered among themselves, and it felt awkward at first. Adelina told me I'd forget the guards were there in time.

"Who?" Adelina cut a slice of an apple and handed one to me.

"Natalia."

"One of Renato's old hoes," Rena joked.

"Rena," Adelina chastised.

"Sorry, Mom," Rena replied and took the plate of food from her.

"RJ can pick up on your energy. Natalia has no control over your emotions unless you let her," Adelina preached, and Renato showed me in more ways than one what they had was superficial.

"How about your relationships in the beginning?"

McKayla helped Savio Jr. out of his coat.

"Calabresi men don't cheat, I didn't raise my boys like that," Adelina insisted.

"Savio would be the first to tell you when I was pregnant I had moments of doubt, because my body was changing." McKayla let Savio Jr. play with RJ.

"Renato never had the chance to experience my pregnancy though."

"Are you guys trying for another one?"

I bit the inside of my cheek.

"Sonya." McKayla called my name.

"Huh."

"You two are using protection, right?" McKayla asked.

"Not exactly."

"That's how you ended up with him." Rena pointed at RJ, and I was embarrassed.

"No reason to be shy now." Adelina pinched RJ's cheek.

"We've had sex twice, and not one condom used. I said I was going to get a Plan B, but I forgot."

"Do you want more kids?"

"Not right now. I like my job, and classes just started online."

"Then you need to talk to Renato. I would love more grandkids, but as a woman, first you have to do what's best for you," Adelina explained.

"Adelina's right. One day you'll wake up with a football field of kids, stuck in the house and your goals slipped away," Rena remarked.

"RJ would like a sibling, but I have dreams before another pops out." I laughed at Savio Jr. pushing the train up McKayla's leg.

"Talk to your husband," McKayla said.

"What is she doing here?" Rena sassed and stood. I looked behind me, a lump forming in my throat.

"Sonya, you really married him?" Brilynn pointed at my ring finger.

With rolling eyes and a pinched nose, I shook my head.

"Why is she here?" I focused on my mom.

"You two need to talk."

"No we don't."

"Sonya, she's your best friend."

"And?"

"You let him come between us," Brilynn complained.

"Did you forget someone tried to kill me and my son?" I chided.

Brilynn looked away.

The guards started to close in on us, and I waved them off.

"How many times will you ignore the fac that your husband is the problem?" Brilynn screamed.

"I have nothing to say to you. If you're smart, you'll stay away from me."

The look of surprise on Brilynn's and my mom's faces was vivid.

"How dare you treat us like that?" Mom stomped her feet.

"Mom, I love you, but she can no longer be around me."

Brilynn chortled. "See how he controls her, lies to her. I tried to tell you," she spouted.

"How much is Tulio paying you? Whatever it is will only get you killed."

Smack!

My mother hit me across the face, and the girls ran over to separate us. I felt my eyes start to water.

"Either you two leave on your own or they will help you." Adelina motioned at the guards that marched toward us.

"Sonya, let me talk to you alone," Mom asked.

"No, I need time."

Rena wrapped her arm around me, and I turned away.

"Give her some space." Adelina rubbed my arm.

"Thank you."

Rena changed the subject, and we laughed about stories of Savio Jr. interrupting McKayla and Savio's alone time.

———

Renato watched me in my outfit, and I pressed a kiss on the side of his jaw. He rested both hands on my waist, sliding them down to grip my ass.

"Nope, I'm leaving."

"You hung with them all day today."

"And you had business, so what's the point?"

I rubbed the plum lipstick off his bottom lip.

After our park date, I went to get my hair styled in long spiral curls and trimmed my bangs. I had on a leather corset and short set. I needed a drink and to be off mommy duty for a little while. Renato promised to watch the baby so I could have a girls' night out if we stuck to the directions Renato gave.

"Fine, just follow the rules."

"Yes, sir." I licked his face.

He grunted. "You know what that does to me."

"Down, sir."

He tried to pick me up, but I dodged out the way.

"Any problems…"

"Call you immediately. I promise."

"Stay in Remo's line of sight."

"Yes, Daddy."

Smack!

"Ouch!" I rubbed my butt, then grabbed my purse and sauntered to the door.

"Sonya!"

With my hand on the doorknob, I looked back at him.

"Brilynn and I have to have a conversation."

I sighed and nodded. There was no way to keep the

conversation from him, and his mother would never trust anyone that felt like a threat to her family. I wished I had been the one to tell him, though. Brilynn had plenty of chances to stay loyal, but Renato wouldn't spare her anymore.

"Renato—"

He held a hand up to interrupt me.

"Go have a good time."

Forty minutes later, I swayed to the beat of a Doja Cat song, the Patron shots we'd had making me feel warm inside. We'd started to drink as soon as we arrived. After the first bar, Rena wanted to hit up a club and got us into a VIP section. She used Sante's name, and they treated us to the best drinks in the house. Rena clinked glasses with McKayla, and I took another shot.

"How many drinks have you had?" I laughed when Rena bounced her leg up and down.

"I need to go pee." Rena stood and ran over to Remo, and he pulled a man to walk with her to the bathroom.

"Are you having fun?" McKayla asked.

"Yes! Thanks for coming tonight." I spoke over the loud music.

"We're sisters."

Brilynn and I used to be close like sisters, and now I barely knew who she was.

"Renato said he has to have a conversation with Brilynn."

"Adelina told him," McKayla suggested, and I nodded.

"Damn."

Rena came back from the bathroom, and I saw one of the dancers I used to work with.

"I'll be right back."

"Where are you going?" Rena looked out to the crowd of people.

"A friend I used to dance with. I won't be long."

"Let me go with you."

"No, stay, it won't take long. Besides, the guards are right there."

Rena sat back down and grabbed another bottle of merlot.

"Hurry back," she yelled over the music.

I jogged over to the entrance of our section.

"Remo, I see someone I know. Can you let me through please?"

"Sorry, Mrs. Calabresi, you have to stay here."

"Remo, where am I going to go?"

"We can bring her to you."

"How about you have someone walk me to her?" I placed my hands on my hips and poked out my lip.

"Give me a second." Remo waved to his man, and he came quickly.

"Stay here with them." Remo motioned at Rena and McKayla.

"Thanks, Remo." I grinned. He helped me down the stairs, and we pushed through the crowd, then I tapped Crystal on the back. She turned around with a wide smile.

"Sonya!" she screamed enthusiastically.

"Crystal!"

Crystal and I hugged each other.

"Where have you been? All the girls miss you at the club," Crystal asked and locked her arm in mine. Remo followed next to me, keeping his eyes on the crowd.

"Have a drink with me." Crystal pulled money out of her bra.

"One shot." I held a finger up, and she grasped my hand.

"Shut the fucking door! You're married."

Crystal was cool and not as money hungry to sleep with a rich guy as a dancer; we talked from time to time.

"I am."

"How is the baby boy?"

"He's good, getting bigger every day."

"I bet."

The bartender placed two drinks down on the counter, and we chucked them back.

"Let me run to the bathroom, and you should join me and my friends in our section."

"Are you sure?"

"Yes. Remo will walk you to them while I go to the bathroom."

I put the empty glass back down, told Remo where I was going, moved through the crowd, and pointed at our section. Crystal was let in, and I introduced her to the girls briefly before wandering down the hall to the bathroom.

"Oh, sorry."

Someone bumped into me.

I headed into the bathroom, but before I could push the door shut, my hand was jerked back, and I was pushed up against the sink counter.

"What the—"

"Shushhh..." Tulio whispered.

"Let me go before I scream."

The door unlatched, and my eyes ballooned wide as Tulio crept toward me.

"Sonya, sweet Sonya," Tulio said.

"Tulio, Remo is right outside."

"Remo isn't shit to me," Tulio spat.

"Whatever you want, Renato will pay you."

"Renato is too scared to face me."

Tulio grasped my thigh, running his hand up my leg. I slapped him across the face, and he released me. I kicked him in the balls.

"Bitch!" Tulio shouted; the door came ajar, revealing Remo.

"Remo!"

Tulio's guard released me and tried to punch Remo, but Remo cut him off, shoved him back, and punched him in the face. I saw Ian come up behind me and started to grip the guard around the neck, then Tulio pointed a gun at Remo.

"No!" I screamed in panic.

"If you want to walk out of here alive, get out of my way," Tulio demanded.

"You won't live long after this," Remo growled.

Tulio screwed his top lip up.

"My brother can say the same thing about you." Tulio fired a shot in Remo's direction, and I dropped to the floor as Tulio charged past him. Ian dropped the guard and came to help me lift Remo. McKayla and Rena leaped up when they saw us carrying Remo around the corner.

"What the hell!" Rena picked up our purses.

"Are you okay, Sonya?" Crystal questioned.

"I'm fine, we need to leave."

Remo leaned on Ian's shoulder.

"Bring the cars around back," McKayla suggested.

His guards forced their way through and helped us to the back exit; Remo stood against the wall, blood leaking through his jacket.

"Hang on, Remo."

"No worry. It's a flesh wound," he gritted through his teeth.

I really didn't believe him based on the amount of blood, but I tried to not worry.

Ian unlatched the back door, and I climbed in next to McKayla and Rena while Remo went to the front passenger side.

"Don't be a stranger, Sonya." Crystal tapped on the door.

"I won't."

I heard police sirens nearby, and Ian started the car, then

drove off to the end of the block, made a left, heading in the opposite direction when an ambulance and police car pulled in front of the nightclub.

"We need to get him to the hospital." I sat forward in my seat.

"Not at the moment." Ian's eyes glanced from the side mirror to me.

"He's bleeding out."

"Sit back, Sonya."

"We have company," Rena whispered.

I whirled around and looked out of the back window and saw a car speeding up on our tail.

"Is that Tulio?"

"Probably, or Emers's men." Ian sharply turned at the green light; I slid in the backseat.

"Where are we going?"

"Not the house," Remo muttered and sat up in his seat.

"Warehouse?" Ian glanced at Remo for confirmation, and he nodded.

"Tell me what's going on."

"Call Renato," Ian said through the car's Bluetooth.

"Did she drink too much?" Renato tittered.

"Boss," Ian said.

"Is she hurt?" Renato said in a calm, even tone.

"No, Boss," Ian answered.

"Renato, Remo is hurt," I interrupted Ian.

"Bring them to the warehouse." Renato ended the call.

CHAPTER 17

Renato

AS SOON AS I heard the distress in her voice, I knew Tulio had made the decision on his death; now I just had to figure out if I wanted him to have an open or closed casket. Savio, Sante, and EJ stood around the warehouse with me as we waited for the car to arrive. Ian had done the right thing not bringing them to the house. Nothing should interrupt my son's sanctuary, so Remo knew to do plan B.

Knock! Knock!

Dome unlocked the door. Ian helped Remo to the wheelchair we had waiting and pushed him farther into the room where we took care of wounds. I had a doctor on call in case any of us couldn't show up at a hospital without police wanting answers. Sonya ran into my arms, and I checked her back, arms, legs, then stared into her eyes.

"Is he going to be all right?"

"Don't worry about Remo."

"Tulio is crazy." A tear fell down her cheek. I knew she cared about Remo; he'd become a part of her family just like my brothers.

"He's going to pay. I want you to go with McKayla and Rena."

"Where are you going?" She clung to my arms.

I kissed her on the forehead and lips.

"Sante is going to drive you to our parents' house. RJ is already there."

When she'd called, I'd had him transported, and Savio had his son already there because my mom wanted to babysit.

"Let them go, and you stay with me."

"Not how this works. I promise I'll be fine."

I kissed her knuckles.

McKayla and Rena grabbed her hand and walked her out to the bulletproof Hummer.

"I can see it in your eyes. As a husband to a wife that was disrespected in the worst way, you do what you need to do," Savio announced.

"Already started."

Savio knew how calculating I could be, so I'd had Tulio followed; I knew he'd show himself eventually like the fool his parents raised him to be. I walked over to the room where Remo was being treated and tapped on the door.

"Are you heading out?" Remo tried to get off the hospital bed. Ian pushed him back down.

"Listen to what the doctor says."

"I'm going with you," Remo answered.

"Stay here."

"He shot me!" Remo scoffed.

"Payback is coming." I shook hands with him.

Savio, EJ, and I piled in the car. Vincenzo wanted to come, but I needed my brother to stay with the family as backup. He was trained like us, but as the youngest, we never put him in situations that could harm him.

Ian drove, and I closed my eyes, fighting my thoughts of how Sonya was scared of Tulio and that was something I refused to let slide. She should never have to look over her shoulder, and I'd played the good guy long enough. Emers was going to have to see us.

Ian turned the lights off as he slowly crept up on Costa's territory. Tulio had done the dumbest thing ever and came back to his home like he was untouchable. He didn't live like his brother, under twenty-four-hour security, even though his home was a mansion in a predominately quiet neighborhood. I grabbed the bulletproof vest and shotgun from Savio; EJ placed his two guns in the holster.

"Are you ready for this?" I asked him.

EJ rarely got out to do action like me or Sante.

"She's family." Anger darkened his eyes.

"Like this side of you."

We looked behind us; it was only our cars lined up on the block. I led them up to the small gate and checked my watch, then heard a click.

"Dome, override the security cameras." I slid the gate wide. A few men went to the right, and I motioned for a small team led by Sante to come from the back. The place sat around six thousand square feet. I touched the top of the car in the driveway, and it was still warm.

"He's home," I whispered.

Ian passed me the night goggles, and he held the dynamite.

I waited five minutes for everyone to get in place, then raised my foot and kicked the door twice; when it broke ajar, I tossed a smoke bomb inside, and I heard shouts and screams.

Pop! Pop!

"Go!" I shouted to my team. They split up, and I heard the back door crash, followed by loud yells. I sent a shot between the eyes of two of Tulio's men.

"Renato, you clear?" Sante called in my ear.

"Clear, going upstairs." I slid behind the wall.

Rattata! Rattata!

I poked my head out, looking up to the top of the arch-way. Two of his men opened fire.

"Put your guns down!" Savio yelled.

Pop! Pop!

Savio ducked down, barely missing his targets. I closed my eyes, calmed my breath, and aimed my gun, sending a bullet to his leg. Both guards dropped the gun and fell to the ground.

"Come on, Tulio, show yourself." I ran up the stairs, dodged a bullet, and hit a guard with the butt of my gun.

"Arghhhh!" He tried to take the gun from me, but I wrapped my hand around his neck and swung him over the banister.

"Don't move" I heard from behind me.

I grinned, holding my hands up in the air. Savio stood to the side, and I shook my head no.

"Tulio, decide."

"Shut the fuck up," he spat.

"Decide if you want an open or closed casket."

"Fuck you, Renato!" Panic lanced his voice.

I started to walk toward him, and he backed up.

"Stop moving."

"Emers know you came after my wife tonight?"

His eyes looked right to left.

"I bet he doesn't. That means you made a move on a wife of a fellow mafia family without permission."

"That bitch owes me!" A desperate gasp clipped the silence.

I snarled when he called her a bitch.

"Put your gun down."

He cocked his head to the side, lowering his gun.

"I don't need this to finish you off," Tulio bragged. He balled his fist up and tried to hit me on the jaw.

"Wrong move." I dodged and quickly removed the gun

from behind my back, knocking him across the face. He fell to the ground.

"Uggghhh!" he moaned in pain.

I beat him in the face with my gun three more times, then shot him in the head until I ran out of bullets.

"Renato!"

"Renato!" I heard my name called, swinging the gun in that direction.

"Relax, it's over," Savio calmly spoke.

"Piece of shit deserves to die again." I spat on him.

A week later, they held Tulio's funeral. Everybody in the city talked about how he was robbed and killed. I changed the channel on the TV in my office at the Calabresi building and turned toward the documents in front of me.

"Have you had a break yet?" Sonya stood at my door with a bag of food.

"No, but I could eat." I licked my lips. She shut the door, sauntered to my desk, slipped on top, and crossed her legs.

"For food only." Sonya giggled, opened the bag, and pulled out what looked like sandwiches.

"How are you feeling?"

"Feel fine, just busy."

"I mean about the Tulio situation." I unwrapped the sandwich and took a bite, cleaning my hands with the napkins.

"No nightmares if that's what you're thinking." Sonya uncrossed her legs, and I gripped her thigh.

"Sounds like you're normalizing this world, and I never want it to taint you."

"I don't want anything to happen to Brilynn," she blurted out.

I removed my hand and sat back in the chair, staring at her.

"I understand what she did, but Tulio is dead now."

"You can't protect her."

"Renato, I'm not. She won't make a difference to us either way. But enough bloodshed has happened."

"Have you talked to her lately?" I adjusted the lapels of my jacket.

"Not since the park." She stared at me blankly while chewing the inside of her mouth.

"Keep it that way."

"Never had plans on contacting her, but Renato, your request sounds like a demand."

I clenched my jaw.

"Brilynn means you no good."

"She would say the same thing about you." She leaped off my desk.

"Fuck Brilynn," I muttered.

"Too much death, Renato, that's all I'm saying." Her breath hitched.

"Have you finished your work for the day?" I changed the subject.

"Are you kicking me out as the boss right now?"

"I have work to do."

"I'll get back to my desk, Mr. Calabresi."

She started to grab her food, and I extended a hand, grabbed her wrist, and pulled her in my lap, caressing her cheek.

"Look at me."

Sonya pouted, and I smiled.

I tapped her nose.

"Dinner tonight."

"Is this work-related, Mr. Calabresi?" She wrapped a curl around her finger.

I chuckled at her joke, then slapped her thigh gently.

"Can I talk to my wife for a moment please?"

A smile spread across her face.

"Dinner tonight." I jammed my hand in my pocket. "Then a little movie."

She gave a nervous laugh.

"I wasn't talking about that type of movie." I hung a lopsided grin on my face.

She had a shock-filled expression on her face.

"A sex tape." Biting her lip, she turned away.

"All I want is dinner with you tonight."

"A charmer." As she fixed my tie, she chortled.

———

After work, I called and had the restaurant reserve a table for us; we didn't have to wait hours for a table. I had a taste for a big bloody steak, so we booked Aphonso's, a well-known eatery that some high-profile celebrities stopped at. Sonya sat in her chair while I sat across from her, unbuttoned my coat, and placed my cell on vibrate.

"Anything special you have when you come here?"

Our waitress came to the table. "Hello, I'm Charlene and I'll be your waitress. Can I get you started with drinks?"

"Can we have the red wine?" I ordered for the both of us.

"Sure, and would you like to hear the specials?"

"Actually I already know what we want. Do you mind if I order for you?"

"I don't mind." Sonya grasped my hand.

"We will take two steaks, rice, and baked veggies."

"I'll have your drinks right up." Charlene took our menus.

"What did you do after I left you after lunch?"

"Vincenzo has me working on some cool projects." She rubbed her stomach.

"What projects?" I brushed my palms together.

She fidgeted with the silverware.

"I never told you, but my goal is to become an art buyer one day."

"I'm listening."

"It's my second love, besides RJ."

Charlene brought the wine out, and we thanked her.

"I knew you started online classes."

"Vincenzo said that you guys own a few art galleries."

She seemed nervous to ask.

"The company owns a lot of business."

"He stated I could possibly have a job with that side of the business."

If that meant she would leave the company and work longer hours, then it would mean less time for me and RJ.

"Based on the look on your face, you hate the idea."

"RJ is growing. He needs us both around."

"Our family is always top priority." I quirked a smile.

"When that time comes, we can discuss it further."

"You're not turned off by me wanting a life outside of the family business?"

"At first I was hesitant, but the gallery is still under our portfolio."

"That's true."

Charlene approached our table with the food.

"Thank you," Sonya said, a smile returning to her mouth.

"Enjoy your meal," Charlene responded.

I picked up my napkin and laid it over my lap, while Sonya started to talk about RJ and his latest tricks to pretend like he was asleep.

At the end of the night, we came back home. Our evening concluded in the Jacuzzi as I smoked on my cigar, holding a glass of Hennessy in my hand and watched Sonya sip on her glass of white wine.

"Thank you for dinner." She placed the glass down on the side of the Jacuzzi, plucked her arms out, and locked them behind my neck. I watched her low eyes drip with want.

"You're welcome." I studied her face.

"Tomorrow I'm taking RJ to the mall. Since Tulio is gone, we don't need to be locked away as much." She rubbed the back of my head.

Emers was still lurking but hadn't confronted me.

"You have a closet full of clothes."

"Please. If it makes you feel better I'll take McKayla and Rena with me."

I blew out a breath. She started to trail kisses down my chest, and lower until she disappeared in the water; my head fell back in a trance when her lips wrapped around my shaft.

"Fuck, Sonya!" I groaned, and my eyelids fluttered shut. Beads of sweat popped out on my forehead as I gave myself over to the sensations.

CHAPTER 18

Sonya

I WHIRLED around in my dress, stood in front of the mirror, and looked at the extra weight I'd gained after giving birth. Plus, all the delicious food Renato had introduced me to since we'd been together.

"Where are you going in that?"

"Out." I shoved my bracelets around my wrist.

"Sonya," McKayla grumbled.

Rena pushed the stroller back and forth with RJ inside; he kept trying to eat his stuffed bear.

"I want to surprise Renato." I smoothed the short, V-neck dress with spaghetti straps.

"Where are you taking him?"

I looked around the store, to make sure no one was listening to our conversation.

"I want to dance for him." I flipped through to a light green Chanel bodice and skirt.

"Stripping?" McKayla asked.

"That's how we met."

I picked through another set of dresses and held up a leopard print.

"When are you planning on giving him a show?" McKayla grabbed a dress for herself.

"Tomorrow night. I want to cook for him and show him how much I appreciate him."

"Then we should go to Victoria's Secret next," Rena noted.

She was right; no point in having a full outfit when I knew he'd rip it off me the minute he saw me.

"Maybe you're right."

Rena pushed RJ while I went to change. I went to meet them outside but saw a woman blocking them from leaving.

"Brilynn." She looked like she hadn't slept or eaten in a few days. She seemed jittery and unfocused.

"Why are you keeping RJ from me?"

"Brilynn, not today." Renato would only hold out for so long before he made her disappear, and I was doing my best to keep them separate.

"Brilynn, I found these shoes for him." I heard my mother's voice. She held shopping bags from the kids' closet.

"Brilynn, I can understand you, but you're my mother," I grumbled, pointing a finger at myself.

"One could say the same about a daughter that throws away her friend she's known for over five years," Mom argued.

"Sonya, we should go," McKayla insisted.

The girls and I started to walk off, and Brilynn grabbed my wrist, but I jerked away.

"Don't touch me."

"He's only using you!" Brilynn yelled; I ignored her words and continued heading to Victoria's secret. After browsing for a short time, I picked up two sets for my surprise. Afterwards, McKayla wanted something to eat, but I had one more store to check for shoes and told them I'd meet them at the food court.

"Don't take too long," McKayla announced and threw a thumbs-up in answer.

The shoe shop had a sale. Even though Renato had given me a credit card with no limit, I liked sales, so I grabbed two pairs to try on.

"You walk in a room with those shoes, he might not let you leave," a smooth voice hinted, and I shifted around toward it. A tall guy with dark gray eyes, a shaved head, and a business suit that reeked of money.

"That's the point." I chuckled.

He laughed.

"So you are taken?"

"I'm afraid so." I held up my ring finger.

"If you were my woman, I'd never let you out of my sight."

I started to take off the shoes and try another pair.

"Sorry, he snatched me up."

He slipped his hand in his pocket and passed his business card to me.

"What's this for?" His name was Phillip Costa, and I froze.

"Just wanted to meet the woman that caused my cousin's death."

"Stay away from me." I dropped the shoes on the ground, picked up my purse, and turned to leave. He gripped me by the arm, and it looked like an innocent situation. I didn't want to cause anyone else in the store to get hurt, so I didn't grab my guard's attention for help. He released my arm.

"Emers is coming. I suggest you tell your husband Costa wants revenge." He picked up a pair of shoes and walked to the counter, paying for them. Finally, I got my bearings together and left the store, walking to the food court.

Rena and McKayla held bags of food in their hands.

"You didn't get the shoes." Rena poked through my bags.

"Oh, no. I decided to wear what I already have."

"Are you all right? Are you still thinking about your mom and Brilynn?" McKayla checked.

"Kind of. I think I need to take RJ over to see her."

"You need us to go with you?" Rena shuffled the bags from one hand to the other.

"I can handle my mom." The girls didn't need to be in between my drama, and Renato would stick me back in the house with around-the-clock protection. On the other hand, he and I had promised to not keep anything from each other, and Tulio's family had it in their minds to continue this war.

"It is getting late. I want to meet with my designers before they get busy," Rena informed me, then trailed beside McKayla and me to the car.

———

As soon as our driver dropped the girls off at home, I had Dome bring me to my mom's house so we could talk. I didn't know how the conversation would go, but it would be the last straw before I completely cut her off like I had Brilynn. Dome got out of the car with me and scanned the traffic while I knocked on the front door.

"Sonya, why didn't you call?" Mom wiped her hands on a towel.

"Are you alone?" I held the car seat in my hand.

"Yes, just preparing dinner." She stood to the side, and I stepped in with RJ. Dome waited outside. I carried RJ over to the couch, taking him out of the seat. He started to get fussy since we'd been out all day.

"Everything going well with your appointments?"

She smiled at RJ and sat next to me on the couch.

"You are not here to talk about my cancer treatments."

"You're right. I love you and want to keep a relationship with you."

"But." Mom grabbed RJ out of my arms.

"I can't—no, I refuse to allow Brilynn to be brought around my family."

"Brilynn's like a daughter to me." She patted RJ on the butt to calm him down.

"That's all well and good, but I'm your blood child, and he's your grandson. Our safety should come first at all times."

"I guess I've been trying too hard to push you two back together." She got up from the couch, heading to the kitchen.

"Extremely hard."

"After your father died, you know we didn't have a lot of family, but Brilynn and you became good friends, so I knew you'd have someone with you in case..."

She placed RJ on her hip and opened the fridge to grab some mashed fruit she kept for him.

"You can't think like that." I grabbed her free hand.

"Life is short, and I love you, Sonya, but the minute those people came here, I pictured you without me, and I got scared."

"Renato's not perfect, but he loves us, and his family is a supportive, Mom."

"Renato's crazy." She blew out a breath, and I couldn't do anything except agree.

"His mom says the same thing," I jested.

"Are you staying for dinner?"

"Din... Dinnn," RJ babbled.

"No, I made plans to cook dinner for my family tonight."

"How is school going?" Mom queried.

"Fine, I'm thinking of moving to in-person classes."

"How will you navigate that with him and work?"

"Renato knows that my passion is art buying, and his younger brother has me helping out with a few of their galleries."

"Gosh, the families are really rich." Mom remarked, smiled at RJ.

"Billionaires," I muttered.

RJ clapped his hands together.

"Billionaires, seriously." Mom gasped.

"They are, but his money doesn't matter anymore. I've tried to tell him plenty of times, but he insists on spoiling me," I replied.

"I taught you well. I'll stay away from Brilynn." She leaned her head on my shoulder.

We stood at the counter as she washed off some vegetables.

"Thank you. Brilynn can be manipulative. For your safety, it's best to call and tell her you can't see her again."

"I saw on the news the guy that threatened me is dead."

"Brilynn worked with him, and my gut is telling me she's still working with his people."

"Your father would be proud of you, Sonya. I hope you know that."

"I do." I kissed her on the cheek.

"Little one, I'll see you soon. Bring him by so I can babysit one day." She kissed his hand and held him out for me to take.

"Yes, ma'am."

"If you want to do in-person classes and you need someone to watch him, I'm here." She waved around the house.

"Maybe when you feel up to going out, we can find you someone."

"No one will ever replace your father."

I nodded but turned and sauntered to the front door. She unlocked it for me.

"Dad would want you to be happy."

"As long as you are happy and I have my grandbaby, nothing else matters." She reached for a hug, engulfing me and RJ.

"Say bye to Granny." I held RJ's hand up to wave goodbye.

———

RJ finally fell asleep around nine, so I planned to have the food ready thirty minutes later, and Renato texted he was on his way home. The wine bottle was chilled, I was showered, and candles were set up in the living room near his fire. Renato told me this was our home and he'd made me feel welcome to the point I could redecorate as much as I wanted. All I did was make sure RJ had a room he was comfortable in because most of his life we'd shared a room. I did tell him about putting a fence outside to surround the pool. Then the guest room I stayed in when I first arrived was changed into my office.

The locks on the door clicked, and I heard the alarm chirp. I moved to the mirror to check my makeup and the dress I'd picked up from the mall today. I went to meet him at the door and noticed the polished marble flooring gleaming in the full light.

"What's the occasion?" Renato asked.

I smiled. "I made you dinner," I replied, pointing at the rectangular walnut table.

He smirked, stepped down the entry stairs, and came farther into the room.

"Any reason for the dinner?" He hiked his brow up in suspension.

"A way to show my appreciation, and then I have a surprise after."

"I hate surprises, Sonya." He groaned, sliding his hands around my waist.

"I can promise this surprise will make you very happy."

He dipped his head to the side of my neck and sucked on my ear.

I raised my hand to his shoulder to slow his excitement down.

"Dinner."

"No."

I busted out in a laugh.

"Never had someone refuse dinner."

He grabbed my hair. "I love when you change your hair up like this."

Today it was in a simple braid, styled into a halo, but we'd mixed in the colors pink and blond. He trailed kisses along my collarbone.

"There is something I need to talk to you about."

"Will it make me mad?" he mumbled through his kisses.

"Possibly, but don't let it ruin our night, please."

He pushed me back gently, dropping his hands to his side.

"Speak." He walked around me to the table and sat down.

I cleared my throat and sat across from him and picked up the bottle of wine.

"You know I went to the park and the mall with the girls today."

He stopped moving as I lifted the covers off our plates, waiting for me to continue.

"Brilynn and my mom showed up."

The napkin fell on the table as he leapt up in a hurry, and I grabbed his wrist to stop him.

"Why didn't you call me the moment they showed up?" He slid a hand in his pocket and removed his phone.

"Wait! Renato, calm down."

"Calm down?"

"Just listen."

He held the phone out to dial who I assumed was his brothers.

"I kicked them out both times, and I went to talk to my mother alone and we resolved our issues."

"Sonya, I don't like to be in the dark when it pertains to my son." The room was silent.

"He's my son too."

"Which you've seemingly forgotten."

"That's not fair, Renato."

He rubbed his temple.

"That's not the only thing I need to tell you."

"What?"

"Sit down first." I pivoted, leaned in for his glass, and poured some wine.

"Are you trying to get me drunk so I won't blow up?"

"What I'm going to tell you might."

"Are you pregnant?"

"No, but we should discuss the lack of condoms."

"You're my wife. I don't need condoms." He took the glass out of my hand, placed it back on the table, slid his hand around my throat, and pecked me on the lips.

"You want more kids?"

"Maybe, but don't change the subject."

"Sorry, ummm… I went into a shoe store, and a guy came up to me."

"Did my men not secure the location?"

"It's a shoe store, Renato. People come and go."

"Get to the guy, Sonya."

"He gave me his card after he tried to hit on me." I reached in my pocket and pulled out the business card and slipped it to him.

Renato flipped it over and balled it up in his hand.

"Anything else?"

"What are you going to do?"

"Nothing for you to worry about."

His nonchalance about the whole thing has me scared; it was like the calm before the storm.

"What other surprises do you have for me tonight?"

"In the bedroom."

"Show me."

"Shouldn't we eat first?"

"You are my full-course meal." He pulled me up and smacked me on the ass.

I grinned, took his hand, and escorted him up the stairs to our bedroom.

"Close your eyes."

He snarled, and I placed my hand over his eyes, opening the bedroom door to a stripper pole and rose petals on the bed.

"Open your eyes." I removed my hand, and he scanned our bedroom in awe.

"You did this for me?"

"Even though I don't do this professionally anymore, I can still bring out your dirty dancer to please you." My hands cupped his large shaft, and my mouth sucked on his neck.

"Sonya, you are playing with fire." He groaned, stopping my hand from moving.

"Have a seat."

He removed his suit jacket and sat on the edge of the bed. I turned the lights down low as Beyoncé's "Naughty Girl" began to filter through the room.

Renato pushed his sleeves up and kicked off his shoes.

My right hand went on the pole, my legs separated, and I slowly dropped down to the bottom.

I timed the movement to perfection and released my hair from the tight crown, letting it flow down my back.

"Shit," Renato muttered, and I laughed. I came up the pole until I stood to face him, then gripped the pole with both hands and pulled myself up to the top, whirling around until I came back down.

"Can I be your naughty girl?" I seductively begged, crawling over to him. I threw my head back so my blond and pink highlights fell into his lap. He tried to touch me, and I slapped his hand away.

"Not yet."

"The longer you make me wait..." he grumbled.

"What are you going to do? Punish me?" I rose up, then turned around so my back was to him and bent over; my dress coming up to show the bra and panty set attached to stockings.

"Sonya," he groaned and tried to reach out for me, but I pushed his hand away and slipped the zipper of my dress down slowly before taking it off.

CHAPTER 19

Renato

HER HAIR, makeup, and the little dance show only made me want her even more than before. Sonya bared her soul and kept my attention more than any other woman I'd ever had sex with, and it had more to do with her kindness, presence, and snappy attitude whenever we disagreed than her looks. She wasn't afraid to demand respect from me, and I happily gave her anything she wanted. The moment she slipped off her dress and showed her black thong and bra connected to stockings, my dick came alive.

"Can I be your naughty girl?" she probed; I nodded with my mouth open.

"Come here." She met my unrelenting stare.

"You want to slut me out tonight?" Her eyes darkened.

"Fuck yes." I emphasized each word.

She stood in front of me and stuck her foot encased in the red heels over my dick.

"Who do I belong to?" She rested a hand on her hip.

"You're my bitch," I grunted and pecked a kiss to her leg, running a hand up her thigh to the back of her ass and pushed my nose toward her, smelling her arousal.

"Perfect, can I have you?" I looked up into her eyes; she

knew all along she had the control, and I was made desperate to have just a simple taste, to give her the world if she let me.

Sonya lifted my chin.

"Take them off, slowly." The heat from her hand burned my skin.

"Yes, ma'am." Thinking about it gave me sharp palpitations.

I glided my hand over her knee-high fishnet stockings, rolling each one down to her heels on the floor beside us. I trailed kisses across her stomach, stuck my tongue in her belly button, and extended a hand up to caress her breast.

"Ohhhhh… baby!" she squealed, holding the back of my head.

"Ready for me to eat, Sonya." I made eye contact with her, then ripped her thong apart.

"Yesss." She tried to hump my face.

My eyes were riveted to her nipples.

I picked her up, adjusted our position, and laid her on the bed. My tongue stretched out to suck on her full breast as I hovered over her warm body.

"Ahhh! Ahhh!" she bellowed; I did the same thing to her left breast.

To get her wet and ready, I continued my assault, then moved to my favorite meal of the day, pushing my finger in and out, then rotating them as she squirmed and tried to lock my hand between her warmth. Her juices made a wet spot, and her moans filled the room. She clawed at my hand, and I moved down her body before I stuck my nose in her nectar and smelled heaven.

"I'm a filthy motherfucker." Warmth spread across my chest.

She nodded, and as I relentlessly sucked on her clitoris, she tried to run from me, but I sped up my attack, and she arched her back.

"Renato!" she panted with tears in her eyes, and I sucked on her bud while hurriedly unzipping my pants and boxers to invade her walls.

"Ughhhh," Sonya gasped. I fed her more of me, and she locked her legs around my waist.

"Many nights I tried to find you," I informed her of the past.

"Baby, I'm here," Sonya breathed, making eye contact with me.

"Tell me you'll never leave me." I pounded aggressively, and the bed started to shake. Usually I'd play longer with her, tease her even more, but my hard dick was ready to feel home again.

"No, I'll never leave you, Renato," she screamed. I lifted her arms beside her head and captured her mouth, circling my hips. Sloppily, she kissed me back, and I could hear her ready to explode.

"I love fucking you raw, baby." Desire burned hot in the pit of my belly.

"Don't stop!" Her voice was a bare whisper in the night.

"Fuck! Shit... Shit!" Either I was delirious, or I heard ringing in my ears. She had the best pussy in the world, and I'd kill anyone that tried to take her away. My head fell back, and my heart rate sped up. I was close to coming or having a heart attack, which meant I would die from the best sex in the world tonight, and I had no regrets.

"Come with me, baby," she begged, and I felt her rub her essence, then push her finger in my mouth to taste her, and she grinned.

"Swear I'll kill over you again." My body draped all over her.

"Arghhh! God! Right there."

"Thank God you're all mine!" My gaze devoured her beauty.

She shook in my arms. We both came at the same time, and I fell on top of her again, out of breath.

"I have another surprise," she whispered, then nudged me to the side of the bed and crawled down to engulf my entire dick whole.

"Sssss... Fuck, Sonya." Her tongue gave me a teasing lap.

My dick hit the back of her throat, and I reveled in the fact this was the first time she'd given me oral sex. I made plans to have this every night before bed if she'd allow it.

"Mmmm..." Sonya moaned, sinking into my body instantly.

"You can have whatever you want," I promised and felt her tonsils at that moment before I blacked out.

———

Sonya sat next to me at the café breakfast bar near Montrose Beach on a lightly busy day with foot traffic. I peered around the room, a habit of mine to watch who comes and goes, while I sat at the end of the bar with my back to the wall. I'd taken the day off from work, and she'd called Vincenzo to take the rest of the day off for herself as well. Our night together played over in my mind all morning, and I woke up early to spend quality time together. RJ sat next to us cloaked in his blanket away from prying eyes. Photographers would still follow us, even though I never went out of my way to be a public figure, but somehow they found us no matter where we went.

The waitress placed our breakfast down on the counter. I watched as Sonya played with RJ, and I couldn't believe he was growing so fast.

"Tell me about your plans for school."

Sonya lifted her orange juice, taking a gulp.

She planned on getting back to in-person classes, so I

told her as long as things weren't disturbed at our home, I would be fine. Our son's birthday was the top priority for me, and I wanted to go all out to show him that he was the most important person to me.

"I spoke with a counselor at Chicago University. My studies will be art history."

"You end up with a bachelor's degree?"

Her head shook as she picked up her knife and cut into her pancakes. I rubbed the knuckles of her free hand.

"RJ is my concern, though."

She lifted her gaze to me.

"He can go to daycare."

The thought of RJ in someone's care beyond my parents or brothers gave me great anxiety.

"RJ will never be in daycare."

"But he needs to be around other kids."

"He has a cousin."

Her eyes lingered on me.

"You can bat your eyes, but my mind is made up."

"What are we doing for his birthday?"

"A party just for the family."

"I'm fine with that, something simple, with cake and ice cream." She cooed and pecked RJ on the nose.

I had a sudden impulse to take her to the bathroom and bend her over to take my girth in her mouth.

"You're not hungry?" Sonya glanced at my plate of omelet and sausage.

"Not for this." I pushed the plate away from me.

"Da da." Both our eyes spiked high in shock.

"Did he…?" I pivoted off the chair to pick up RJ.

"That's the first time he's really said anything remotely like that."

I grinned, shifting him in my arms.

"Little man, you say it again."

Some of the customers peered in our direction.

His eyes scanned my face, and he smiled.

"Da da." He drooled.

"Say Momma," Sonya coerced.

"Are you jealous?"

"Yep. I'm the one that carried him for so long. I was around before you, and he says da da first." She pouted.

"Come on, let's take a walk."

"Where?"

"Along the beach."

Sonya finished off her drink; I'd already paid for our meal. RJ angled to his mom, and I let her take him.

"Really beautiful out here today."

I slid her hair away from her face and kissed the side of her neck.

"Costa family."

"Nothing for you to worry about."

"Now that Tulio is gone and his cousin made contact with me at the mall."

"You should never be afraid." I curled her into my arms.

"As long as we're in your arms, I know you'll keep us safe."

"Good that you recognize that." I pressed a kiss to her forehead, then her nose.

"Have you looked into the mayor any further?"

"Leave that to me. Focus on our son and school, but remember my men will drive you to and from school or I will myself."

"Like a hostage." She sucked her teeth.

"I can't have you driving yourself."

"Table this discussion before I blow up."

Her attitude was apparent, but I ignored the pinched brows and watched the cars pass. One black sedan with tinted windows lagged behind, and I touched my right hip, then remembered I'd left my gun in the car.

"Walk on my right side."

"Huh… Why?" Sonya looked from me to the traffic.

"Stay calm, just follow my lead." I pushed the walk sign at the corner of the traffic light, and the black sedan stopped behind two other cars. I clenched her hand, led her across the street to the local art boutique nearby, and pushed the door open.

"This is so cute."

"Check it out." I nudged her inside, then stared out of the door at the car I'd spotted earlier. I relaxed once it drove away and sent a text to Remo to park outside for a few minutes so she could shop.

"Vincenzo would love to come here." Sonya smiled at the diverse paintings on the walls.

"Da… da…" RJ started to cry in her arms.

"Let me take him."

"We can go. I saw an ice cream place next door." Sonya leaned her head on my arm, and I placed my hand on her waist.

"Renato, I want to come back here and pick some stuff up for the house."

"Don't we have enough art in my house?"

"You can never have too much art."

"Maybe."

"Besides, all you have is family photos and art from your family on the wall."

"Are you saying I'm obsessed with my family?"

She slumped her shoulders and giggled. I unlocked the door and followed her inside of the ice cream parlor.

———

We finished our day with shopping for RJ and had dinner together, then we came home, gave him a bath, and put him to sleep. Sonya decided to watch a movie. I curled up next to her after she popped some popcorn, and we relaxed.

Knock! Knock!

I lifted my wrist and saw the time was around nine p.m. and Sonya started to get up, but I pulled her back behind me.

"I got it." I brushed our lips together.

Climbing up the steps, I checked the monitor to see Remo and Ian at the front door.

"We have a problem."

Sonya tried to stretch her neck to see who was speaking. I stepped out and closed the door behind me so she couldn't listen.

"What's going on?"

"Costa hit one of our buildings."

"Remo, get everyone rounded up just in case we need to have a meeting with all the families."

"Tonight?" Ian's grimace was hard.

"Tonight he has overstepped. The mayor, what happened to him?"

"He was seen leaving Costa's home," Ian confirmed.

"Give the mayor another little update to let him know we're not playing around. Let me know when the cars are ready."

I turned and stalked back in the house and kissed Sonya on the cheek.

"I have to leave," I said.

"It's bad?" she asked

"Hopefully nothing, but I need to take care of something really quick. You're fine. We're fine."

Sonya grasped my wrist. "Be careful."

"Nothing will take me away from you and RJ."

She released a breath, and I squeezed her cheeks between thick fingers, leaning her head back.

"Don't stress."

I looked back at the house as the car drove us away, and Remo told me Costa and the mayor were last seen at

Naked, a Costa strip club. A few people were outside, and I watched the bouncers let some women in without checking their ID.

"Stay here."

"Boss, we might need to walk with you," Remo remarked.

"Emers won't do anything at his place of business."

I shuffled out of the car and strolled to the front door. The bouncer looked like he'd seen a ghost and removed the velvet rope, allowing me entry without checking my ID. The place wasn't as upscale like the place Sante owned, and some of the women looked addicted to more than just pills. I scanned the room and walked up to the bar.

"Is Emers here?"

"Who wants to know?" the bartender questioned, placing an empty glass down and pouring wine for a guest.

"A friend."

"He left already."

"Thanks." I angled toward the stage and watched a woman come down off the pole; she reminded me of Sonya with long hair and full breasts. I shook my head and crept near the front door when someone yanked me back. I shook them off quickly.

"Mr. Calabresi, you look stressed."

"Do I?"

"You do. Maybe I can help you with that."

"My wife is already taking care of my stress." I lifted a hand away and blew her a kiss.

CHAPTER 20

Sonya

"Don't wait up" I heard him say as he walked out of the door.

His words played back in my mind. Something happened, and I couldn't put my finger on what it was because he refused to talk to me about it. I slid RJ into his new outfit with a shirt that said "birthday boy" on the front. It was the weekend. I was thankful that Adelina had taken over the party planning from me since I'd started back in class. My schedule consisted of three days a week at campus. I worked the other two days at the Calabresi office, as well as Fridays after class. I had bodyguards with me all the time, even outside of my class, and I had to apologize to my professors that my husband was overprotective. Brilynn, I think, got the point about us not being friends anymore, as she hadn't called or showed up anywhere I went.

"Happy birthday, RJ!" we cheered together; he tried to climb off the bed, and I pulled him back.

"Mrs. Calabresi, the car is ready," our nanny, Deborah, informed us.

"Thank you. Is he here?"

"No, ma'am."

"Thanks."

He wanted to make a big deal of RJ's birthday and he was nowhere to be found. He came home last night, but ever since a month ago, he started coming in late at night. I tucked a strand of hair behind my ear and rose to take RJ with me to the car.

"Probably already at his parents' house."

"I definitely think Renato is running around buying up every toy in the store." She gave a faint smile, closed the door after me, and laughed at RJ when he tried to pat me on the jaw. I smiled at him and rubbed his back.

"RJ, you ready for your party?" She held her hand up for a high five.

The door opened, then closed, and Renato stood there with a large arrangement of flowers in his hands.

"How about I take him to the car?" Deborah placed him on her hip.

The smile on his face could make me melt, but it dripped with manipulation after a continued lack of communication.

"You're late."

He tried to grab me, and I jerked out of his hold.

"Sonya, I'm sorry." I was enclosed in his arms with my back to his chest. He pressed a kiss to my shoulder.

"Okay."

"You don't sound like you accept my apology."

"You're right."

"What can I do?"

"Where were you?"

"Work."

"Tell me why I got this on my phone last night." I

decided to remove my phone and show the photo of him in the strip club with naked women.

"*Your husband's not home*" was the accompanying message.

"That doesn't mean anything."

"Explain it to me, Renato. We've been good for a while, but I feel like you are hiding stuff, and I don't like it."

"Work."

"Stop being an asshole."

A deep crease formed on his forehead.

"You like this asshole." He stared into my eyes.

"Okay." I dodged his kiss, leaned back, and opened the door to leave.

"I had Kennth followed, and he showed up at the club," he blurted out.

"Was that so hard to tell me?" I reached the car and hopped in, shutting the door, then put my seat belt on. Renato locked our hands together and rested them on his thigh. Ian reversed out of the driveway, heading toward Renato's parents' home.

"Rather you not worry about my business."

"I understand, but you can't always be with me, and your guards need me to be prepared, correct?"

The sun beamed through the window, and the limo eased through the neighborhood.

"How many people are coming to this party?" He changed the subject, but I wouldn't keep quiet like other wives.

"Adelina invited about ten kids."

"Do you know these kids or their families?"

He frowned, and I smirked at the annoyed expression on his face.

"Not like you have to watch them."

"Are you up to something?"

In mock pity, I held my hand to my chest.

"Next time, answer me when I call."

Finally, the car stopped at the gate, the guard buzzed us through, and we saw cars lined around the water fountain.

"Are you ready for cake and ice cream, RJ?" I removed my hand from Renato's leg and cupped RJ's feet.

"Da... da..."

"Here we go." I chortled and removed his seat belt and climbed out with Renato next to me. The front door displayed a sign that said "Happy birthday RJ" with his picture, and as the door swung agape, Marilyn, Adelina, and McKayla smiled and clamored for RJ.

Renato stood off to the side with his brothers and laughed about something Savio had said. Adelina had outdone herself to have an animal theme in the backyard. She hired a clown and had a face-painting section and a train the kids could ride around on. Some of the kids were from the neighborhood, and a few mafia members had brought theirs. SJ and RJ were running together to hide from the donkeys.

"Having fun?" Rena bumped me on my hip. I held RJ's cup of juice, watching him laugh with his cousin.

"He is growing so fast, Rena."

"He reminds me so much of Renato, but much sweeter," Rena jested.

"Renato's been in and out of the house late for the past month."

"Did he tell you why?"

"No, and I avoided it when he came in today, but that didn't last long."

Rena poked her hip out.

"If he's like his brother, that means something is going on, and we need to be prepared." Rena pulled a box of party hats over to the side of the table. The food was a buffet style of hamburgers and hotdogs, with a candy table and an open bar.

A feeling of someone watching came over me, and I looked behind me and caught Renato's stare. He lifted the beer to his lips and winked.

"Class going well?"

"Yeah, I love it and Vincenzo is amazing to let me work part time."

"Happy you've focused on yourself outside of all this." Rena waved a hand around the family.

"Same. How is the fashion business?"

"Good. I might have another fashion show soon."

"Sante agreed."

"Still early, but if I do, plan for New York."

"Time to open presents." McKayla brought a few bags over, and Marilyn grabbed RJ to sit at the head of the table.

"Who bought him a Jeep?" I quizzed through an exasperated breath.

"Leave my nephew alone." Rena stuck her tongue out at me.

I picked up a box of smaller gifts and sat them next to him.

RJ didn't pay any attention to the presents and stared at the donkeys. I tried to get him to look, but he snatched his hand away.

"Let him go play." Renato walked up on us, and I wanted to argue but thought better of that in front of his family.

"He can open them later." I let Marilyn take him back over to the animal enclosure.

"Come talk to me," Renato challenged, planting his fingers on the back of my neck and rubbing small circles.

"I'll be back, Rena."

Rena took the box out of my hands; my eyes slid from RJ, and I followed Renato to the house.

"What's up?"

He shoved me up against the door, out of view from our guests.

"Before you get pissed, I need you to know this is nothing but work."

"I know."

"How is school going?"

"Either you really want to know or you are trying to gauge my attitude."

Hesitation laced his eyes; I looked away, and he pulled me back to face him.

"School, Sonya."

"School is fine. I like my professors."

"My guards tell me you've made a few friends."

His jaw twitched, and I knew that look of jealousy. A few men had tried to talk to me at school, but I'd turned them all down, showing them my ring. Also, the big, burly bodyguards with visible guns indicating they get away from me made the bigger impression.

"What do you have to tell me, Renato, that's so important?"

"After the cake, I need to leave."

I tried to shove him away from me, but he placed both hands on my waist, digging his fingers into my hips.

"On his birthday!" I shrieked.

"Listen to me. It can't wait."

"Just go."

"You know if it could be avoided I would, but we're closing in on ending Costa."

"Whatever makes you feel better."

"I won't be gone long."

"Lie to me again." My lip was tucked between my teeth.

He brushed a hand down his face. "Costa set fire to some of our business."

My head snapped, and I put a hand on his chest.

"Was anyone hurt?" I softened at his touch on my wrist.

"It was retaliation for what happened to Tulio. As far as I know everybody is fine."

"Go do what you need to do."

"You won't ignore me when I come back?"

I smacked him gently on the chest, leaned forward, and hugged him.

"Just come back safe." He buried his face in my neck, then our lips connected in a sloppy long-held kiss.

"Renato, you have to come see this." EJ crept near us. Renato went in the direction of his brother's loud grumbles.

"Breaking news from the mayor's conference. He stated that the Calabresi family is being indicted for criminal activity…"

"Shit!" Savio yelled, stomping out of the room.

"…The list of what is being charged is stemming from a Renato Calabresi." My eyes ballooned in surprise.

"He's made his choice." Renato's deep, raspy tone was disturbing. To think he could get rid of the mayor and nobody would notice.

"What can we do?"

"Our family lawyer will be here soon," his dad said.

"Take care of RJ, and I'll handle the rest."

"But Renato, they have your picture across a screen."

"It's all a game, Sonya. Let me handle myself and you look after our son."

"He's right, Sonya. Emers must have figured the mayor is running out of time and they took the bait," EJ remarked.

"What bait?"

"You."

"Huh?"

"Renato would be off his game if you're upset and distraught," Sante explained.

"Renato is stuck here to comfort you and not notice how our territory is being taken if we are distracted by Renato in jail," EJ finished his theory.

"We need to make a move now," Renato insisted; all the guys started to move in sync to the front door.

"Please come back to me." I gripped his shirt.

"Take care of RJ and get video."

"What if the police come by here while you're out?"

"Sante is checking with our contacts at the station, promising nothing will happen tonight." He rushed a kiss to my lips, then my hand.

Adelina carried the cake out of the kitchen; I soaked up my tears and put on a smile to continue my son's party without a clue if his father would end up in jail for the rest of his life. The Calabresis liked to think they were untouchable, but I had a feeling something bad would happen and hit too close, causing a ripple effect.

CHAPTER 21
Renato

WE SPED AWAY. I had Savio on speakerphone while he was in his car heading to our second warehouse, closest to his bar. A month ago, we'd hunted Emers's people throughout the night and each one was too scared to give up his whereabouts, plus Kennth Sanchez had it in his mind we'd play nice after his show of force. It only made me want to kill him even more.

"Where are you headed?" Savio asked.

"To take care of a last-minute thing."

"I need you to get here as soon as possible," Savio demanded.

"It shouldn't take long."

"No games, Renato."

"Soon as I wrap this up, I'll come there." I sighed.

"Something you're not telling me?"

"It's safer this way."

"Something that will put you in a position to lose your family?" he probed.

"My family will be protected."

He sighed. "All I ask is you get here fast."

"Savio." I needed him to understand, the same way he'd fought for his wife.

"Yeah."

"I won't stand down."

"I get your feelings," Savio replied.

"I want a meeting with all the families."

"Tell the guys to get everybody, whoever is not with you, it's on them," Savio expressed.

"Emers hit more than one location. Our construction site," I responded, wiping a hand own my face in aggravation.

"Keep me updated. I'm on my way, Savio."

Ian coasted by her house. All the lights were off, and two cars were in the driveway. If Costa was here, he wouldn't make it so easy for me to catch him. I rolled my window down and watched for any signs. The window was flung agape, and a young guy that looked no more than twenty years old checked the surroundings.

"We'll come back." Ian pressed the gas, then rushed to the warehouse.

———

The entire room was quiet. Savio stood at the head of the table and ran his eyes over each boss of all the families. As the Don in the city, no one could do a thing to another family without his permission and the votes of the other bosses. Everything had to pass through him and get approval. So If I made a move, we needed him and all the families to agree.

"What are we doing here, Savio?" Alize questioned.

"I called this meeting because Costa has stepped out of line."

"Yes," Alize answered.

"As you know, a few months ago, Tulio made a move on my brother's wife. We cannot allow that to happen."

"And he was taken care of," Tommaso Gallo hissed.

"We didn't take this lightly. All families try to peacefully coexist." Savio explained his reasons, and I didn't care to give an explanation.

"But he wouldn't listen. On top of that, the mayor has decided he wants to go behind our backs and do his reelection with Costa backing," Savio informed them.

"Force us out. I'm here because we need approval. Well, technically, I'm here because I wanted you all to be aware," Sante remarked.

"This is my brother's family. So he is taking the lead on this. And I back him a hundred percent," Savio followed up.

I stood, staring each man in the eye and spoke in a calm tone.

"The Costa family has to end," I said.

"We make a lot of money with them, though," Alize responded.

"If you're with Costa, you're against me. And when you're against the Calabresi family, you are no longer welcome at this table," I said.

"Renato, we can't just throw them out because of some bitterness over a woman," Gallo spat.

"That *woman* is my wife. You need to figure out whose side you're on. Because I'm not waiting."

"He hit our place a few nights ago. And there's no telling where else he's going to hit before he needs to be stopped." EJ passed photos of our business burnt down.

"He's right. There's no more playing by the rules. This is beyond cordial conversation," Sante insisted.

"If it makes you feel better, we can tell him you did not vote because we made a move on you," Savio said.

"When you become integrated in the family, all bets are

off and and you cannot step over that line. And Tulio did. And now his brother had his cousin reach out to my wife. That was a sign of disrespect. And each of you knows I don't handle disrespect well," I argued.

"Okay, Renato. If we do this, what do we get out of agreeing?" Gallow inquired.

"If the mayor doesn't go along with our plan, we take him out. And we give you a piece of Costa's land." Savio shifted in his chair.

"We give you Tulio's territory. The entire land, all of it," EJ disclosed, and their eyes lit up. Their area was close to downtown Chicago, and money could be pushed in for local business.

I looked at Savio for confirmation, while each man looked at another and nodded their heads at me.

"You made the right decision," I said.

I stood and made my exit.

I headed straight back to check on RJ at the house. When I arrived, I watched him talk with his uncles and stood back in the light at my son. My namesake.

"What do you think about if we have another one?" I said.

"How about five years from now?" Sonya slid her hand around mine.

"Thank you for throwing the party." I placed a hand on her lower back.

"He's having a good time."

"He is. What did you do for his first birthday party?"

The smile left her face.

"I don't want to make you miserable today. Especially after what came about."

"I'm not miserable. I'm okay. What did you do?"

"We just had a cake and ice cream little party, just Brilynn, my mom, and me."

Her mention of Brilynn caused a lump in my throat.

"Do you have class on Monday?"

"I do."

"How's that going?"

"Going fine, talked to the counselor and got leads on potential internships. Everything's going great, only two classes right now."

"I need to come up there and meet your classmates."

"No and I still have time to take care of the household and work with the family. Not too overwhelmed," she said.

"Then that's great. How about I take you to school on Monday?"

"What? Like we're a high school couple, you're gonna drop me off and pick me up during lunch to take me off campus?"

We both burst into laughter.

"Something like that. But I just want to let you know, some things might be coming up that you should be aware of after today's announcement."

"You really scare me, Renato."

"Nothing to stress about. But just be aware of your surroundings and the people you talk to."

"Costa is still missing?"

"It's about everything. Just be on alert if I'm not around," I said. I grabbed a beer from Sante when he walked up next to me.

The meeting for approval went according to plan, and the family surrounded RJ with love and happiness today. Even EJ got along with Cora. She was able to be around him, and they did not get into a spat. I finished my beer.

"You handled yourself in the meeting."

"I know. It's weird."

"Finally started to control your temper."

"RJ's rubbed off on me."

"What if we all have sons like us?"

"I know, it's like a whole other generation of Calabresi boys." I chuckled at my joke.

"Yeah, it would be, but everything's set in place." Sante tossed his empty beer in the trash.

"Press conference didn't help."

"Look into our assets."

"Not worried. All of our stuff is legit," EJ said as he texted on his phone.

"But he's trying to turn the public against us. It's all about perception. If we look bad enough, they assume we're guilty with no evidence," Sante snipped.

"But I'm gonna take care of him. Costa was at Brilynn's or his people are. He's not hiding, so he thinks he's safe, we got to make a move."

"I agree we need to go tonight. EJ, you stay here," Sante demanded.

An hour later I was strapped into a black bulletproof vest. Dome pulled up to Brilynn's place. It was me, Sante, Savio, and Remo, then in another car was the rest of the team. I checked the time, and there was now only one car parked outside. It was just going on nine.

I got out of the car and walked up to her house to knock, and not a few minutes later, the door unfastened.

"Why are you here?" A flicker of fear swept over her face before she pursed her lips together.

"We need to talk." I pushed my way through the door. She stumbled back and fell.

"Get away from me!" she screamed.

I kicked the door closed behind me; she just couldn't keep quiet. I cocked my head as she tried to reach for her phone. I lunged at her.

"Women like you disgust me." I gripped her face firmly. Brilynn tried to push me away, forcing herself to the floor.

"You're pathetic." I dropped down to my knees and

stared at her. "My wife is ten times a better woman than you will ever be."

"Let me go," she begged.

I pushed her head back and scanned my eyes around her living room.

I saw a couple photos of Sonya and her together.

"Where did you get the money for the house?"

"None of your business."

"You were just living in an apartment with Sonya and now all of a sudden you can afford this house."

"Fuck you, and Sonya will see soon. Get out of my house."

I chuckled. "How much are Emers and the mayor paying you?"

Her eyes ballooned wide. "Emers and my business has nothing to do with you."

"None of my business? Really? Because I saw his car here earlier and a few weeks ago."

"You make me sick."

"It was late. Did you know he's married? Still has a couple of girlfriends on the side. So you're like number three or four?"

She smirked. "I knew you wanted me."

"Bitch, I would never stoop that low. You're not my type."

I removed my hand.

She stood, ready to slap me across the face. I grabbed her wrist, pulling it behind her back.

"You know I gave you a chance to leave."

I covered her mouth as she screamed.

"I like when they scream," I whispered.

I kept her head in a chokehold and pulled out the needle. I spun her around, and her eyes clouded in fear as I clasped my hand around her throat. Then I pushed the needle into her neck. I didn't always have to have blood. I do prefer to see the sight of blood from my victims. But this time, since she was Sonya's friend, I decided to keep it clean and just have it look like an overdose and tasked my men to set it up with needles and drugs around the room. I placed her on the couch slowly with her arms still out. They would find her immediately. I retreated back the way I'd come, progressing to the car.

I monitored her neighbors' homes as I climbed into the car, and we drove off when my phone rang and Sonya's name showed under my favorites.

I placed the phone on speaker.

"Hello."

"Where are you?"

"Out with my brothers."

"When are you coming home?" she whined, and I adjusted my shaft.

I smiled and took her off speakerphone.

"Is RJ asleep?"

"Yes, he was knocked out as soon as we got him in the bath."

"Did he love his gifts?"

"You know he did, and that ridiculous car he's constantly tried to play with."

"He can have anything he wants."

"Renato, we shouldn't spoil him."

"That's a promise I can't keep." I heard a splash of water.

"My mom showed up to the party before it was over."

To hear that her mom came surprised me, but I wouldn't try and get in between their relationship. I'm close to both of my parents, and I grew up with my grandfather; RJ should have a piece of her family around.

"Are you in the tub?"

"Yes, with a glass of wine."

"Ughhh…" I grunted at the thought of her pouty lips and fat ass on my face.

"Hurry up and maybe I'll think of a way to relieve your stress."

"Teasing me only makes me do what I want to do to you even longer."

"How do I tease you?"

"Tease me with your fat pussy that smothers my tongue. Tease me when your moans sound like I've taken you to the highest of highs. Tease me when you wrap your pouty lips around my dick and make me come."

"How long will it take you to get here?"

"Is the bathroom door locked?"

"Yes, why?"

"Unlock it, I'm outside." I heard the dial tone and pressed the end of the call and tossed it on the nightstand as the door yanked ajar. She stood on her tiptoes, linked her hands to the back of my head, and pressed into my chest.

"Are you in for the night?"

"Yes." I slipped my hand around to sink my nails into her left cheek.

"Come let me tease you then." Sonya took my hand, led me into the bathroom, and shut the door behind us.

CHAPTER 22
Sonya

MONDAY MORNING CAME AROUND, and the day started off all wrong when I woke up late and almost missed the start of class. Renato twisted me in all different angles, and I was happy to enjoy his tongue all over my body; it relaxed him to see me pleased. His eyes bored into mine when I pleased him right back.

"Fuck! Sonya, suck me clean." Renato grunted, bent my head back, and watched me swallow his cum down my throat.

"Sonya!" the professor called out.

"Huh?"

"Did you hear the question?" Professor Kirk probed.

"Sorry, no I didn't." I sat up straighter.

"I asked if you've found an art gallery to intern with."

"My brother-in-law is helping me secure an internship."

"All right, please make sure you stay awake during class."

A curt smile formed on his face, and I nodded.

Class ended, and I grabbed my backpack, heading to my next class.

An hour later, I ambled out of class to grab something to

eat. Dome came toward me and took my backpack out of my hands.

"Dome, I can carry my bag," I joked.

"No, ma'am."

"How long have you worked for Renato?"

Dome and I had become friendly, but we've never had a full conversation about his life outside of driving me around and being cordial.

"A few years."

"Do you only work for Renato?"

"We rotate between each family if they need extra protection." He opened the door of the cafeteria.

It was kind of sad that everybody was already connected as groups at each table. It felt like back in high school; I wanted to have friends. Brilynn and I had talked about being on campus together, but now our lives were separate.

"Are you hungry, Dome?" I turned to check, and he watched the crowd.

I tapped him on the shoulder.

"I doubt you'll have trouble here," I jested.

He cracked a smile and patted his jacket. I looked to his waist and saw a gun.

"Always prepared," he answered.

"After class can we run by my mom's?"

"Boss said he's going to come pick you up."

"Crap, I forgot."

I recalled how my mom came to the birthday party later than expected, but I enjoyed how happy RJ was to see her and the other kids and take pictures together.

"I hate to admit, but you two made a beautiful baby, Sonya." *Mom held my hand.*

"Even though it's with a guy you hate." I leaned my head on her shoulder.

"We've come a long way, but I will give him credit."

"Thank you."

"Courtney, are you hungry?" Adelina came near with a tray of food.

"No thank you, Adelina. Sonya stuffed my face already when I got here," Mom kidded, taking the stuffed bear out of RJ's hand.

"Yeah, I told her you don't let anyone leave without eating, so she might as well pig out now." I pointed out how Adelina treated everyone like family when she met them.

"Glad you and Sonya are back on track. I know how it feels to lose a relationship with your child," Adelina confessed, and I was curious who she was talking about.

"You have a lovely home." Mom trained her eyes on the mansion that sat behind us.

"Thank you. My husband wanted a place to raise our kids, and grandkids one day." Adelina tickled RJ.

"He's getting tired, Sonya," Mom brought up. I looked into his eyes and saw the restlessness from all the running around today.

"He sure is. I think we've had enough fun for the day."

"I'll need to call her and reschedule," I told Dome and picked up a bottle of water and a salad and went to the cash register to pay.

"How many more classes?"

"Just one after lunch. I need to go by the office to check in with Vincenzo."

"Should I tell Renato? I know he doesn't want you out all day," Dome replied, lifting his phone up.

"No, I can tell him when he picks me up. RJ is home with Deborah anyway."

Dome stood at the edge of the table, and I felt anxious with him hovering over me.

"Can you sit down, Dome? It's weird, I have people staring at me."

"My job is to protect you."

"Can't you do it by sitting down though?" I poured oil

and vinegar on my salad, then unwrapped my fork and knife. He didn't move and scanned the room as I complained.

"Be happy Boss didn't want more men on you."

"That's true, He talked about putting you guys in the class with me and I had to plead with him to cut it down to you and one person outside the building.

"Emers is slick, he's nothing like Tulio."

"I wish I'd never overheard him that day."

"It'll be over soon." Dome patted my shoulder.

I finished my lunch and went to my next class.

"Hey you're new, right?" A guy approached, and I froze. He sat next to me in my art history class, and we'd never talked, so I was surprised he made a move today of all days.

"I am."

"I'm Sean." He held a hand toward me, and I reciprocated.

"Sonya."

"You're married." He zeroed in on my left hand, tossing his blond ponytail, then his blue eyes pierced mine.

"I am." I gleaned at my wedding ring.

"He's a lucky man."

"Thanks."

"You don't look old enough to be married." He removed his book out of his bag.

"How should a married woman look?" My right brow quirked up at his statement.

"I picture someone at least in their late thirties, short hair, long dress with a jacket, carrying a notepad to keep up with the schedule."

I burst out in laughter. "Sorry to disappoint you."

"Not disappointed at all." Sean winked at me.

His cocky demeanor reminded me of Renato, and I chuckled when he passed me a note.

We should have lunch sometime as friends.

I balled the note up and focused on the professor for the next hour. After the professor added a pop quiz and relayed the homework we needed to study, Sean and I chatted, peeling out of the building while Dome held a grimace as we laughed together. He tried to push Sean away, but I demanded we were just making friendly conversation.

"How old are you?" Sean asked, holding his backpack and books.

"About to be twenty-five."

Honk!

Sean and I stared forward; my stomach clenched at Renato standing outside of his car, then he started toward us.

"Uhm, Sean I'll see you in class." I tried to end our conversation.

"Let me get your number so we can study together." Sean pushed his phone toward me. Renato snatched it out of his hand and scrolled to get his number and send to his own phone. "Aye, that's my phone, man," Sean fussed and tried to grab it back.

"Renato, it's not what you think."

"Did she tell you she's married?"

"Yeah, we weren't doing anything," I snapped, planting my hand on my hip.

"Dome, take her to my car." Renato ignored me.

"Renato, leave him alone. He's in my class." I stood in between them, glaring into his eyes.

He growled, looked from Sean down to me, and smirked before pecking my lips.

"For you." He slipped his tongue in my mouth.

"Thank you, can he have his phone back please."

"Remember when you think of her, picture my face and fist. She's married." Renato tossed his phone back to him, took my hand, and headed to his car. He unlocked my door, and I piled into the backseat. Dome took my backpack and tossed it in the trunk as Sean stared at us.

"Embarrassing me is not in my plans for our agreement."

He shrugged his shoulders, and my head whirled around.

"You think it's funny, don't you?" I shifted in the seat and saw out of the corner of my eye his smile grow.

"I know what guys think about when they see a beautiful woman."

"Duh, I was a stripper, I know as well."

The veins in his knuckles popped as he gripped the steering wheel.

"Whatever his name is—"

"His name is Sean, and you have some making up to do, mister, for embarrassing me."

"Happily do anything to get that pretty smile on your face."

"How about you run me by the office. I need to talk to Vincenzo."

"I wanted to take you to dinner."

"Can we push it back? I haven't been in the office for the past few days, and I need to check in with him."

"You really like your job."

He turned on the signal.

"Yep, my professor wants me to get an internship, so I need to make sure I can get in at the gallery."

"I'm sure you have it in the bag." Renato put his hand on my thigh as he drove.

"How was RJ when you left the house?" I texted Deborah to check on him earlier.

"He was up playing in his room."

"After I leave the office, I promised my mom we would hang out. Do you mind if Dome takes me?"

He scratched the back of his neck. "Remember you have a family."

"Let's not go there. I'll be home before dinner."

"All I ask."

"What did you do all day?"

He pulled up to the front of the Calabresi offices.

"I hung out with RJ for a little while, then handled some business."

"Do I want to know what that business is?"

He put the car in park and leaned over the console to crash our lips together.

"Go work, and I'll check in with you later. Don't stay too late, or I'll have Dome come get you," Renato demanded, touching the door handle.

"Same to you."

He stared as the doorman held the door ajar for me and finally went on his way. I got on the elevator and rode it to Vincenzo's floor. Checking the time, it showed two p.m., and I had plenty of time to see my mom afterwards and make it home for dinner.

"Hey, Sonya." Vincenzo's assistant, Krissy, waved at me.

"Hi, is he with anyone?"

"You came at the perfect time."

"Great, I won't hold him too long." She buzzed me in, and I tapped on his door, poking my head in. He was in the chair with his eyes closed.

"Working hard." I cackled, and he opened one eye at me.

"I thought you had class."

"I'm finished for the day."

"Usually you don't work on school days midweek."

"You're right, but I feel bad I haven't been around in a few days." I plopped down in the chair.

"Education is more important. Don't feel guilty."

"How can you be related to Renato and be so sweet?"

He cackled, and I really wondered how all of his older brothers were such rude assholes, especially Renato.

"The mask comes off sometimes," Vincenzo teased.

"That's something I can't believe."

"True, after being treated like a baby all my life I had to show I was tough, and I'd get into fights at school because I was known as the little brother."

"Please never change. We need a sane brother out of the bunch."

"Wish I could keep that promise."

"Is something wrong?"

"No, how can I help you?"

"Are you trying to change the subject?"

He chortled, then turned his attention to his phone.

"Since you won't tell me what's going on, can you please talk to your brother?"

"Renato?"

"Yeah, my crazy husband."

"Tell me what he did."

I gave a rundown of how Renato made a big deal of Sean and me talking, and all Vincenzo could do was laugh.

"That's not funny." I threw my hands up in exasperation.

"Renato has no home training."

"Now you tell me."

"Be happy he didn't shoot him."

"That's your solution?"

His lips formed a straight line.

"Anyway, did you find out if I could intern at the Prism Art Gallery?"

Prism was owned by the family, but they didn't manage it like they did the company, so I'd have to report for work like a real employee, unlike here, where I could make my own schedule to accommodate my class and home life balance.

"Agnese knows you'll be interning."

"She knows I'm married to Renato?"

"Yeah, but she won't give you any problems."

"Thanks, Vincenzo."

"You are welcome."

"Anything I can do here to help out?"

"No, go home and be with my nephew."

"I will after I check in with my mom."

"I remember she showed up at the party. How is that going?"

"Good, her treatment for cancer is going well, and her weight is coming back."

"Happy to hear she is doing well."

I took the piece of paper with Agnese's number and double-checked my emails and messages before I left for the rest of the day.

CHAPTER 23

Renato

"WHERE ARE WE WITH THE MAYOR?" I rubbed the top of RJ's head, and he smiled a mostly toothless grin. I looked at Remo, Ian, and Dome at the kitchen island.

My phone started ringing, Sonya's name flashing on the screen. I put her on speaker.

"You said you were going to pick me up from my mom's."

"Aren't the guards there?"

"No."

"Shit," I cursed.

"Don't bother, Mom is bringing me."

"I will be there in a few minutes, got stuck in a meeting."

"No reason to leave now, she is taking me."

"No, you two need to stay put."

"Are you sure everything is all right?" she asked.

"Everything is fine. Just stay at your mom's house. I'll be there soon."

"Okay, hurry up, I want to get ready for dinner." Sonya ended the call.

I made eye contact with RJ and nuzzled my nose in his

neck. Dome had been called back to the house because we got word Emers had made a move, and I had to do what I had to do to make sure my family stayed out of harm's way. So we came back to the house and worked on a plan, but I left a team at her mom's home. I jumped in my car and drove up to get her while Dome rode shotgun, leaving Ian at the house with RJ and Deborah. It took me less than twenty minutes to reach her with light traffic. When I pulled in, she stepped out of the house. I wiped the sweat off my forehead as I got out of the car and unlocked the passenger door for her, then kissed her on the cheek. She lifted up and kissed me on the lips.

"What have you been doing?"

"I hung out with my brothers and had a short business meeting. Got a little sidetracked, and I forgot."

"Are you sure that's all?" Sonya intertwined our hands.

"Why do you ask?"

"Usually you're on time or you'll send the guys."

"I need to look into why they didn't show up." I scanned the area, and Dome was already texting on his phone.

"Do you think Emers has something to do with your men not being here?"

"I will pick you up myself; if not, it'll be Remo or Dome going forward."

"Okay."

"What do you want to do for dinner tonight?"

"I'm exhausted. You want to just order in?"

"Whatever you want." She caught sight of me out of the corner of her eye.

"Why do you seem jumpy, Renato? Normally you're not."

"Told you just business, so tell me how class was and your mom."

"It was good. Vincenzo gave me the number to the

manager of the Prism gallery. Professor gave us a quiz earlier."

I listened to her talk until we finally made it home, and she got out of the car. I waited.

"Are you coming?"

"Yeah, just give me a second. I just need to make a phone call."

"All right. That means I get to order whatever I want."

"But I never stopped you before," I joked. She stuck her tongue out and switched her hips. I stared at her ass. Dome followed her inside.

"Did you make sure Brilynn was cleaned up?"

"Yeah, Boss. The ambulance came and didn't ask any questions." Remo relayed the situation.

"They got an anonymous tip that a woman died of a drug overdose."

"Good. Good. Just make sure if you see anyone come to her house, you let me know. Emers will come eventually, and I need you to follow him. "

"Already on it, Boss." Ian stood at the car door.

I got out of the car, then went to talk with Dome.

I strolled through the house then jumped in the shower, cleaning up for the night. I came out of the bathroom and dried my hair, switching the TV on. It played the news.

"*Breaking news, Mayor Sanchez is giving a speech on the steps of City Hall,*" the News Nine reporter said.

"*The authorities are looking at the Calabresi family possibly being indicted for embezzlement and illegal gambling funds.*

"*The mayor has stated the family has too long been into nefarious affairs. We will report live at six. Make sure you join us then,*" the reporter stated. I turned the screen off and changed into jeans and a shirt before I headed downstairs to eat dinner. Sonya was at the counter, removing the takeout cartons of rolls, and putting them on the counter.

"Hungry, RJ?"

He raised his hands to be picked up.

"Dinner is almost ready." Sonya poured soup in a bowl.

"Is that my mom's famous spicy potato soup?"

She held the spoon up to my lips so I could taste it.

"Amazing." I kissed her on the back of her neck, sliding my arm around her waist, and she giggled.

"Not in front of RJ." She tried to nudge me away; I whirled her around to face me.

"He wants us to work on a sibling."

Sonya narrowed her eyes at RJ.

"RJ, you want a sibling?"

"Momma... Momma," RJ expressed, and Sonya moved a hand to her mouth, tears appearing in her eyes.

"He finally said Momma." Sonya picked him up, and he locked a hand on her face as I chuckled at them with excitement.

"He did. Can we eat and put him to bed so I can enjoy you tonight?" Sonya placed him back in the highchair; she fixed our plates and we sat down to eat dinner.

———

While drinking my coffee in the kitchen, I listened to the conference the mayor had decided to have. Assuming Emers had been playing him like a puppet, Savio had revoked our deal to keep him covered, and we scheduled a meeting with our contact to work things out. I put my coffee cup in the sink, wanting to head to the office. Sonya walked into the kitchen, looking disheveled. After checking my watch and knowing Savio was talking to the staff, I decided to talk to my parents to work out what to do.

"Why didn't you wake me?" she grumbled, pulling her hair up into a high ponytail on her head.

"I thought you needed to sleep. It looked like you had a long night." I poked her on the nose.

"You mean after you held me up against the shower and fucked me senseless." Sonya smacked her lips. I planted my lips on the back of her palm.

"Where are you going off to?" Sonya asked, grabbing the coffee mug and cream.

"Business."

"Of course. Is it business business or mafia business?"

"If I tell you I'd have to kill you."

After she smacked me on the arm, I groped her ass, threw on my jacket, and gestured to Remo to get in the car. Within minutes, Remo was at the headquarters, and there were a lot of reporters waiting outside.

"Mr. Calabresi. What can you tell us about the accusations by the mayor?"

"Don't know anything about what he speaks of. You know the mayor hasn't been well lately. Ever since his affair, really can't trust anything he says." I smiled at the camera, eased through the crowd, and took the elevator, heading to the main conference room. While a few employees lingered around the break room, I pushed open the door to our small team of board members, who were listening intently to what Savio had to say.

"Listen, everything is under control. This is just another bureaucratic stronghold to try and put us back in the hole to make us look weak."

"What about the books?" Carter, an older board member, probed.

"Vincenzo has managed to look at all of our books, and everything is in the clear," Sante breathed.

"We have nothing to worry about. We just need to let this blow over," Savio said.

"What about our parents? Are they up to date?" Vincenzo asked.

"McKayla has talked with her own bosses at the newspaper to see what they know right now. It's just a wait and see if anything comes about this morning."

Ring! Ring!

I saw my wife's name scroll across and decided to answer.

"You have to get home quickly," she hysterically cried.

"Calm down and tell me what's wrong."

"The FBI is here."

I leaped out of my seat.

"What? The FBI is there?"

Sante and Vincenzo stood next to me.

"No. There's a lot of men here. They have FBI and ATF jackets saying that you are being investigated for the murder of Tulio Costa," Sonya whispered over the phone.

"Just stay calm. Where's RJ?"

"He is with the nanny."

"I need you to stay calm. I will be there soon. There's nothing to worry about."

"Cops are taking a lot of stuff out of the house."

"There's nothing in our home that would make us suspects. You don't have anything to worry about." I ended the call and blew out a breath. "Emers must have given a tip to someone in the FBI. He just wrote a check for his own funeral."

"We need to play this smart," Sante said, stepping on the elevator beside me.

"Who do you have to take over? I'm sending the information to your phone now see if they can draw the papers up," I announced. Sante and I jogged to the car, and Remo sped us back to my house, taking the freeway to cut down on time. Finally, EJ pulled up right at the same time with our family attorney, and I slammed the door behind me.

"What are you doing at my house?" I growled at the FBI agent.

"Mr. Calabresi, we have a warrant to search the premises."

He held a piece of paper up; I snatched it and tore it up.

"On what grounds?"

"Witness states you killed Tulio Costa."

"What witness?"

"We have evidence, a lot of proof to bury you." He pointed in my face.

"What proof?"

"Don't talk to anyone, Renato." Vaughn, our family attorney, picked up the torn paper.

"It'll be shown at trial."

"That's if it makes it."

"Excuse me." He tried to get up in my face.

"I said that's if it makes it to trial."

"Is that a threat?" he snapped.

"It can mean anything, Officer, or should I say, Agent Gallagher. Whatever you think you have on me, it's been fabricated."

"That's a cost of the criminal life, finally coming to an end."

"Our family businesses are legit. I have no idea who is lying about us."

"You can lie to me. Or you can tell me the truth. But either way, you're going down, Renato Calabresi," he snarled at me. Giving him my back, I walked over to Sonya.

"Did you find anything out?" she said as soon as I came into the house.

"No."

"As soon as you left, I tried to shower and get changed, but I heard a loud knock."

"It's okay. Don't worry about it. The FBI is just sniffing around."

"They came in and out of our house."

"Are you sure?" I held her close to my chest.

"Positive."

"They're going to try and do whatever they're going to do. Pack some clothes; we're going over to my parents' and let them finish with EJ and Vaughn here."

"Who's going to clean up?" Sonya glanced around the now-ransacked room.

"Gonna stay to make sure they don't fuck anything up."

She leaned her head on my shoulder.

"All right. This is crazy. As soon as we figure stuff out, more shit happens."

"Don't worry. It all works itself out."

Thirty minutes later, we rolled up at my parents' house. Sonya yawned and took a sleepy RJ to his bedroom that my parents kept for him.

"Are you coming?" Sonya held her hand out for me to take.

"In a little bit. I need to talk to my father."

She saw Rena and McKayla get out of their cars, and all three looked exhausted as they stood at the front of the house.

I grabbed our bags and shut the door. Angling around the girls, I climbed the stairs and placed our things at the door of the living room.

"Your room is ready, Renato." Marilyn leaned in for a hug.

"Thank you. Is my father in his office?"

"He's waiting for you."

Canvasing the kitchen, I saw workers preparing dinner for the night before edging up to my father's office door and knocked.

"Come in!" He waited for me to sit.

"Did EJ call you?" I shut the door behind me and stood near the window in his office.

"Him and Vaughn," he said with a down-in-the-mouth demeanor.

"And?" I sealed my lips.

"Let the FBI twist the lies. It will be fine." He pulled on his mustache.

"She's more nervous." A reminder that I had someone to keep safe now.

"As a wife and mother, that's expected."

"I took care of one problem." The progress I'd made about Tulio replayed in my mind.

We made eye contact.

He lit his cigar.

"No choice in the matter."

"Growing up, I would think I was a monster for how easy it was for me to kill someone."

"Never raised a monster. You're my son, Renato."

"But our conversations weren't normal."

"I raised all of you boys the same. You might not think it's true, but I saw something different in you."

"That I lacked a soul."

"No, you have a soul, but you care so much for your family that sometimes you get irrational and have to focus that energy in the best way we know how."

"Killing."

"Each of you came with a unique ability. My father wanted to carry on our legacy. At one point, I thought about normalcy as well."

"You mean in Italy."

He sighed and moved to stand next to me at the window.

"After he died, I became the Don of the family and then moved to America."

"Why didn't you try hard enough?" My nostrils flared. All of our lives stemmed from old wars.

"Because they'd never let us leave." His annoyance showed in his upper body as his shoulders tensed.

"Who are they?" The questions rolled off my lips.

"Five families."

"Costa is impulsive now."

"I heard." Worry darkened his puffy eyes.

"The night of our warehouse fire, I tracked Costa's men to City Hall in the back alley arguing with the mayor."

"That wasn't part of the plan!" Brilynn shouted.

"Why is she here?" Emers's henchman groaned.

"Because my neck is on the line if we get caught."

"She's not worth keeping around," the mayor grumbled. Brilynn tried to smack him, but Emers pushed her away.

"Stay focused," Emers gritted through his teeth.

"Renato is little by little going to feel my pain, I need him to get buried under the jail sentence," the mayor muttered.

"What about my money?" Brilynn went on.

I looked through the window and watched her eyes shift from the mayor to Emers.

"When he's arrested, you will get your money."

"I want him dead," Emers rebutted.

"We agreed to get him locked up," the mayor remarked; Emers shoved him against the wall.

"Mayor, I don't take orders from you."

"This is the closest you've been able to get to Renato, don't forget that." The mayor pushed him back.

"How long were they out there?" Dad questioned.

"Long enough that I could have killed all three of them, but Savio told me not to take the shot."

"He's right. It would look suspicious if all three were dead together. It would point right back to you."

"I know."

"Where's my grandson?"

"Sonya is putting him down for a nap."

"Does she know?"

"Not yet."

"Never keep things from your wife."

"She's upset about the raid. I'll let her know."

"Just make sure she understands."

"She knows."

"As her husband, you need to understand the fear she holds if something happens to you."

"She's been on her own with her mom, ever since her father died."

"Which means, if something happens to you, it will only send her in a destructive direction. I won't have my grandson toyed with, Renato."

My parents were old school in every way, and even though Sonya and I had a modern relationship, she was still in a relationship with a man that was part of a dangerous world. Father had seen his closest friends and family betray him, so he'd do anything to protect his grandson.

"I need a drink."

"Talk to EJ and see what the next move is going to be." Father dismissed me and I went to go find something to eat.

CHAPTER 24

Sonya

MY MIND WAS RESTLESS. I kept remembering the smooth and quality bedding I shared with my husband, the plush carpet and rugs, the feel of his arms running up and down my back to help me sleep. Everything could be gone.

"He won't tell me what's going on." I touched the embroidered towels.

"They never do." Rena drew the bottle to her lips.

"Agreed." McKayla set her glass down.

"I just think it's crazy. The FBI showed up at our home."

"That's part of the lifestyle. We all have to go through it at some point," Rena countered.

"But all I want is normalcy."

"We're not a normal family."

"I know that. You guys are just so calm about this, numb even," I complained, picking up a water bottle.

"Sonya, we've all been through it. This isn't the first and won't be the last," McKayla replied.

"Maybe I should call my mom."

"No, keep her out of the family business. Realign your relationship, don't add more drama." McKayla pursed her lips.

"Maybe you're right. I just think it's such bullshit that we have to deal with threats every second and Sanchez on television? What was that?"

They both looked at each other.

"What do you know?"

"Nothing," Rena answered.

"No, tell me, Rena. I would not have kept anything from you, I feel like I'm left in the dark."

"The mayor was working with Tulio."

"I know."

"Yes. Well, basically, he was trying to sell or trying to get the Calabresi family territory to double-cross with Tulio. Then run for reelection, then governor, and he could have, but he wanted to play both sides.

"And that can't happen. He was meant to stay neutral between the families."

"No, okay. Well, once Tulio died and Emers connected with Brilynn…"

"What are you saying, Rena?"

"Don't know how to say this without hurting your feelings, but Brilynn is dead because she tried to betray the family."

My mouth opened, then closed. "She's dead?"

"Based on what the mayor did today set off another chain reaction. It's just a matter of when Savio plays his card," Rena explained, and I felt sick to my stomach.

"He already blew up part of the family business and robbed another, so the mayor basically just set us out to dry."

"And how was Brilynn involved? Wait, did the mayor have Brilynn killed?"

They looked at each other.

"I feel like you're telling me something without telling me."

"We just want you to think about this. Because you're

gonna have to live with the answer forever." Rena placed her hand on top of mine.

"No. He promised he wouldn't."

"I'm sorry, Sonya. But it needed to be done."

"He said as long as we stayed away from her. She wouldn't be a threat."

"Brilynn and Emers were together with the mayor. They were all working together," McKayla confessed.

"You're lying."

"We're not," she insisted.

I stumbled back in shock and ran to be alone, bumping into Renato in the hallway.

"What's wrong with you?"

"Tell me the truth."

"Okay, what's wrong?" He hovered inches from my face.

"Did you have her killed?"

"Who?"

"Stop playing dumb." I inched forward.

"I don't know who you're talking about."

"So you get a lot of people killed." He pushed his hands in his pockets.

"Did you forget that's my job, I never pretended to be a post office man. I never pretended to be a nine-to-fiver or a cook. I'm the fucking enforcer of a mafia family. Get that through your head," he argued.

"You disgust me." I weaved around him.

"And you married me." He ran a hand down his face.

"I'm leaving."

"You're not going anywhere." He moved to block me.

"Tell me what the problem is." Silence enveloped us.

"Did you kill Brilynn? It's a yes or no."

"Yeah." His voice was gruff.

He studied my reaction, and I felt a few tears run down my cheek. "You promised you wouldn't touch her."

"I promised that I would protect our family."

"She would have left us alone."

"You don't know that, Sonya." His head shook from side to side.

"I could have talked to her family."

"You can't talk to them. You have to understand they would have never left us alone."

"I don't believe you, but we're not going to do this here. I need some air."

I walked out to the backyard.

"I told my son he probably couldn't handle the situation properly."

I looked to my left, and Mr. Calabresi sat on the patio deck with a cigar in his hand.

"Excuse me, what did you say?"

"The life of this family, I overheard you, he made a decision..." His words trailed off. To be at odds with his lifestyle like specific values in raising our child I could handle, but killing was another level.

"So you knew."

"I know everything that goes on in this family. I like you, Sonya. You bring Renato happiness."

"He kills people." A shutter banged against the frame, making me jump.

"We have to protect our family at all times. Is it ugly? Yes. But it happens."

"I don't know. I just think this is all surreal. She was my best friend at one point."

"Yes. A friend that betrayed you, betrayed your trust. Think about that. If she would have been alive, she would have gone to the police or worse, sold your location out to Emers."

"Has to be a different way."

"Do you remember who the enemy is?"

"Please don't lecture me. I'm not a child, Mr. Calabresi."

"I know you're not. For both my grandson and son, I will do whatever it takes to protect them."

"Oh, like the agreement. He told me about that. I didn't sign it."

"Then you know you can never leave."

———

"Sonya is going to stand next to him with RJ in her hands," EJ announced, and I dropped my fork down.

"No."

"Come again." A perplexed glare filled his eyes.

"You won't have me standing next to my husband, like those women that stand next to her cheating husbands."

"Sonya," Renato grumbled.

"Renato, save it."

"Sonya, can I speak with you in the other room?" Adelina rose out of her chair. All eyes watched, expecting me to disagree, but I'd never disrespect his mother. She walked into the living room away from prying eyes.

"You feel betrayed." A shadow came over her face.

"Yes."

"You feel blindsided."

"Yes." Fear clogged my throat.

"You feel like your entire world is imploding."

"Yes." Bile bubbled up my stomach.

"Good, because that's what Brilynn has done." A twinge of anger laced her voice.

Her words tightened my chest.

"Adelina." I chewed on my nail.

To stop me, she raised her hand.

"Being in your position, I completely feel your pain, but you never let that come between you and your husband. Outside forces will try anything to bring you down."

"I wish I could change the past."

"And I wish I'd seen my grandson being born."

Her words stung.

"You would do anything to protect your son, right?"

"Yes, anything." My eyes widened.

"Same for me. Renato is my son. Is he perfect? Hell no, but he loves hard, and he did something to protect us all."

"He could have found another way." The ceiling fan whirled.

"Possibly, but when a problem is brought to his attention, it needs to be dealt with permanently."

"I think I need to be alone." I held her gaze before I looked away.

"Understandable."

"RJ will not be a part of any plans."

"What do you suggest?"

"Not sure. Tell EJ he needs to figure something else out."

"Are you scared he's going to jail?"

"Yeah, I'm getting anxious. At any moment a knock will come, and they'll arrest him."

"He's told you we have people on our payroll."

"How are you so calm about all of this Adelina?" She looked so put together; she wore a pair of simple leather pants, knee-high boots, and an air of confidence.

She laughed. "Because my husband and I are on the same page. I know the plans before they happen, and I'm comfortable with what is done to protect our foundation." Her words bore truth.

Our arms encircled each other.

Ring!

"Who's that?" We examined my phone, and I saw my mom's name pop up.

"Hey, Mom."

"Thank God you answered."

"Are you all right?" I scratched my head. My mother was already opposed to Renato and me together; she didn't need more ammunition when I felt hesitant at the same time.

"Yes, I just saw the news and worried about you."

"I'll give you some privacy." Adelina left me alone, and panic engulfed me.

"Renato is innocent." A chill coiled up my spine.

"Are you sure?"

"Yes, what have you heard?"

"Nothing much besides what the news talks about."

"News lies all the time."

"Where are you?"

"At his parents' home."

"Do you need me to come to you?"

"No, I'll be fine, McKayla and Rena are here with me." My posture went limp.

"Before you go to bed, let me hear your voice."

"You'll be asleep by that time." I chuckled.

"I can hear it in your voice, you never have to put on a strong shield with me, Sonya, I'm your mother."

I glanced up and saw McKayla poke her head in the living room.

"I have to go."

"Okay, if you need me..." She held her breath.

"I'll call you." I disconnected the call.

"How is your mom doing?" McKayla clasped her hands behind her back.

"How did you know that was her?"

"Your face lit up with a broad smile." She sat next to me on the couch.

"She called to check in on me."

"Dinner is getting cold." She tucked one leg under the other on the chair.

"Is Renato looking for me?"

"He tried to come in here, but I told him to let you breathe for a minute."

"Thanks, he has a way of..."

"Making you not be mad for long. I have the same problem with Savio."

"How did we end up with crazy men like them?"

"Who knows, but I wouldn't change him for anything."

She laughed, and I smirked.

"Hey, do you mind if I stay at your place for a few days?"

Her smile dropped from her face.

"Sonya," she groaned and laid her head on the back of the couch.

"Just a few days to clear my head."

"Are you crazy? Renato won't like that, especially with everything going on."

Knock! Knock!

"Who could that be?" McKayla stood, and I watched Marilyn go to the door before a few men in suits came into view.

"Renato, we need to go down to the station," Vaughn explained, and I rose from the couch and saw Renato with a blank expression.

"McKayla, take Sonya upstairs," Renato said, and Adelina held him back.

"No, why are you taking him?"

"Ma'am, stay out of police business," the officer stated, and I watched Renato clench his fist; I was afraid he was going to hit him, and I didn't need him doing more damage.

"Vaughn, we can follow you," EJ said.

"Come on, Sonya, we need to check on the kids." McKayla nudged me out of the room. ***

As soon as dinner was over, I left for McKayla and Savio's home because I couldn't take the people coming and going all night. The place felt like we were on lockdown, and nobody would give me any answers on Renato. I lay in bed while RJ slept in the crib in SJ's room. Savio wasn't here either, and McKayla tried to stay up as long as possible with me while we drank and discussed what could be going on. If they didn't have any evidence, he wouldn't still be locked up. For a second, I thought back to the time when he gave me a choice if I wanted to sign an agreement, leave with twenty million dollars, and never have to worry about anyone or anything that had the Calabresi name.

I scrolled through social media and most of the posts and pictures were of me, Renato, and his brothers from the charity event.

@lisahenry: *Can you believe it, the Calabresi brothers are hot!*

@poppyjones: *I'd be his pen pal.*

@Juliebecker: *Marry me Renato Calabresi*

"Desperate." I closed it out and tossed my phone on the nightstand, then rolled over, turned the light off, closed my eyes, and pulled the blanket over my head to fall asleep with my life in shambles.

CHAPTER 25

Renato

"I DON'T FISH, RENATO." *She pretended to vomit when I pulled the worm out of the bucket and placed it on her hook. After our time on the water, we explored the area more, had dinner, and then I decided to let her see what I like to do when I'm out here.*

"You don't look like you fish."

"It helps to calm me down."

"How? They're disgusting."

"It's quiet."

"Big bad killer Renato likes to fish." She laughed, and I joined in, wiggling the worm in her face.

"Stop, Renato!" She tried to move away from me.

"After we fish, we can watch a movie."

"Did you check on RJ this morning?"

"Stop worrying, he's fine with my parents." I snuggled up behind her as we stood on the dock.

"Do you really believe we could have it all?"

"If we try, we can." I planted my chin on the top of her head.

"My father would like you."

"You think so?" She linked our hands together.

"Yeah, he was a fisherman—well he liked a lot of outdoor

things, but he had a daughter and I wasn't really into sports or camping," she recalled with a giggle.

"I wish I could have met him."

"Me too."

I massaged the back of my neck.

"Can we go and watch a movie? This is not my style of entertainment." She raised the pole up for me to take.

"You're giving up?"

"Sorry, but I'd rather you fish for something else." She turned around in my arms, squeezing my waist lightly.

"What do you have in mind?" A smile broke on my lips.

"Mhmmm… something warm, long, and hard."

"Playing with fire, baby."

"I like my odds." She blew me a kiss, pushed me back, stripped out of her clothes, and dived into the water. I looked over my shoulder at my men and they'd all turned their backs to us. I was happy because a bullet would have been in their head.

"Sonya!"

"You gotta catch me first!" She giggled, swimming on her back, and I dropped my pants, left my boxers on, and caught up to her, wrapping my arm around her waist.

"You crazy woman."

"Yes! For you I am." Her breasts pushed up against my chest.

"If my guards would have seen you naked..."

"Stop being an asshole and kiss me."

We engaged in a heavy make-out session. I gripped her hips; she wrapped her legs around my thighs.

"I'm ready to go back inside." I pulled back.

"I can tell."

"Didn't bring any of my toys this time."

"Doesn't matter. We'll make the best of our night."

She squeezed my dick, and I lightly bit her ear. We swam back to the dock, I helped her up, and then I climbed up and carried her back inside.

"Renato, are you listening to us?" the FBI agent grilled

me; I faced forward while my attorney advised me to not answer any questions.

"He's answered that one already," Vaughn stated.

"He seems to be ignoring me." Agent Gallagher slid forward in his chair, staring at photos of me and my brothers.

"Why was I brought in again?"

"Don't get cocky, motherfucker!" he spat, hitting the desk.

"How many times are you going to bring us in here and try to pin a crime on my family?"

"You're all criminals."

I chortled at his words.

"How is your family, Gallagher? I heard your mother is dealing with your father's death pretty hard."

"Son of bitch, shut the fuck up about my family."

"Renato," Vaughn chided me.

I sucked my teeth, rolling my eyes.

"Funny you want to bring up a family, where's your little wife? Maybe she can talk some sense into you."

I cracked my knuckles.

"Can we get on with the interrogation?" Vaughn asked.

Desperately, I tried to not reach out and pull his heart out of his chest; I needed to calm down. Gallagher grinned and pushed another photo in front of me. It was Sonya with RJ and her mother at her house.

"Sonya Eden, how did you two meet?"

"What does this have to do with the Calabresi finances?" Vaughn cut him off.

"We've searched into your bank accounts, and multiple transactions look suspicious that go to an offshore number."

"No idea."

"Stop playing stupid with me and tell us what you did

with Tulio Costa, God damn it!" He leaped forward, and other agents pulled him back.

"If you're done with the circus act, Agent Gallagher, I'd like to get back to my family."

"I agree with my client. This seems like a setup," Vaughn hissed, pushing the folder of pictures back toward the agent.

"Probably Mommy and Daddy could come down here and talk to us," Agent Gallagher continued his taunting.

"Try it and see what happens," I threatened, and Agent Gallagher balled his fist up to hit me, but he was shoved out of the room.

"Stay out of trouble, Renato. I mean it." Vaughn drove away from the police station, and I stomped to my brother's awaiting car.

"You ready?" Sante looked over his shoulder.

"Time for Kennth and me to have a one-on-one meeting."

"Did you get everything forwarded to him?" Sante checked in with Remo.

"All cleared on our end," Remo answered.

"Take me home first." My shoulders slumped.

Sante shifted nervously in his seat.

"You hear me?"

"Ugh, I heard you, but we need to talk first." His face sagged.

"About?" A groan accompanied the roll of my eyes.

"Sonya's not there." Pain funneled into my heart.

"Where is she?"

"I'm not sure."

"The fuck, Sante!" I bellowed and tried to open the door

while he was driving. He swerved and pulled me back inside.

"Are you out of your mind?" He shoved me in the arm.

"Where is my wife?" I glared at him and Remo.

"We need to handle the mayor and Emers first."

"I recall Rena left you when she went to New York and you didn't wait it out."

"That's a different situation."

"Fuck this." I removed my phone and dialed Sonya's number.

"You've reached the number Sonya Eden—"

"She's not answering," I whispered, hung up, and dialed my mother.

"Hello, Renato, have you spoken to Sonya?" my mother asked.

"No."

"She hasn't answered my calls either."

"Do you mean something's wrong?"

"We haven't spoken since she found out about Brilynn's death. She went over to McKayla and Savio's. But I was trying to call to see if she needed anything."

"All right, I'll swing by there." I hung up the call.

"That Mom?" Sante quizzed.

"Change your plans. Go to Savio's house."

Sante quickly made a U-turn and a few cars honked their horns. I dialed Savio's number.

"Hello," Savio said.

"Are you at home?"

"No," he replied.

"Have you talked to Sonya?"

"Been at the office all night ever since you left." He made a tsking noise.

"Did you talk to McKayla tonight?" I grew frustrated, and my legs started to shake.

"She was holed up in the guest room, all I know."

"The interrogation ran late, and bullshit Agent Gallagher tried to provoke me."

"Call me if you need me, but McKayla would know more."

"I think she has me blocked and Mom."

"Probably not talking to anybody."

"I'm on my way to your place now." Blood drained from my face.

"Try not to kill each other."

"I can't promise that." I slammed my hand on the dashboard of the car, closed my eyes, and prayed I got to Sonya before she did anything crazy.

A few minutes later, we showed up at Savio's home, and I told Sante to stay in the car. I stalked up to the door, pounded as loud as I could, and waited for it to open. McKayla was holding SJ on her hip, rolling her eyes.

"Why are you mad at me?"

"Because Sonya is not speaking to me. Because of your decisions."

"How is that my fault?"

"You don't think before you act."

"I did my job. You know this, she'll learn."

"She's not a child." McKayla pushed me in the chest.

"McKayla, are you going to let me in or not?" I grew annoyed with the speeches, and she softened a little.

"Renato, you have to speak with your wife and make decisions together."

"We're not you and Savio, don't need your approval on how to go about my marriage."

"It's not about approval. It's about understanding that your decisions affect her and your family."

"McKayla, what are you saying? I should just not do my job? Let us get screwed?"

"That's not what I'm saying."

"I'll think about it, McKayla."

"She was in the guest room."

"Thanks." I pivoted around her, stalked up the stairs, banged on the door, then pushed it open. It was empty. I angled toward the bathroom, then closets; her purse and keys weren't there. I rushed back downstairs.

"McKayla!"

"What did you do to her now, Renato?" she spat, shifting my nephew to the floor.

"She's not up there."

"How? RJ was just with her."

"No, he wasn't there." I dashed back upstairs to check the adjourning door and saw RJ asleep in the crib.

I ran back to the front of the house.

"He's here." I relaxed a little.

"Where does she go?"

"She probably went to the only place she could, her mom's, because she knows she wasn't supposed to go anywhere."

"Again, she's not a child, Renato."

"McKayla, I get that, but we have too much going on to have her running around alone with Emers out there."

"Just stay calm. We can call her phone."

"She has blocked me."

"Let me try." McKayla tried her number. No answer.

"Have Rena try. I'm gonna go look for her."

Sante started the car when he saw me rush out of the house and climb in the backseat. I told him to check her mom's place first. Courtney would only use her disappearance as an excuse to hate me even more, and we could argue about it later, but right now, I wanted to make sure Sonya was safe and protected.

I ran up to her door and banged as loudly as I could; no one was out this late, and her neighbors were mainly older couples. Courtney's door flew open.

"Sonya here?"

"No, why, Renato? Is Sonya in trouble? You lost my daughter?"

"Courtney, I don't need a fight right now; it's not the time."

"She and I talked earlier." We both knew Sonya was headstrong and didn't need her mother's permission to live her life, but the two of us not getting along played on her distrust after I'd snatched her up.

"Sonya is not answering her phone."

"Let me see if I can dial her number." Courtney turned, shuffled to the landline she had near the couch, and dialed Sonya's number.

"Yeah, Mom." A hushed tone wedged itself between her words.

"Sonya! Where are you?" she barked.

"I don't want to say," Sonya mumbled.

"Sonya, I'm your mother, tell me what the problem is so I can fix it, honey."

"I needed a break."

"A break from what? You have a child and husband worried sick."

"Brilynn was killed."

"She would have tried to kill you."

"Renato," Sonya grunted over the phone.

"He's right here, Sonya, stressed." Courtney held the phone up for me to listen.

"Leave my mother out of this, Renato."

"Where are you?"

"I'll be home when I'm ready."

"Where are you now?"

"None of your business."

"Either you tell me where you are or—"

She cut me off. "What, you're gonna threaten to kill me, or my mom? You can't kill everybody."

"Actually, I can." I chortled.

"Forget you, Renato. I have to go."

"Wait."

Sonya ignored me, and her mother shook her head at the sound of the dial tone.

"What happened to Brilynn?"

"She's right. Brilynn is dead. I didn't kill her, though," I lied; her mother could sense my annoyance with the barrage of questions.

"Brilynn worked with some people that wanted to kill me and your daughter."

"I can see both sides, from Sonya and your perspectives. You need to understand that we were her only friends for years."

"Should I have let her weaken my family and hurt my wife! Hell no, and now we have the mayor as a bigger problem."

"Not necessarily. I think you need to give her space."

"We don't have space in my world."

"Then you'll lose her forever. Just FYI, you may think I don't know anything, but I know my daughter."

"Thanks for the advice." I turned to leave.

"Where is RJ?"

"Call McKayla, she's watching him." I shut the door behind me.

CHAPTER 26

Sonya

ASSHOLE, he's always functioning as though his rules are the only things that matter. I sat at the lake and smiled at the birds flying around. I was confident I could relax here. We'd had fun times here; I guess I wanted the old Renato back. Not sure what I was gonna do or how to teach my son this was our life, without consequences. Even when I became a stripper, I knew that it wasn't going to be a day at the park type of situation and to not get so caught up in the glamor and money to let it overwhelm who I was at the core. I would be a fool in his eyes if we stayed together knowing he went out to kill all the people that could possibly hurt his business. I was surprised Renato's father hadn't threatened to take my son away after our conversation at the house. I loved them, all of the brothers and Adelina, but the lack of empathy for the victims really felt like a gut punch.

I glanced up and saw Renato. "Ughhhh, I need space, Renato. What are you doing here?"

"Figured after I went to see your mom, you'd be here."

"We have nothing to talk about."

"How did you get past security?"

"I told them you were meeting me here. I guess I learned from you on how to lie."

He chuckled.

"What do you want?"

"I want you to stop."

"I can't. What else do you want?"

"You're crazy, the family is crazy."

"I know, baby. That's my life, but you knew that when you decided to marry me."

"You're right. I don't regret it. If I had to choose between you and Brilynn, I'm gonna choose you. A part of me knows deep down you're right. I just don't know. I feel like she could have maybe had a second chance possibly."

"That decision and everything else I do, I have to be calculated in my world. Either you are right the first time or you die, no in between." Renato sat down next to me on the dock.

"And the mayor?"

"He's being taken care of right now."

I stared with wide open eyes, shocked.

"Ki-kill the mayor?" I stuttered.

"Don't always just kill. I have other ways to get my point across."

"Basically I won't get rest or space from you."

"Can have space in our home when we're together. That's it, that's all I can give you. This is my life now, this is our life, this is the way we do things."

"Did you bring RJ?"

"He's still with McKayla. She's worried about you."

"Yeah, I stopped talking to her and Rena. They were just so nonchalant about everything. I don't know, I just feel stupid naïve."

"I mean they're used to us." He placed his palm over mine.

"I'm not. I never want to get so used to your world I lose my mind."

"You won't. I don't want you to become like the other women. You're my wife, you're my escape from all the bullshit."

"So you say."

"We will take a vacation together after this."

"Just the two of us? I guess I'll go back with you."

"Good."

"Do you have to kill the mayor?"

"I told you I'm not killing him."

"Oh I get it, that's code for something." She did an air quote with her hands. I grinned and pulled her close to my chest.

"I'll never let you get used to this. Make sure you call my mom because she was worried about you."

"I know I left everybody in the dust and left in the dark, but I just needed alone time."

"Sonya, you ran to the place that you knew I would find you."

"I guess I did."

He stood, extending a hand to help me up, then his fingers ran up and down my back. Renato leaned down, took hold of my bottom lip with his teeth, pulled it into his mouth, and I felt wetness in between my thighs.

"Ohhh, please, sir."

His hands caressed, then gripped a handful of my hair, and his eyes darkened with passion. He nipped at my neck, and I slid a hand under his shirt and down to the dark curls that surrounded his dick.

"For taking off like that, I should spank your ass." His husky voice in my ear turned me on.

"Spank me, then fuck me, sir."

"Shit, Sonya." He bent down, lifted me up, placed my legs around his waist, and carried me up to the cabin, while we continued to kiss. I ripped his shirt open, popping all the buttons off.

Smack! Smack!

"Arghhh! Shit." I felt his rough, callused hands smooth over the sting, and I wanted more.

Renato carried me to the top of the stairs, closed the door behind us, and placed me on the bed. He slowly removed my sandals, followed by my shirt and pants. In order to torture me, he had me wait for my punishment before he delivered my pleasure.

"I've never had to be vulnerable or scared in my life, Sonya." Renato sensually kissed up my left then my right leg.

Smack!

"Yes, oh… baby." I took a deep breath.

"You did this to me, made me love you." He grabbed my hand and brought it to his mouth, pressing a soft kiss to my knuckles.

Buzz!

I looked behind me and saw he'd removed a vibrator out of the nightstand.

"Renato." My brain fizzled.

"Shut up; this is your fault, that I would kill anything that hurts you or my son." His dark liquid eyes memorized every part of me.

Renato spread my legs and climbed onto the bed.

"Don't move," he demanded, and I felt another slap on my ass, followed by his tongue.

"Please, give me more," I begged when I felt his warm tongue slither to my pussy. He pressed a kiss to each butt cheek, kneading them, then I heard the buzzing get closer.

"Renato! Fuck, yes." The vibrator took my breath away. Pushing against my lower lips, he spread them apart, burying his tongue next to the vibrator, and I felt myself start to tear up, then all of a sudden, it stopped.

"The fuck! Keep going," I screamed, trying to push his head back in place.

He laughed, and I flipped him off, but that only motivated him to torture me further. He latched on to my clit with thick lips, and his hand kneaded my ass. I started to move my hips back and forth to catch the high.

Renato licked, then sucked, and I was aching to feel him inside of me.

"Baby, you're so sexy like this." Renato grunted and climbed over my back, kissing me on the lips. He started to push his hard dick against me, while clothed.

"Take these off and fuck me." I reached my arm around his neck, pulling his tongue farther into my mouth.

Buzz!

The buzzing increased; his finger joined in, and the sobs started to overpower me as I felt my orgasm creep up.

"Yeessss, keep going." My cheeks burned, hot and scarlet.

"You'll come on this dick." Renato threw the vibrator across the bed, flipped me over, kicked my legs wide, and plunged his dick inside. The weight of his body on top of mine had my heart feeling grateful he forgave me and let me see him at his lowest moments. I loved this man, even with the things he'd done.

My face was buried in his neck. He bucked against me, playing with my pebbled nipples, and I felt we would explode together as one at any moment.

"Fuckkk! I love you, Sonya Calabresi."

"Arghhhhhh! Renato, I feel it coming."

His groans and grunts were almost overshadowed by our bodies clapping together. Sweat and tears spread on the bed, and I'd never squirted twice in one night until him.

"See what you do to me, huh!" He flung a growl at me.

He pushed my leg further up; I'd never known how flexible I could get until him either, and I trembled when his tongue slid from my thigh up to my toes. I was delirious by this point and forgot my own name, trying to claw my hair out.

He spit on my pussy and slapped it a few times, and I squeezed my breast when his hand reached around my throat. His pumps turned into hard thrusts.

"Don't you ever leave me! You are mine," he growled.

"Never, baby! Can I come, oh shit!" He fell on top of me, breathing heavily.

"Come." He sucked on my neck, and I shook in his hold, almost passing out. He released instantly, veins popping in his neck. I struggled to breathe when we rolled to the side of the bed. I placed my leg over his thigh, kissing his chest.

He played with my hair, his eyes closed, and I dreamt about our new beginning, after he got rid of our enemies for good.

"I want to take a trip."

"Where?"

"Anywhere, long as you and RJ are with me." I leaned up to stare at him.

One eye flickered open; he puckered his lips for a kiss.

"I will set something up soon."

"Should we invite the rest of the family?" McKayla and Rena probably hated me for ignoring them, and I wanted to make it up to them for defending their husbands.

"If you want them to come."

"Okay, let me think it over."

"Long as we have our own room, so I can fuck you any time."

"If we don't have a room, I can take you anywhere, sir." I seductively crawled up his body and pecked him on the lips.

"Get some rest. We head back tomorrow."

"Take a shower with me first."

I rose off the bed; he pulled himself up, lifted me off the floor, and walked us to the bathroom. We showered, without a round two, and fell into bed afterwards.

The next day, we drove back to the city and stopped at Savio and McKayla's home first. Renato held my hand as we trekked into the kitchen and the boys surrounded the table with Rena and McKayla laughing.

"Morning," I said, bashfully waving, and the girls jumped up and came around the table toward me.

"I knew he'd bring you back." McKayla pulled me into a hug.

"He's very convincing."

"Aren't they all." Rena tapped her lip, glaring at Sante. I didn't know what that was about, but I'd hear the story later.

"Is RJ still sleeping?" I released Renato's hand and went around the table to kiss Savio Jr. on the head.

"He's almost ready, Marilyn is giving him a bath."

"Is he all right?"

"He has a little fever, but he's doing better," McKayla informed me, and I felt bad I hadn't been here when he got sick.

"Let me go check on him." Renato didn't wait for me and rushed up the stairs to the boys' bedroom. I was right behind and saw RJ asleep in Marilyn's arms as she sat in the rocking chair.

"Sorry, Marilyn." I bent down to pick him up out of her arms.

"He was a little fussy, but I gave him a warm bath." Marilyn rubbed his back; Renato felt his head before sitting on the bed and motioned for me to take a seat on his lap.

Renato glided his hand over my thigh.

"He's going to be fine. Babies get sick sometimes," I reassured him.

"Has this happened before with him?"

"Yeah, early in the beginning. Of course I panicked like any new mom."

He allowed me to continue.

"Doctor explained it's nothing serious."

"I wish I was there to help."

"You being here now is more than enough." I grabbed his chin.

"Possibly, but I hate he has to be sick." He rubbed my back.

"Big, strong mobster can't handle his son being sick," I kidded and got off his lap.

"Do you need me to get you anything before I go?"

"Come home safely."

"Sure you don't want to stay at my parents'?"

"No. I'd rather go home to our bed." When he heard the idea at first, he shook his head and refuted it.

"Walk me out."

He held my hand as we descended the stairs and to the front door.

"Get some rest, and I'll check in on you later."

"Be safe." I stood on tiptoes to kiss him.

I shut the door behind him and headed back into the kitchen, where Marilyn, McKayla, and Rena were at the table eating.

"They leave?" Rena picked up a biscuit with honey spread on top.

"Yes, not only is RJ being sick stressful, but Renato is out there fighting for his life; I need to do something."

"Way to help is by taking care of his son."

"I hear you, Rena." I rocked RJ back and forth in my arms.

"Are you planning on staying tonight? We can watch movies and catch up."

"I really want to get him home in his own bed, plus I need to figure out when Brilynn's funeral is."

McKayla and Rena paused at my statement.

"Sonya, that's not a good idea."

"Brilynn made mistakes, but she was in my life before anyone else."

"At least tell Renato when the funeral is."

"Honestly not sure."

"We will go with you when you find out."

"Your husbands will kill me if they knew you were with me at her funeral."

"They will understand, family supports family." McKayla put a bottle for RJ on the table in front of me.

"Thank you."

"Welcome, he's going to wake soon and need to eat."

McKayla finished up breakfast, and we talked more about my plans with school and the art internship.

It was going on past five in the afternoon when I felt it was best to pack up our things and head home. To cook in my own kitchen would help me relax and clear the thoughts of what Renato was up to. I threw my bags in the back of the car, strapped RJ in his seat, and hopped in next to him, closing the door behind me.

"You don't have to leave, Sonya. We have plenty of room."

"Thanks, McKayla, but I need to be home in my bed, in my kitchen."

"Please let Renato know you're heading home," Rena suggested.

"Dome is doing that right now. So long as we have protection around the house, it will be fine."

"I don't like this at all."

"Emers isn't a wild card like Tulio. Renato has said that plenty of times."

"Call me when you make it inside and don't leave."

"Thanks, *Mom*, I promise," I joked, and Dome reversed out of the driveway, taking off to our place.

The way I deal with stressful situations is different from everyone else, and they couldn't see that being around people was the last thing I needed. My son and I would be fine in our own home together. RJ slept peacefully, and I wished I could be a little girl again with no responsibility or worry.

"Boss said he doesn't like that you left, but to make sure we keep tabs every thirty minutes." Dome spoke from the front seat.

"Thanks, Dome."

"No problem."

The Town Car moved along the road steadily as cars whizzed by. I stared out at the beautiful trees and soft colors of the different flowers that bloomed. Chicago, my home and birthplace, held me together through it all. I'd finally become the person I was meant to be; an unlikely person—besides Renato—did that, and it was Brilynn. I'd go pay my respects and close that chapter in my life and start a new one. No longer would I sit and wait for other people to dictate my thoughts and wants. Time for me to become Sonya Calabresi, a person of value.

CHAPTER 27

Renato

Savio sat at the edge of the table and watched the monitors with all the news channels on regular programming. At the same time, we sent a package to be dropped, and I watched the minutes tick by before life for Kennth would be blown away.

"Are you ready?" EJ passed a blue binder to Jason Thompson, our new interim mayor of Chicago.

"Been ready to take him down." Jason was our secret contact at the mayor's office and City Hall. His father was one of the lawyers at our family's attorney office. Vaughn made the introduction when he found out Jason was into politics, and he'd stayed on top of it when things came through City Hall that could potentially help or hurt our business. I warned Kenneth that anyone could be easily replaced, and he never knew when we'd strike. Now our biggest test had played out in our favor once again.

"We have confirmation." I talked over the speakerphone to Remo.

"Outside of the station now, I gave the package to Channel Nine reporters like you said," Remo confirmed.

"Time for you to go back to City Hall." I motioned for Jason to leave with our guards. He worked as deputy mayor and would seek a full term, and we would make sure he won the race when that time came; right now he was to place himself as the one to comfort and reassure the city that people like Kenneth Sanchez would never get into politics again.

"Thank you again, Renato, and you, EJ," Jason expressed, and I released his hand, noticing the sign of "*Breaking News*" scrolling across our monitor. The video Remo dropped off was a recording of Tulio, Emers, and Kenneth exchanging money outside of Tulio's restaurant.

I laughed.

"*We have breaking news. The mayor of Chicago is seen on camera with local mobsters Emers and Tulio Costa. The video is clear that something is being exchanged, correct, Patrick?*"

Another reporter was displayed on screen, speaking toward the camera.

"*That's right, Janine, and if you zoom in close, you will see him pull out a handful of cash. The mayor now has police at home so we can report.*" The footage cut to a video of the mayor being escorted out of his home with his wife crying.

"*Just got word that charges have been brought against him, on money laundering and mafia dealings. We don't know where this video came from, but we are looking into confirming.*

"*At the moment, the mayor has stated he is not guilty, and he is going to be working with authorities and that he is being framed by the Calabresi family,*" Janine announced.

Savio turned off the video. I sat back, smoked the cigar, and watched the FBI agents set up outside his house. I hadn't decided if I wanted to take care of his family; I wasn't too heartless of a man, but if he didn't step down and plead guilty, get them off our backs, Savio would give the green light to take care of him.

"Where should we go now, Boss?" Remo spoke over the phone.

"Time to take care of him."

Leaving Savio and EJ behind, Sante followed me, and we drove to Costa territory, then my phone rang.

"You think I'm going to take this bullshit lying down!" Sanchez barked through the phone.

"Surprised you got your one phone call so early," I taunted, listening to Sante direct Remo to head to the freeway.

"If I go down, you're going with me."

"Kenneth, I thought we were friends."

"Only used me to get where you are."

"Mayor Sanchez, I recall we used each other. You wanted to be mayor, and we needed someone to look the other way."

"My lawyers will get me out before dinner tonight."

"Sure about that?"

"Positive."

"I suggest you turn on the news."

"Why?"

"Something I think you should watch instead of me telling you."

Before he could reply, I ended the call and opened the phone to the local news app and watched Jason take the podium at City Hall.

"What can you tell us about Mayor Sanchez?" a reporter grilled, and I turned it up loud.

Jason looked calm and composed. He was about my height with a low fade and dark brown skin, and the cocky smirk he tried to hide turned into a somber, angry expression.

"Today is a terrible day for our city and the staff here. We, like everyone here in Chicago, trusted Mayor Sanchez to work for us and not for some sick mafia family that would help destroy our homes and business." He pounded his hand on the podium.

"Can we know how much was in the bag he took from Costa?" another asked.

"At this time, not sure how much he was paid off, but there had to be a lot for him to turn against us."

"What happens to the mayor's office now while his charges are pending?"

"I'll step in as the interim mayor, and before you ask, I will run for his seat after the term is up. Because Chicago deserves to have someone working for them."

Remo arrived outside of the conference Jason was giving. I glanced at the reporters, and they ate up everything EJ wrote for him to talk about.

"Emers's men are there," Sante observed.

"Fun time begins." I waved for Remo to keep driving, and he sped up into traffic, taking the side streets to make it to Costa territory. We followed closely behind. Cars lined up around the bars, clubs, and restaurants he owned. I stepped out of the car and headed to the same bar where I'd beat up one of his men, then slipped in by myself.

"Renato." I turned to the left and saw a new friend at the bar.

"Crystal."

"He's not here, but I overheard them talk about him going to your part of town."

"Thank you, you should find a new crowd of friends." I slid four hundred out of my wallet and passed it to her.

"Tell our girl I said hello." Crystal winked, and I marched back out to the car.

"He's not there?" Sante asked.

"Check with Dome and make sure we have things ready." I grabbed my phone out of my pocket and sent a text to Sonya.

Me: RJ okay?"

MyGirl: He's sleeping.

Me: I'm heading in that direction.

MyGirl: Everything okay

Me: It will be once I see your face

MyGirl: Dome just came into the house to look at the cameras.

Me: Work is getting close to home.

MyGirl: Work like Costa?

She made an intriguing comment and I smiled.

Me: Grab RJ and go to my office.

MyGirl: Should I be scared?

Me: Never, I'll always protect you.

MyGirl: I'm calling you now.

Ring!

"How much time do we have?" Sonya checked with me.

"Not long. I want you to take RJ and go to my office and lock the door until I come for you."

"You don't sound nervous."

"Emers won't get through the gates."

Pop! Pop!

I heard a loud crash and the phone dropped.

"Sonya! Sonya!"

"Remo, fuck the traffic lights!" Sante shouted. Remo pressed the gas and ran through the lights.

Pop! Pop!

"Sonya! Sonya!" I shouted her name.

Remo was five minutes away from our home, and I had to think Sonya was safe in the house rather out in the open.

"Here it is!" Sante jerked the wheel, careening onto our street and came up through the back, where Remo had already parked. I jumped out, reached in the back for my shotgun, and ran up the backyard to the guest house, scanning the area. No one was in sight when I heard footsteps behind me.

"It's me!" Sante shouted, holding his hands up.

"Take Remo and go find Dome," I demanded and started for the main house. Before going inside, I looked in the back window and saw it was empty. I slid the key in and unlocked it, then slowly walked in from the hallway.

Boom! Boom!

"Ahhhhh!" Emers's hitman was shot in the arm and then forehead. I turned toward the living room and saw someone rambling on the desk in the corner. I whistled to get their attention.

"Hey!"

The guy spun and raised his gun.

Boom!

He slumped forward on the desk.

"Put the gun down," I heard a voice say.

"Get out of my house."

"He's not here to save you, Sonya." Emers was outside of the office door.

"Fuck you, Emers," Sonya spat.

"That's the plan." Emers raised his gun up to shoot; I started to run at him.

Pop! Pop! Pop!

I froze when his body dropped to the ground, then turned to look up at Sonya with a gun in her hand.

"I remembered the gun in the top drawer, and before he came in I grabbed it and tried to get him to leave. I had no choice," Sonya muttered, eyes drawn together in confusion at what she'd done.

"Baby, put the gun down." I slowly moved in closer to get it out of her hands.

"I remembered the gun in the top drawer, and I tried to get him to not shoot. I had no choice."

The front door opened, and I raised my shotgun, but it was Savio and our men.

"Check the rest of the house," I demanded and ran to Sonya.

"Renato." She gripped the sleeve of my shirt; I peppered kisses over her forehead, nose, cheeks, and lips.

"I'm here."

"Is he dead?"

I looked behind me. Remo checked his pulse but didn't comment.

"He's gone."

I wiped the tear from her cheek.

"Never killed anyone before."

"You won't have to do it again, promise."

"RJ!" She jerked out of my arms and ran out of the room and up the stairs, yelling his name.

"He's fine." Sante came out of his room holding my son.

"Oh, thank God." Sonya grabbed him and rocked him back and forth. He looked to be crying from all the noises and gunshots.

"The cleanup crew is outside." Savio came from the backyard.

"Take her to our parents' for the night." I slid my arm around her shoulder.

"Did you call them?" Sonya checked, and Sante and I looked at each other.

"It's being taken care of by our people. Grab your phone and purse so we can go."

"We need clothes and RJ's medicine."

"Remo will have it delivered to you later. I want you out of the house right now."

Sonya looked around at the dead bodies on the ground; she covered RJ's eyes, and I escorted them to our Mercedes, helping them inside.

"Take her straight to the house, no stops."

I watched as Dome drove out of the front gate and down to the stop sign at the end of the block.

"He's still alive," Sante told me as I reentered the house, and I felt a little relief she didn't really kill someone. At the same time, I needed this release of torture I was going to expel on him.

"Get him to the warehouse."

Emers was dragged out of the house by his arms and placed in the back of a black van.

"Are you going to let her think she killed him?" Sante grilled as I hopped in the front seat of the van.

"For now." I slapped the side of my door, and Remo drove us in the opposite direction of Dome.

"Keep me updated!" I shouted to the guys in the back with Emers.

"Ughhhh…" he moaned in pain.

"He's going in and out of consciousness."

"Don't let him die."

Remo ran over a bump in the road, and the van jumped and swerved.

"Ahhhhh, fuck!" Emers screamed, and I chuckled.

"Party is just getting started." I picked up my phone and saw Sonya had sent me a message.

MyGirl: Made it to your parents safe.

Me: Get some rest.

MyGirl: I love you.

Me: Love you more, call your mom.

MyGirl: Yes. Sir.

Her comment pushed my erection through my trousers, and I wanted to tell Remo to turn around and take me back so I could fuck her, but Emers needed to be handled before anything else.

Pulling up to the warehouse, I rushed out and held the door open so they could carry the unconscious Emers inside.

"Tie him up on both ends."

Remo grabbed him by the shoulders, put him in the chair, and locked his hands and legs in chains.

"Bring out Sumba." I rubbed my hands together.

The chainsaw started up, and I took it out of Remo's hands and approached the table, smacking Emers on the face to wake him up.

"Time to get up, sleepyhead."

Blood seeped from his mouth, and his breathing was shallow.

"Please, take me to a hospital."

"Something you should have thought of before you trespassed on my property."

"I can pay you, whatever you want," Emers tried to plead; Remo gripped the back of his head to make him stay awake.

"Already have your money, taken care of by hacking into your accounts." I took out my phone and showed his bank account with zero dollars.

He growled and tried to charge at me, but the chains held him down.

"I'm going to kill you!"

"Emers, we had mutual respect, but you allowed your brother to hurt and threaten my wife." I pushed the saw to his wrist and cut it off.

"Ahhhh!!! My hand, you son of bitch!" His eyes welled up in tears as blood spattered everywhere.

"Just kill him, Renato." Sante held his stomach, and I laughed at his queasiness. This is what I loved, but my brothers stayed out of this part unless it was necessary.

"Go to the car. It might take me a few minutes."

"Please get me a doctor, I can't... Sante," Emers begged my brother.

"We could have done business together if you would have told your brother to stand down, but now you're going to follow him to hell." The chainsaw went to his other wrist, cut it off. His eyes rolled to the back of his head before he slumped forward.

"Grab him up."

"He's out, Boss." Remo tapped his cheek multiple times.

"Can't even take a little pain."

I placed the saw to his left foot and cut it off; he popped up, screaming.

"Mhmmmm… arghhhh." It sounded like he choked on his blood and Remo let his head go, dropping it to the table. I checked his pulse.

"It's faint."

"What do you want us to do?"

"Grab the trash bags, cut him up and burn him. Keep the bags close to grab the ashes." The final pleasure came when I cut into his neck, slicing it straight off. It rolled forward on the table, and I heard my brother vomit.

"You can finish the rest. I have a trip to plan." I passed the saw to Remo, checked on Sante, and headed back to the car.

"Fucking crazy, Renato." Sante wiped his mouth.

"Crazy maybe, but you pay me the big bucks to handle that crazy."

Another car, driven by Savio, was next to the black van, and we hopped in his ride and headed home. Sonya was probably still upset and crying about what happened, and I wanted to be there to comfort her; I hope she didn't feel guilty.

CHAPTER 28

Sonya

I BRUSHED MY HAIR, stared in the mirror of the bathroom, and slid earrings in my ears. Three days after I shot Emers, I thought I would have some type of nightmare or nervousness with the police about what happened. But honestly, I had never felt so good and ready for the next step in my journey. I was dressed in a blue pencil skirt and white long-sleeved blouse for my first day at the Prism Gallery as an intern. Renato didn't think I should quit my job at Calabresi Holdings, but I needed something where I could focus on my goals and not feel obligated. The gallery was the perfect place. Even though they owned it, none of the family worked there, so our working lives would be separated for the most part.

"I'm quitting."

"Quitting what?" Renato sat on the back patio with RJ nearby, playing with his toys. The events of yesterday over, I needed to make it clear what I'd planned.

"Working at the company."

"Why?"

"It's not for me, and I want something I can build on, that I earn."

"You got the job on your own merits. Why can't you do both?"

"Because I still have school and juggling both, plus spending time with my family, was a lot, I realized."

"Not liking how you've already decided to quit without talking to me first."

"I am talking to you."

"No, you've made a decision and forced me to agree."

"Sounds familiar," I mumbled under my breath.

"Come sit down."

"I need to get dinner ready." I pinched his nose and went to the kitchen to cook.

The memory of our conversation replayed in my mind, and it only continued for the rest of that day until we went to bed. Once we had sex, he understood the reasons I wanted to go in this direction.

Ring!

I placed the curling iron down on the counter and grabbed up my phone.

"Sonya?" I heard the sweet voice.

"Hi, it's Brilynn's Aunt Esther."

I tipped my head in the bedroom looking for Renato, but he wasn't around. I turned the curling iron off and sat on the edge of my bed.

"Sorry for your loss, Esther."

"Thank you. It came as a shock to us. Hard thing to cope with since she was so young," Esther muttered, and a small tear escaped my eyes.

"If you need anything, please let me know."

"The funeral is happening tomorrow if you want to come, I know you two were close."

"Uhhhh, did you and Brilynn talk much lately?" I struggled to ask.

"Not really. I hadn't talked to her in over a year."

"Sorry to hear that." My words felt shaky.

"Family sometimes can be complicated."

"Yes it can." I bowed my head.

"I won't hold you up, but I'll text you the address and time."

"Thank you, Esther."

"Of course, Sonya. I think of you as my niece as well."

I quickly hung up and dialed my mother's number.

"Sonya, you all right?"

"Yeah, I just got off the phone with Esther. Brilynn's aunt."

"What did she want?"

"Tell me about the funeral."

"You're actually going?"

"What choice do I have? Brilynn hadn't talked to her in almost a year, and she told me she was strained from most of her family. I'd feel bad if no one comes to pay respects."

"I'll come with you then. I was fond of Brilynn."

"You don't have to do that, Mom, especially if it makes you uncomfortable."

"Stop worrying about me. I will be fine. Send me the time and you can pick me up."

"Thanks, Mom. I need to get to the gallery."

"Today's your first day?"

"Yes, I'm excited. I already quit the company to work as an intern."

"Renato is fine with you quitting?"

"He had no choice, but I did tell him what I was doing."

"As long as you talk, on the same page."

"Believe me, I won't be stealing anything any time soon."

She laughed, and I cackled, standing to slide into my heels, then picked up my jacket and purse.

"Let me get out of this house before RJ wakes up."

"Bring him over to see his grandmother."

"We're planning a trip if you want to come."

"With Renato?"

"Yes, my husband. At some point, you two need to become cordial or friends hopefully."

"Friendship is a long way off, but he and I are cordial, especially when you run away."

"He's fine with you, I promise."

"Call me if you get a break."

"Probably not on my first day, but I will try."

Mom and I said our goodbyes, then I dropped the phone in my bag and checked on RJ in his room. He wasn't there, which meant his dad had woken him up before it was time. Renato, for the last few days, had stayed home. It was a surprise to see him so focused on our well-being, and not run out to handle business like before. I made it to his office and heard the TV up loud. I nudged the door open and saw RJ on the floor with his toys and Renato's feet kicked up on the desk.

"I made mistakes and I want to apologize to my family, staff and all of my fellow Chicago citizens." Mayor Sanchez was reading from his speech.

I felt bad for his wife, standing there with her children as their father basically confirmed all the things he'd done to the city, from stealing to giving breaks to the mafia. It was sickening. There was no chance based on the charges that he would be out anytime soon. Then get out selling a book, go on tour. But that's politics for you. I went to sit down on Renato's lap.

"What are your plans for today?" I rubbed the back of his head, then fixed the collar of his shirt.

"I'm taking him to the park."

"He looks better today."

"Think I want to take him to Dr. Wraith to make sure."

"You're overthinking it, honey. He is fine. You don't need to worry. Make sure you call me if you need anything."

"Today's my first day at the Prism Art Gallery. I have everything I need." I held up my purse and computer bag.

"Make sure you stay with Dome. I don't want to have to come up there."

"How do I look?" I ignored his request.

"Like you need to not leave. Maybe we could do a revisit of our time at the cabin."

I slid out of his lap.

"I don't think so." I bent down and sucked on his lip. He pulled my head in forcefully, slapping me on the ass.

"You should be exhausted from the past couple of days." I pushed a piece of her behind my ear.

"Never be exhausted from having you. Oh, I do have a surprise for you." Renato informed.

"Your surprises, never could I get used to them." I smiled.

"I'm planning a trip for us." Renato expressed.

"A trip? Where?" I folded my arms.

"New York."

"Oh, I've never been to New York."

"I already know you're going to tell McKayla and Rena."

"Are we taking RJ?"

"Up to you and the girls."

"All of the kids and wives should go. But what's the catch?"

"How do you know there's a catch?"

"You just all of a sudden want to go to New York, out all other places out there. It just seems a little suspect."

"Like there is a catch, nothing for you to worry about."

"Okay. Remember, we're in this together. I want to know what's going on."

"All about celebrating your birthday, and your accomplishments."

RJ strolled over to me and held out a Lego toy, and I dropped to my knees and squeezed him to my chest.

"Mommy loves you."

"Wahhhh." RJ giggled wrapped his arms around my neck.

———

Dome held the car door open for me, and I slipped inside, dialing McKayla's number and waiting for it to connect. I heard a baby scream in the background and clicked the phone over for FaceTime.

"Savio Jr. sounds like he's not in the mood for you." An impish smile made her mouth twitch.

McKayla rolled her eyes.

"He's spoiled." She smiled beautifully.

"Same as RJ."

"You're all dressed up."

"First day at the art gallery."

"Awww, I forgot."

"Yes, I'm supposed to connect with Agnese." A sigh escaped my lips.

"She sounds old." McKayla flashed a huge grin.

"Maybe, but Vincenzo told me she's stern, but fair." My forehead creased in worry.

Dome stopped at the traffic light.

"Renato told me about a trip to New York and he said I could invite you guys."

"A trip out of town, no kids? I'm for that."

"Actually I want to bring RJ."

McKayla groaned, and I giggled at her response.

"That means Savio will want to bring his son."

Dome arrived at the gallery a few minutes later. The building was a standalone, trimmed in white and gold, with a large sign in gold labeled *Prism*.

"Thanks, Dome."

"Let me help you out." He reached for the door handle, but I stopped him.

"I got it from here. You don't have to stay."

"You know that's not going to happen." Dome came to my side of the door, helping me out.

"McKayla, I'm here. I'll call you later."

"Have fun and enjoy yourself."

I sauntered in; my eyes wandered around the space, taking in the eclectic pieces on the wall. A young man who looked to be in his late twenties stood at the front counter.

"Hi, I'm Sonya Calabresi, interning here."

"Nice to meet you, Sonya, I'm Rocky. Agnese is in the back. Let me grab her for you."

"Thank you."

"I'll be in the car."

"Okay."

Rocky returned from the back area with an older, gray-haired woman, probably in her late fifties.

"Hello, I'm Agnese." We shook hands.

"How are you? I was telling Rocky my name is Sonya, the new intern."

"Welcome aboard, I spoke with Vincenzo, and he spoke highly of you."

"That makes me nervous, but excited."

"To be expected as your first day in the art world. Don't let it be too intimidating, but you'll be fine."

"You're closed right now, correct?"

Agnese picked up a few pamphlets from the counter and went through the employee area, and I followed.

"We're in the process of reopening the gallery, but I have enough time to kind of show you around and let you get acquainted with a couple of things."

"Oh, great."

"We have this office over here so you can put your

things down. And basically, it's a couple like three or four of us that work here."

I laid my purse and computer case on the desk. It wasn't a large room; it held a computer desk and chair. I could decorate with pictures and a few flowers to brighten it up.

"Our interns start with studying the background of the Prism Gallery, what we bring in and curate for our clients."

"How long does it take to get in the position to make purchases for the gallery?"

"You'll assist me on appointments and learn the ropes. Normally, it would take years for interns to get to that status. I know you're studying and almost done with school."

"The complexity of paintings speaks to me."

"I normally curate at least once a month, and you'll get to sit in on bidding."

"Anything new coming in today?"

"Today is slow so you'll just do reading on these and catch up."

She pointed at the stack of folders on the corner of the desk.

"Get familiar with our database and learn about our clients, shipping and purchases. We make up to twenty million in profit a month."

My eyes glanced at the stack of papers.

"Hopefully it won't take too long. Can I take some of these home with me?"

"Sure, just make sure you bring them back. Confidentiality." She headed out of my office.

"Thank you."

"You're welcome. I'm not too bad to work with no matter what Vincenzo says." She smiled at me, and I smiled back. I logged into my computer and set up my password and opened the client portal of the Prism Gallery and scrolled through the names.

"Multimillionaires, Giosuè Calabresi." I whispered the name I came upon that had to be related to Renato and his family.

"Interesting." I continued to study all the past works they'd taken in and read the history of how it came about from the beginning in Italy. Four hours later, my stomach growled, and a knock on my door pulled my attention.

"It's open." The person on the other side twisted the knob, and I saw a vase full of red roses with a large smirk on my husband's face.

"Are you checking up on me?" I dropped my pen on the table and stood to greet him with a kiss and hug.

"I knew this would be the perfect time to take you to lunch."

"You're right; I really didn't eat breakfast today."

"Come and let me take you out."

"I have a lot of studying, though."

"That can wait. You have to eat."

"Hey, Sonya, we're closing up early. Agnese wanted me to let you know." Rocky stepped into my office, and I felt like Renato had something to do with us leaving early.

"She just happened to want to close early on my first day?" I crossed my arms over my chest, staring at Renato.

"Don't look at me."

"Renato, did you force her to let me leave for the day?"

"No, I just suggested it would be a good idea to have a spa day on me," Renato remarked, and I felt annoyed at him going behind my back.

"It never ends with you." I moved back to turn off my computer and grab my purse and the folders I wanted to take home with me to study.

"Stop being a brat." Renato extended his hand for me to take.

"Whatever."

"Boss, we have company," Dome said, and I looked

behind him and saw a black Honda parked a few blocks from my workplace.

"Who is that?"

"No one. Get in the car." Renato helped me get in the passenger seat of his car, and Dome trekked to the car that he'd driven me in earlier.

"Should I be worried?"

Renato shifted the car across a lane of traffic.

"Not with me. Put on your seat belt."

"Tell me the truth."

"I think that's Gallagher following you."

"How long?"

"Not sure, my first time seeing him."

"How do you know it's his car?"

"I have a file on him with that car's description."

"Try not to get pissed. RJ and I don't need you going to jail for killing an FBI agent."

"You're right." He leaned across the seat and placed his hand on my thigh.

The Honda did a U-turn into the street and followed a few cars behind Dome. It was apparent that Renato had another enemy waiting in the wings to strike, even though we'd hoped to bury everything in the past and start fresh. It might be for the best that I pushed my dreams to the side and stayed home.

CHAPTER 29

Renato

THE NEXT DAY

I stood in the back and watched as they put her in the ground as faint cries were heard through the graveyard a few feet away. I wanted to comfort and protect Sonya from any pain, but she needed to handle this moment on her own. Sonya hooked a hand with her mom and wiped a tear from her cheek. After we left the gallery, I drove us straight to a nice restaurant like a normal couple as best as I could without wanting to snap at Gallagher while he continued to spy on us.

Brilynn had very little family besides Sonya, her mom, and a few others, which made it about ten people total that paid respects. Sonya put on a brave face, and I admired her strength and tenacity with everything that comes being the wife of a mobster. Even though we left in separate cars, I did hold her hand when she got out of the car and walked her to her mom, then fell back in the shadows. Gallagher had it in his mind that I would do something to interrupt the funeral, so he came and brought a few police cars for protection. He refused to move on, determined to place Brilynn's death on me.

Sonya tried to force me to be okay with RJ being at the funeral, and we were fighting for a while last night. I didn't want my son exposed to any of the fake bullshit that Brilynn came from.

Sonya started toward her car with her mom, then my phone rang with a name I hadn't talked to in a while.

"It must mean money is involved." I left and motioned for Dome to help Courtney and Sonya into their car.

"No reason to speak on fruitless things, cousin."

"Don't let my father hear you say that." Both of us chuckled at my admission as I put the key in the ignition and shut the door of my car.

"We might have a problem."

"Giosuè, you know I don't like to hear that, as your cousin, hearing that makes me suspicious."

"Well, it should because it's my fucking money."

"I was coming for a visit, not to do business."

"Business is always a priority for me. Are you getting soft on me, cousin?"

"Fuck you, Giosuè."

He laughed, then cleared his throat.

"I had a deal not go through."

"Is this something you need my services for?"

"Possibly, but I have another potential one that could benefit us both."

"How?"

"When you come to New York, we can discuss."

"What am I missing?"

"Art, my dear cousin, art."

"Then EJ can help with the paperwork of handling the shipment. You know he and Vincenzo run that area."

"I do and I will speak with him next, but I can't move forward until we lock in what I want."

I checked my watch. "I plan to go there next month."

"When you get here to New York, we can have a cigar and catch up with the family."

"My wife is coming."

"Why would someone be that desperate to marry you, cousin? A death wish?" he joked, and I started to curse him out, but out of the corner of my eyes, I saw Gallagher on my tail.

"Listen, we have a lot to talk about when I get there."

"Something that could hurt the family?"

"If we do it right, the family will be fine."

"I heard about the situation with Kennth Sanchez out there and some FBI agent."

Giosuè and I had a lot of heat on us from the police, but it's a different type of heat when an agent is basically stalking your family.

"Give EJ the information you have."

"I know more than you think, cousin."

"Meaning?"

"Talk to Mayor Sanchez."

"You know that's not happening."

"He has the answers you seek."

"Stop talking in riddles, Giosuè." I sped through the yellow light. Gallagher had to stop, and he lost my tail when I turned down a side street.

"Cade Gallagher has long roots in the police field. His father was a cop."

"Send me the information, and I'll get EJ to look into your situation."

"Only fair. Tell Aunt and Uncle I said hello." He ended the call, and I tossed the phone in the passenger seat and focused on the road. No way I could show my face at a prison to speak with the mayor and not become suspicious. EJ could pull strings and maybe have Jason get some information on Cade, but Kenneth Sanchez hated my guts. I turned at the gate and motioned for my guard to open it. I drove up and parked, turning the car off. Finally, I looked up and noticed my father's and EJ's cars in the driveway. Family visits rarely happened without the rest of my brothers, so it had to be bad if I only saw two cars.

Entering the front door, I shuffled to the kitchen but didn't see anyone, so I angled to the living room and saw my father and EJ playing with RJ.

"Where's Sonya?"

"Upstairs studying." EJ tossed a ball to RJ.

"Must be important for you two to be here."

"We got off the phone with Vaughn," Dad said.

To hear our family attorney's name could only mean someone was in trouble.

"Tell me."

"I didn't tell you too much about my past," Dad said.

"What did Vaughn say?"

"The mayor clarified some things that could answer why Cade Gallagher has been watching all of our homes," EJ grumbled.

I lifted RJ up and called for our nanny.

"Let's go to my office. Deborah, can you take him while I talk with my father and don't disturb Sonya while she studies."

"Yes, Mr. Calabresi. Are you hungry? I have dinner ready."

"Not right now."

The three of us scrambled to my office, and I shut the door and locked it behind me and waited for my father to speak.

"Vaughn only got a visit because he needed to get the mayor's signature on some papers," EJ announced, and I waited for my father to elaborate.

"Tell us the truth."

"Years ago when I was in charge as the Don of the

family, I made some choices. I don't regret them all, but some I do," Dad remembered, closing his eyes and clasping his hands together. Whatever he was about to spill could only be bad for us now.

"You killed Gallagher's father," I remarked, and EJ's head whirled around at me.

"Come again."

"That's what the mayor was using against us."

"It became a closed case about a beat cop in the wrong place that was caught up in a deal that went bad."

"Shit." I sat in my chair and slammed my hand on the desk.

"So all this time he might have worked with Sanchez to fuck with you," EJ explained. It would make total sense because if he hated my father, what we stand for, then it would be easy to work underhandedly to take us down.

"Will Sanchez confirm all this?"

"If we get him a deal," EJ said.

"He doesn't get the special treatment," Dad snapped.

"Did you help cover up his father's shooting?" No matter how it played out, I would back my father up, but there had to be a reason behind the shooting.

"His father was crooked and wanted more. I don't give in to people that like to blackmail me," Dad complained in his thick Italian accent.

"Giosuè called me today." The words flew out of my mouth.

"What did he call about?" Dad grilled, pacing in front of my desk.

"A potential deal that he got ripped off on and wants my help."

"You have too much on your plate," EJ reminded me.

"I suggested you could help since it dealt with an art collection."

"Our hands can't touch that right now. Call him back

and say no," Dad insisted, alluding to us trafficking drugs. My cousins were known as bigtime drug dealers. If he needed our help, there had to be a lot of money involved.

"We're going to New York for Sonya's birthday celebration next month and bringing the kids and McKayla."

"Does Savio know about this trip?"

"EJ can tell him." I went to the door and unlocked it to leave.

"Call him yourself. I have enough shit to handle." EJ flipped me off, and I let them out of the house.

I started to head upstairs to check on Sonya when my phone rang in my pocket, and I pulled it out to see Alvize Brambilla's name spring up.

"Has to be good for you to call so late." I continued up the stairs.

"Tell me why I have an unmarked car outside of my house and a package with a picture of me and you together that was left on my doorstep." Alvize's statement made me freeze in place.

"Who was it from?"

"Just said Gallagher on top."

"Fuck."

"Tell me, Renato. I don't like surprises."

"Savio will have a meeting called in the morning," I said and hung up.

"Hey, we need to talk." I shut the door behind me, removed the folder out of her hands, and lay down on the bed across her lap.

"You made an appearance at the funeral."

"Just as a precaution."

"Okay, I think I know what this talk is going to be about." She rubbed her fingers through my hair.

"Have you eaten?" Her eyes caught my attention.

"I ate already, now I'm studying and tried to watch a movie before you disturbed me."

"How are you feeling about the funeral?"

She shrugged.

"Sad, content it's over, but I do miss our old friendship."

"You know the trip is coming up next month."

"Yeah, I already spoke with McKayla."

"There's something I need to tell you about."

"Besides us being followed?"

"Avoided the conversation long enough." Sonya stopped her movements in my hair.

"It has to do with my job. I knew it wouldn't take long before I ended up having to quit, but I refuse to just go back to the family business." Sonya tried to push me off her.

"It's not that. The trip to New York won't just be about your birthday."

"Explain."

"My cousin has a business he runs with his family in New York, and he needs my assistance."

"Let me guess, Giosuè Calabresi."

"How did you know?"

"He's a client of Prism Art Gallery."

"Shit, I never kept up with the books like that, it's a separate business that Vincenzo and Savio check in on from time to time."

"Why does he need your help?"

"A few deals went bad."

"He thinks you can rectify the situation how?"

"For now, EJ will help him, but when I talk with him, I hope to learn more of what the situation could be."

Sonya rose out of bed and grabbed her nightgown off the back of the door and went to the bathroom. Her silent treatment was the worst, and she knew I hated to be ignored.

"It won't touch you. I promise."

"You can't promise that. Does Agnese know?" Sonya wondered.

"Yes. But you will never handle things like that."

I sat up and picked up my boxers under the sheets.

"She doesn't handle it besides an auction purchase," I informed her.

"Giosuè probably needs to recoup what he lost and plans on you agreeing to ship through the gallery to make it legit."

"We haven't gotten that far, baby." I kissed her shoulder and wrapped my arms around her as we stood in front of the mirror.

"Birthday trip to close a mafia deal, great."

"Sonya, I'd never let it ruin your trip."

"I want to help." She turned in my arms.

"Huh?"

"Your cousin Giosuè needs someone that's familiar with art, and I'm that person."

"Sonya, we were not at that stage, and even if we were, no."

Sonya planted her hands on my chest.

"He called for a reason, and besides, you have no choice; we are going to New York. So it's bound to come up."

"That's not reason enough to be involved."

Sonya held her hands up in mock surrender.

"Ready to shower and go to bed." She shuffled around me, and I heard RJ's voice call for me.

"I'll check on him and come back to join you in the shower."

"Hurry."

Deborah helped RJ out of the tub and dried him off.

"He's ready for bed. I can take it from here, Deborah."

"Thank you, Mr. Calabresi."

"Are you giving your nanny a hard time?"

"No!" RJ clapped his hands together, and I tickled his stomach.

"Time for bed."

"Go bed, Daddy," RJ muttered, and I helped him change into his pajamas and removed his favorite books to read.

"I thought you were going to join me?"

Sonya stood at the bedroom door in her robe.

"He's too hyper. I'll be there soon."

"I like you in Daddy mode."

The desire in her eyes and the way she submitted had my tongue ready to dive into her pussy.

"Go, Sonya, before I change my mind."

Sonya laughed at me, and I heard the door chime from Deborah leaving.

Buzz!

"Here, hold this for Daddy." RJ took the book out of my hands.

Big Brother: Did you talk to EJ?

Me: Yeah. He just left here.

Big Brother: Why are we just now hearing about this?

Me: Dad keeps his secrets locked up tight.

Big Brother: This could be bad for our business.

Me: I'm handling it, Savio.

Big Brother: Make sure we get concrete information.

Me: I need you to get Gallo and Alvize onboard.

Big Brother: We've asked enough of them.

Me: Alvize received a gift tonight at his home.

Big Brother: From who?

Me: Agent Gallagher

Big Brother: I want this handled.

CHAPTER 30

Sonya

DAYS *later*

"Breaking news… Mayor Sanchez has issued a statement. He is resigning from his position as mayor of Chicago and he is going to be donating all of his money to charity. The Calabresi family attorney has spoken with the interim mayor and decided to drop all charges."

Renato came into the den holding the newspaper with a wide smile across his face.

"Let me guess, you've thought over what I said." I pointed the remote at the TV and relaxed on the couch. Work at Prism was going well, and Renato hadn't told me yet if he agreed about me working with his cousin in New York. They replayed a lot of the Mayor Sanchez's apology on each news station, and the media wanted to have us come and give an interview, but Savio declined to speak or have any of us speak.

He tossed the paper on the end of the table.

"No, but I have to head out for a business meeting soon."

"At Calabresi or something else?"

"Something else."

"Will it take all day?"

"What are you watching?"

"I'm watching the news about the mayor's statement."

"Time to move on, Sonya."

"True, but I have a feeling I will never be rid of him."

"He can't hurt us anymore. Do you have class?"

"Yep, a pop quiz."

"Great, I can drop you off."

"You sure? Usually you let Dome handle my travel to school since you don't like to see Sean," I teased him about my classmate.

"Sean is no threat to me, and I'm going in that direction."

"Okay, then I have the internship afterwards."

"Maybe you can work from home for a few weeks."

"No, that agent doesn't scare me. Besides I know you will have it figured out soon."

"Since I can't convince you, make sure you stick with the security."

"I have no reason to worry."

"Savio and EJ are coming to New York."

"Rena and Sante confirmed. Do we need to get the tickets?"

"Don't leave without protection, and take the private jet."

"I forgot you're billionaires." I tugged on the bottom of his shirt.

"*We* are billionaires. Keep me updated if you finish early."

"I promise."

Renato waited outside while I finished placing my books in my bags.

"Mrs. Calabresi, you're all set," Deborah said, and I

jumped up to take the leftovers from her Cajun rice and beef strudel.

"Thanks, Deborah. Call me if you need anything. I'm going straight to work afterwards."

"Yes, ma'am." Deborah waved goodbye.

———

"This piece has been in the gallery for over five years." Agnese explained the differences between the works of Van Gogh and Monet.

"Gorgeous."

"We could never part with any of his work."

"I understand, beyond the colors and streaks."

"How was class today?" Agnese quizzed.

I skipped lunch and came straight to work after the pop quiz in class. Sean was disappointed I'd skipped lunch, but I wanted to get to work fast. I'd studied every day since I started and learned at least seventy percent of the paintings they housed.

"Excuse me, sir, the gallery is closed," Rocky voiced, and I turned to see the same agent that had done the raid at our house.

"FBI. I need to talk to Mrs. Calabresi."

"Sonya, do you want me to call your husband?" Agnese asked, and I declined. I could help fight his battles, and it was time I showed him—and this agent.

"Can I help you, Agent Gallagher?"

He smirked. "You know my name?"

"How can I forget a name and face like yours?"

As he flushed red, his smirk dropped, and his nostrils flared. "Bit—"

"A talk with me will not continue if you use foul language, Mr. Gallagher."

"Tell that to your husband."

"Again, what can I do for you?"

"When did you start working here?"

"Why?"

He flipped open a small black notepad and brought out a pen.

"For my notes, I need as much information as possible."

"My job status has no bearing on any case that I'm aware of. Am I being charged with something?"

"He has you fooled."

"Who, exactly?"

"Sonya!" Dome charged inside, and I knew that Gallagher took pleasure in rattling people's cages. He didn't understand that me being a former stripper, I knew how to play any man's pleasures or fears against them.

"I'm fine, Dome. Mr. Gallagher was just leaving."

"We're not done with my questioning."

"You know my husband wouldn't like you here harassing me."

"But he can harass and hurt innocent lives."

"Like who?"

"You know the mayor's wife hasn't been seen since he did the press conference."

A lump formed at the back of my throat. I knew that Renato wouldn't harm a woman and child.

"Mr. Gallagher, you will need to speak with our attorney, Vaughn."

The moment I twisted around to walk away, he grabbed my arm, and Dome brushed him aside. Gallagher tried to punch him in the face and nearly hit me when I stepped in between them. Rocky and Agnese helped split them apart.

"Sir, I need you to leave before we call the police," Rocky fussed; I looked up and saw Ian at the door.

"Everything is fine, Ian. Please don't call Renato," I pleaded and blew out a breath.

"He needs to know, ma'am," Ian argued.

"Let me tell him. Please."

Dome watched Gallagher get in his car, and I stayed to finish my work, putting in orders for the grand opening that Agnese wanted me to start with as my first assignment. Hours later, I was driven home. I missed Renato's call because I was slammed. I figured Dome had gone behind my back because I had four missed calls from Renato. I shut the car door and waved goodbye to Dome and opened the front door to RJ running from Deborah.

"Hi, Mrs. Calabresi, I have dinner ready if you're hungry."

"Please call me Sonya and is Renato home?"

"He called and said he would be late."

I shifted my books and purse to the table next to the door, kicked off my shoes, and picked up RJ.

"Thanks, I've got him from here."

"You look tired."

"Long day at the gallery."

"I admire you, not like the other wives that live off their husbands' money."

"I'd go crazy staying in the house all day." I chuckled, changed RJ to my left hip, roamed into the kitchen, and placed him on the counter.

Slam!

"I'll take him to his room," Deborah said. Neither of us wanted RJ around when Renato and I got into a shouting match.

"Go with Deborah." I picked RJ's plate up and helped her take him to his room.

Suddenly, Renato charged toward me, closed the space between us, and gripped both sides of my face, pressing his tongue into my mouth. I moaned and dropped my hands around his waist. In response, he shoved away, nostrils flaring.

"Have you lost your mind!" he barked, lifting the bottle of vodka and pouring a shot.

"I was going to call you."

"When? After he does something to you to get at me!"

"Dome and Rocky were there. Calm down."

"He touched you," Renato sneered; my lips pursed at the thought of Renato leaving to go kill Gallagher. My eyes opened wide when he turned to leave at my hesitation to answer; I blocked him from leaving.

"Stop it and calm down. He didn't touch me. He got in my face, but Dome and Rocky handled everything."

"You're trying to save him, Sonya."

Renato tried to walk away; I cupped his chin.

"No, I'm trying to save you. My husband, the man I love."

"You don't know your husband that well. I don't leave a trace."

Renato jogged to the office, and I followed, locking the door behind us. He went to bend down in front of his safe.

"Think about your son, our family. Don't let temporary anger fuel a bigger plan."

He paused, and I stepped to his back.

"I promise I can handle myself and Gallagher knows you would have gone after him, then he would have the cops after you. All set up."

I welcomed the silence; maybe he'd think more of the consequences if he went off the handle and tried to kill Gallagher.

Renato rose up, went to his desk, and sat back with his eyes toward to the ceiling.

"Tell me why the thought of him near you makes my skin crawl. I want his blood." Renato pounded his fist.

I came around and sat on the edge of the desk.

"Because killing him will only bring more eyes on you and the family."

To dismantle a mafia like Calabresi would take a life-time, and Gallagher didn't seem like the type to be patient. I'd have bet my money on him possibly planting evidence next time.

"Talk to Vaughn and see if he can find something out."

"Enough about this bastard FBI agent. Are you ready for the trip?"

"Yes, I already have plans for us to go shopping, eat at all the famous restaurants, and go see a few plays." Excitedly I jumped into his lap.

"I'm down for the food, but everything else you can do with the girls."

As I jerked back, I pouted.

"That's not fair. It's my birthday celebration, and I want to spend it with you."

"We will."

"Your idea would be us in bed for the entire time."

"Nothing wrong with that." He pulled me to him and buried his face in my chest.

"We can fuck anytime. This is a new moment we're supposed to make as a couple."

"As much as I want to start new memories, I do have work I have to handle out there."

"As long as it doesn't take up too much of your trip."

"It won't. Let's go eat and play with RJ. It's been a long day."

"You're in for the night?" Maybe my plan to distract him had worked and he'd forgotten about Gallagher for now.

"Yeah, you've won, this time. But if he comes near you again, all bets are off."

CHAPTER 31
Renato

"He's not letting up and busted in on my wife at work."

"How's that our problem?" Tommaso thought if Gallagher focused on us then his hands were clean.

"It's your problem because he's coming after us."

"You set his sights on us!" Alvize barked, shoving the photos of his family on the table.

"He's probably watching us all now. The motherfucker won't let up. He showed up at our homes," said Mirella Pacelli, an old family friend.

"Mirella's right; we need to work together. All of our lives are on the line," Savio explained; he gave the last word, and Tommaso had to agree.

"Emers and Tulio we agreed to, the other bullshit I didn't ask for," Tommaso stated.

"The funeral for Brilynn he showed up."

"Why didn't you tell us?" Alvize fussed.

"There is nothing to tell. He's just plain trying to get us to break. He's not stupid."

"I heard it's because of your father's past with his father." Tommaso tried to throw out a distraction.

Savio and I hadn't discussed if we wanted them to know about the details; the more gossip they had on you, the more likely it would lead to a rat to the Feds.

"Whatever it was, we can handle it. Don't need you to get comfortable with him while I'm away in New York. I'll take care of him."

"Are you accusing me of being a rat?" Tommaso stood from his chair.

"Sit down, Tommaso," Savio ordered evenly.

"He's not going to sit there, talk like that about me. Your father and I go way back, and he'd be disgusted by your accusations." Tommaso's words meant nothing to me because my father taught me to analyze everyone's tone and body language. If Tommaso thought there was a chance he could save himself and live, that'd be the day I was no longer an enforcer.

"Sante, find out what you can bring back before you make any moves," Savio directed toward us.

"We have flights to New York. EJ has to work with Giosuè on a deal."

"This is your area. You're supposed to be on top of this," EJ stated. I arched my brow, and my chest tightened because everybody wanted to piss me off, from Gallagher, Tommaso, and Sonya to now EJ.

"Think again. I have another appointment," I said flippantly and ignored my brother. I left soon after to pick up RJ and take him to the park.

———

"Can you climb, RJ?" I coached him, and he slid down the slide. I clapped my hands and he mimicked, then went to do it again.

"Be careful, let me help you," I said.

"Lovely boy."

I was supposed to not drop my guard around RJ, breaking character in public. Gallagher had already made contact with my wife behind my back and now to get this close to my son took my blood pressure up.

"Told you, this is called harassment."

"Why? Because the bureaucrats in the office wanted the case to end that day in interrogation, just be quiet and go away?" Gallagher mentioned, and I perked up at the statement.

"It eats at you, don't it? In that room you were shown to be a little boy. Your boss had to pull you back before you hurt yourself trying to step on me."

"You can't pay me off."

"I know you. I see it." RJ came down the slide, and Gallagher tried to bend down and talk to him, but I blocked him before he came close.

"Nothing like you or your other mobster friends and cops you paid off." Gallagher fussed, sliding his hands in his pockets.

"All right." With nonchalance, I shrugged.

"They're a little upset with you, I heard."

"Playing a dangerous game, Gallagher."

He chuckled. "Really."

"I can say the same about you. But as a clean businessman I won't stoop to your level."

"Only a matter of time."

"Vaughn, my attorney, will tell you I work at my family's company."

"That's a front. We all know that."

"Agent, you can say whatever you want. But we didn't do whatever you think we've done."

"All I know is you're paying people off. I'm gonna find out."

"And how much do you think the new mayor would like you to harass citizens?"

I struck a chord.

"Your boy looks exactly like you. Just hope he doesn't come up with the same mannerisms as his father. You know, killer instincts."

I chuckled. "Is that your way of trying to poke me?"

"Put a hit on me. You have people for that, right?" he taunted, stepping close.

"I blast every night. I got the balls to take you on."

"Try it if you want. I can see the headlines now: *FBI agent goes missing, mobster indicted.*"

I clapped my hands in acknowledgement. "So right. That would be foolish of me. But I don't make foolish mistakes. I'm good at what I do."

"And what is it that you do? Because I heard your four brothers work together."

"You heard wrong, Mr. Gallagher. I am a man of many talents, and sometimes those talents come in handy. When I need to extract a bug—you know, those things that are constantly popping up."

"Killing is your expertise."

"Never said it was, but people pay me the big bucks for a service."

"I looked at those statements. Those offshore accounts."

"Again, I don't know what you're talking about. You could talk to my lawyer, though."

"Yeah, I will leave it at that. I'll be seeing you real soon, Mr. Calabresi. Oh, and tell your wife she looked lovely. The other day at Prism Gallery."

I didn't break a smile at his comment. Remo kept eyes on him as he walked to his car and got inside. I helped RJ back on the swing and continued to play for the rest of the afternoon.

"How was work today?" Sonya removed her blouse and slid a T-shirt on in our bedroom.

"It was fine. I took RJ to the park."

"Oh, that's sweet, Renato."

"Did you see anybody today while you were at work?"

"No. Agnese gave me a stack of stuff to study, but that's about it. Why? What's going on?"

"Nothing. Ready for the trip?"

"I am. I'm excited."

"Good. That's all I care about."

"Is that all?" She rolled the covers back on the bed.

"What are you talking about?"

"I wanted to talk to you about something before the trip."

"Talk." I removed my shirt, then took off my shoes.

"Wondered how you would feel if my mom could move in with us."

I felt myself grow hot at her comment.

"Before you answer, she's doing better with her treatments. But I would like to have her closer. She could help Deborah with RJ," she rushed out.

"As long as she stays out of my way. We're still not buddy-buddy."

"You won't have to worry. I promise."

"All right. I need to go do some work in my office."

"Okay, don't be too long, I need help studying." She raised her notebook up.

I leaned over the bed and kissed her mouth before exiting the bedroom, then went down the stairs to my office.

Her mom officially moving in would be awkward at first, but I needed to support her in this moment. I lifted the phone and made a call to my cousin.

"Still coming here?"

"Already confirmed with my wife and brothers."

"Good, we need to meet up ASAP."

"The FBI might be sniffing around me."

"That's a target on your back."

"I know, but I'm handling it with the family."

"Let me guess, Tommaso is pissed." Giosuè chortled, and I smirked at his statement.

"He's a fucking clown and always brings up the old days."

"It's a new time. We can't have that, cousin."

"Right now, I don't feel we're at the brink, not yet anyway."

"How can I help?"

"We're coming out there for my wife's birthday next month. I just want to get away for a few days so she can be herself."

"Savio called after word got back to your father."

"I think we need to discuss things and how we can help each other."

"I'm open. Is this going to end up with a black limo for a certain FBI agent?" Giosuè muttered; I heard the sound of the ice in his glass swirl around.

"Never be too careful, hopefully we don't have to."

"But you never know. He's seen as a problem, He's not on our payroll. I have his file. No wife. No kids—well, his wife and him have issues. Sounds like this could be fun. Let me know."

"I will. I'll be in touch." I disconnected the call just as someone entered my office.

"What are you doing here?"

"After the meeting today, I thought we should talk." Savio sat down.

"About?"

"I could tell you were irritated with them."

"You know me too well."

―――――

Savio poured himself, then me, a glass of bourbon. I lit a cigar and blew out the smoke while we sat on the patio of my backyard.

"He showed up at the park today, and I was with RJ," I rambled, letting the smoke ease my emotions.

"And he showed up at Prism," Savio remarked, and I nodded, not surprised since he had reports on the entire family's daily activities.

"He's testing me."

"The time will come, but you can't let him see you've been shaken."

"I'm not bothered by him fucking with me, but my wife and son aren't to be touched or frightened."

"Same, and I know we have this trip, so you need to relax, have fun, and let Vaughn handle him."

"Vaughn takes too long, then it's out of my hands."

"Renato, you can't kill an FBI agent."

"I've done worse." I puffed on the cigar, sipped on the bourbon, and continued to listen to him talk about the trip.

CHAPTER 32
Sonya

He tasted delicious on my tongue. I tortured him with a slow pace, causing a low whimper on his lips. It felt powerful to have this strong man release his control. I clenched my hand around his girth and popped him out of my mouth. His hand started to rub up my arms; I spat on the tip and felt the brush of his fingers across my ass. I knew when I woke him up with oral sex, it would make us late for the day I had planned. His eyes squeezed shut, and my nipples tightened.

"Fuckin' sexy on your knees, baby," he growled. The scent of clean musk from his balls, the warmth of his seed down my throat, the wave of intensity in his eyes showed he wasn't going to let me go without being inside of me.

"Get up here," he barked and smacked me on the thigh. I turned around and slid down on his dick, and he slowly pumped from underneath. A fiery hot sting came to my thigh, and I circled my hips while he stretched my legs wide and played with my clit.

Renato had my mind in a tornado; it comes in and destroys with limited warning, and you're left to pick up the pieces.

"Renato!" I tossed my head, hair whipping wildly as he reached out a hand to brush a lock of long hair away from my face.

He snatched my head back and reached his left hand around to cup my breasts, forcing me onto my stomach so he could fuck me deeper into the bed.

Our sweat soaked us, and I felt his hand come around to grasp my neck; he softly spoke praise in my ear.

"You're mine forever." He reached out and bracketed my waist, rubbing the arc of my hip bones with his thumbs.

His dominance made me want to climb the walls and express to him how his love made me feel accepted, wanted, and appreciated, even when we didn't agree on everything. My skin vibrated as my orgasm crashed into me, and his warm body hovered over me and possessed my soul.

"Shit. Can I please come?" I panted, eyes popped wide.

He licked the sweat off my back, and I shuddered in his hold; it felt like I was on a cloud looking down during an out-of-body experience as he came right behind me.

"Get dressed," Renato said.

He rolled off me, and I slipped off the bed on wobbly knees and rubbed our noses together before kissing him.

"I'm going shopping."

"Take Dome with you." He started to pull the covers over his body.

"Are you sure you're not interested in shopping with the girls?" I turned the shower on in the bathroom with the door open.

"Positive. I need to meet with my brothers and cousin."

My lips parted in surprise; I had the urge to question

what they would be discussing, but I knew it wasn't my place.

"We'll meet up for lunch then," I called, pinning my hair up, stepping in the shower, and closing the door.

———

An hour later, I went downstairs and met with McKayla and Rena at the restaurant in the hotel. Both were gossiping when I came around and plopped down next to Rena at the table.

"She's got a glow on her, McKayla. I think someone just thanked their husband for a trip to New York."

"I think you are right." I winked and grinned.

"Is this your first vacation?"

"Yeah, I've always wanted to go on trips, but could never do anything because I was always working and helping my mom with bills."

"What are the plans besides shopping today?"

"Dinner later, but I wanted a favor."

"Does it cost me money?" Rena asked.

"No."

The waitress brought cups and filled each with coffee.

"Tell me the favor first," McKayla pushed. I took a moment to gather my words the right way.

"You know Renato is meeting his brothers and cousin today."

"Yeah we know."

"So I was thinking, I could maybe talk to Gallagher to get him to back off."

"It would never work."

I'd spent the past few weeks thinking of how I could get Gallagher off our backs, and I knew he wouldn't just walk away unless he got spooked.

"Renato thinks we're going shopping." McKayla cleared her throat.

"We are, but he's here."

"Who?"

"Gallagher."

"Where? How do you know?" Rena looked around the restaurant.

I pulled out my phone and showed them a picture of Gallagher outside our hotel. I wasn't sure if Renato knew, but before he made a call, I needed to see what I could do.

"He's outside the hotel."

"Do you have a plan?"

"I need to catch him in the act."

"You want us as witnesses." Rena nodded in understanding.

"Also to record."

"If we agree it'll work, Renato won't like it, and Savio would kill me if I got anywhere near him," McKayla complained.

"He doesn't have to know until it's over."

McKayla hesitated, but Rena helped her to get on board.

Breakfast energized me and helped me to figure out a plan for Gallagher. I told Renato we'd be ready for dinner and spend time with RJ before it got late. I picked up two more dresses and held them up for Rena to give her opinion on what worked. Saks is one of my favorite stores that I'd grown to love since I was in a better position to afford clothes without having to budget.

"Mrs. Calabresi, see, that's your color."

I released a breath and turned around to face him.

"Agent Gallagher. What are you doing here in Saks—let me rephrase, New York?"

"I just happen to be in New York."

"Sounds funny we ran into each other."

"Not funny at all, more confused."

I put the dresses back on the rack, moving around to the opposite of him to put space between us.

"I find your naivety cute."

"Cute? You really need to do your homework, sir."

"How badly do you want to save your husband?"

"My husband is innocent."

"Oh, do you believe that?"

"Yes, I do. It's already been proven that Mayor Sanchez was the one to do the corruption. I don't know why that's so hard for you to understand."

He chuckled.

"Because it's all a lie. Women like you, all three of you, you're naïve, stupid. You let the money blind you to what you think are decent men."

"As far as I know, they were proven innocent."

"You want to look the other way but have the perks and the money to live the lifestyle, while other families are hurting in grief."

"Calabresi does more for Chicago than any other family," I snapped, but there was a little smile on my face.

"From what I see, the Calabresi family has destroyed this city with weapons and drugs."

"Think you're a little delusional, Gallagher."

"Maybe, but I'm watching you."

"Listen, and you listen good. My husband is innocent. I don't know what you think you've heard or seen. But he is innocent. And I won't let you—"

"Sonya!" Renato yelled.

I whirled around to look at my husband and his brothers.

"Agent Gallagher, is there a reason why you're harassing my wife?" He balled his fists up.

"There's a reason I'm watching all of you."

"It won't be so easy. Not this time. I suggest you talk to our lawyer and think about your life."

"Easy to talk about lawyers when they're corrupt. Oh, tell your cousin, I'm watching him too."

Savio stepped in front of Renato and Gallagher.

"You should leave now," Savio said, his deep voice clear through the air.

All of us watched Gallagher leave the store, get in a car, and speed away.

Renato glanced down at me and shook his head.

"I think we need to keep an eye on him," I said.

"We can't go after a federal agent," EJ stated, dialing on his phone.

"I can go after whoever I want, if they're fucking with my family," Renato answered matter-of-factly.

"No, we can't. EJ is right. If there's an inkling of him gone missing, you're the first one they'll go look at," I replied.

"I'm not going to let him intimidate or threaten you." Renato narrowed his eyes on me.

"I wasn't threatened. I can handle myself."

"Let's just enjoy today. It's your birthday."

"All right, but we're going to continue this conversation later. He is looking for a reason to arrest you. Don't give it to him."

The boys got their cars, we all piled in, and they drove us around Times Square and then to the museum of art.

"What time does the play start?" I turned around in the car to look at Rena.

"We have two hours and then we can get dressed."

"Perfect. Are you excited?" I snuggled up against Renato.

"I have other plans I would rather be doing than a stuffy play."

"Well, it's my birthday. And I want to see a play."

"As my spoiled wife, your wish is my command."

"You're such an asshole."

"Heard that a few times."

Hours later, we arrived at the theater, and McKayla and Savio paused in their steps when we get to the ticket booth.

"We have company." Savio turned and raised his head across the room at Agent Gallagher in a suit, near the door.

"He's asking for a bullet," Renato muttered.

"Go inside, you can't do anything here. It'll be too obvious."

"Just let him go," McKayla agreed, pushing our tickets into the hand of the usher, who escorted us to our seats.

He pointed to our seats a few rows down from Gallagher. The play started and the lights dimmed for the *Beauty and the Beast*.

Hours later, the show drew its curtains. We clapped our hands and gave them a standing ovation. As we prepared to leave the building, Gallagher approached once again.

"Following us has turned into a habit of yours," I grumbled; the hate that I held in my eyes could cause a fire.

"A free country, ma'am. I don't care."

"We know what you're doing. You're trying to provoke him, and let me tell you, I won't let it happen. So figure out what your problem is and find somebody else. He didn't do anything. And if he did something to someone, it was to save me."

"Is that a confession?" Gallagher asked.

"Let's go. Sonya." Renato pushed me to the limo; I climbed in next to McKayla and ignored Gallagher as he stared at us with a smile on his face.

———

Next night in New York

. . .

"The entire family, mostly the men," Renato informed me as we ran down to have dinner with his family.

"You're gonna be there."

"The entire family is gonna be there. Giosuè is head of his family here in New York." Renato explained the dynamics of the mafia.

"Did you grow up close with them?"

"During the summers mostly."

"Are they like you and your brothers?"

"The entire family's interesting. You should know that by now."

"True, but what if Gallagher comes tonight?"

"Not something for you to worry about." Renato ran a hand up my leg.

"All an adjustment, thank you for trusting me."

"There's only so much learning before you do what you did earlier and take Gallagher into your own hands."

"Do any cops or FBI on your payroll know what's going on?"

"No."

"Well, maybe it's time they found out."

"I don't think that's a good idea."

"If you say so, but I'm helping you either way."

"I can't get rid of you."

"Either you take me or I take myself." I shrugged.

"You didn't leave much for me in the persuasion department." He slipped his hand under my dress and slid my panties to the side. I peeled his hand away.

"Not in the car with your family around," I whispered in his ear.

The limo arrived at the restaurant and stopped for the valet to open the door.

Renato hugged a beautiful woman and shook hands with three men that looked identical, almost like triplets with their sharp features and chiseled jawlines. All of the

Calabresi men held arrogance about them because of how handsome they were. Women probably threw themselves at these men as well.

"This is my wife, Sonya Calabresi," Renato said.

"Nice to meet you, Sonya, I'm Giosuè and these are my siblings." He bowed to kiss my hand and Renato grunted, and I giggled at his jealousy even with his family.

"It's your cousin," I teased.

"Doesn't matter." Renato pulled me back to his side.

"Ignore my cousin, Sonya, I'm Giuliana." Giosuè's sister hugged Rena and McKayla next.

"Please tell me you're a model." She blushed, and I couldn't help but stare at how her cat-like, smoky eyes, long legs, and athletic build gave a dominant air about her.

"No, I work with my brothers," she said.

"Let's eat. Everyone sit down," Giosuè commanded, and Renato pulled out my chair.

CHAPTER 33

Renato

"HEY, HOW'S IT LOOKING?"

"Deal called for ten crates. It didn't really make any sense, but things had been on the up-and-up with him."

"But…" I responded, eager to know more details.

"I don't like to lose money."

"I get that, Giosuè."

"Either it's someone on my team or the person that we usually sell to ripped us off and stole from me."

"How can we help each other?"

"You help me with this transaction, and I can possibly help with Gallagher."

"He's here in New York."

"I looked into him and told you it seems his father was killed by your father as payback."

"I would just slit his throat, not even care, but with him I have to think, especially being FBI."

"This deal could benefit us both."

"How secure is the location of transfer? My wife comes, I need to know she's safe."

"Secured a jewelry store he owns, and we would look like you're purchasing a legitimate item."

"EJ is going to look into the paperwork and our cut."

"I have no problem with that, we're gonna get protection and Sonya is on board." Giosuè sliced into his steak.

"Keep an eye on your guy. If he looks wrong, I won't hesitate to kill him."

"It goes later tonight."

"Prism Art Gallery carries a few pieces, but Vincenzo and Savio set that up, so you'll need to keep them updated," I informed him.

"Sonya will handle the auction buying and negotiation," Giosuè suggested, and I could barely think past Gallagher being at the end of my gun.

"Then we finish dinner and head to the meeting."

Savio raised his glass of rum.

"I want to give a toast. We haven't all been together since we were kids. To the family," Savio said.

"To family," everybody answered.

Giosuè's driver parked a block from the jewelry store. I held on to Sonya's hand and watched another car draw close and park.

"That's him," Giosuè said.

Giosuè's men patted him down and checked for guns or a wire.

"He came alone?" My eyes bore into Giosuè.

"He's not stupid."

"As long as you know you'll have one less buyer." I showed my gun.

One of Giosuè's men waved, giving the all-clear. Giosuè climbed out of the car, and I watched his brothers Armani and Bosco stroll alongside his store.

"You're nervous, Mrs. Calabresi?" Giosuè asked my wife.

"No, I know Renato will keep me safe."

Taking Sonya by the hand, I helped her get out of the car and led her into the building so she was behind me. He looked around the area and then looked back at my cousin.

"I have a couple of pieces I think will be great for your gallery," the guy said.

"I looked at my cousin for confirmation; he raised his head to go forward, and Sonya smiled.

"I'd love to see your collection." Sonya switched to beside me as we made it to the back of the jewelry store. He typed in a password, and the door opened to a storage room revealing stacks of paintings wrapped in plastic.

"I've been a long-time fan of art and held on to them for so long."

"Mr.—"

"Ernest, call me Ernest." He smiled at Sonya.

"Ernest, you have some fine pieces. The colors and contrast on this one would go great in our gallery."

"Sonya, Ernest would like to sell his entire collection, estimated around fifty million," Giosuè explained, and Sonya listened intently.

"I could bring this back to Agnese and get her opinion. If it's possible, could I take one to get the information on the location and artist?" Sonya asked.

"That can be arranged," Ernest replied; a hint of pride swelled in my chest at Sonya standing on her own.

"Great, I'll wait for your email. Here's my card." Sonya removed her business card out of her clutch, and Ernest thanked her.

"Go wait in the car," I whispered in her ear.

"Be safe." I received a kiss on the lips.

Armani escorted her out of the room; he was the only one I felt comfortable with besides Dome and Remo.

Ernest dropped the smile on his face and popped open

the crate that held the painting and pulled out a bag of cocaine.

"How much?" Ernest quizzed.

"You'll pay a third, unlike other clients, so fifty million stands."

"Monthly?"

"If you can handle that amount and no interruption in payment," Giosuè answered.

"Everything comes through her business, correct?" Ernest wondered.

"The transportation of the product is not your concern, just be ready to pay for the product," I remarked, so he wouldn't think again about seeing my wife. This was a one-time situation where we needed to confirm the authenticity of the paintings.

"Thank you, gentlemen. I'll take the deal," Ernest confirmed. I let my cousin finish his conversation and climbed back in the car with Sonya.

"How did I do?"

"Amazing. It's over now."

The door opened, and Giosuè slid in across from us; his driver started the limo and turned on his right signal and hauled back to Manhattan. We drove a few blocks when I noticed high beams behind us.

"I see him." Giosuè knew what I already thought. Had to be Gallagher, and I wondered how long he was on our tail.

"He has no authority to stop us. Just stay calm," Giosuè advised.

Forty minutes later, his limo arrived at our hotel; I let Sonya get out first and looked at Gallagher parked across the street.

"He won't interrupt our business," Giosuè said.

"Depends, but I'll figure it out later."

Giosuè and I shook hands.

"Enjoy your time in New York, talk soon."

Sonya snuggled up next to me as the cool breeze sent goosebumps up her arm as we headed toward the entry. The doorman opened it for me, and I kissed the top of her head, looking back at Gallagher standing outside his car.

Sonya shifted in my arms to face me.

"What's wrong?"

"Nothing." I patted her on the butt and pushed the elevator button for our suite.

"As your wife, I've learned a few things about you."

"Like what?" The doors slid opened, and I let her step on first.

"When you have time to think and not talk, that means you're brewing in your mind."

I leaned forward as the doors closed and pulled her in between my legs, kissing the side of her neck.

"Glad you know your husband."

"Tell me." Sonya lifted her palm to my cheek.

"You're great, blow me away."

"Glad you learned that about me." She giggled.

"Tomorrow I'm taking you on a helicopter ride."

"Seriously?"

"Yep, Deborah and McKayla will have the kids, so we can spend some alone time together before we head back home."

The elevator pinged, and Sonya pulled me against her back, then walked to our room. Sonya unlocked the door, and I claimed her mouth, pushing her up against it. Plenty of women desired me and wanted affection, but Sonya shook me to the core.

"Bed."

"Yes, you need to be quiet, RJ is just in the adjourning room," I remembered, and she tucked her bottom lip between her teeth.

"Shower." She angled her face toward me.

I nipped at the corners of her mouth, bent down, and lifted her legs around my waist, walking us to the bathroom in our room after I closed and locked the door. Tonight she was in my atmosphere with my family and then at a mafia deal which filled my chest with hunger.

Gallagher would be dealt with, even if it came up as an accident.

Who would miss him?

CHAPTER 34

Sonya

"LOOK OVER THERE." Renato pointed out the helicopter's window, and I glanced at the Statue of Liberty. We were on our second to last day in New York. Today was sightseeing, and I didn't think we'd get to see all of what New York had to offer. We'd already seen the Museum of Natural History, and I'd even gotten him to do a carriage ride, but it didn't last long because he thought he was too cool.

"I am starving. Can we have lunch?"

"Anything you wish."

The helicopter touched down, and he helped me out, gripped my hand, and typed on his phone, heading toward the car.

"Are Savio and the other guys coming to the club tonight?"

"Not sure."

His face screwed up in a harsh line.

"Talk to me."

"Work. Nothing serious."

"Are you sure? We can go back to the hotel."

"Lunch with RJ and then we get dressed for the club."

"Are they meeting us when we get to the hotel?"

"Yeah, Deborah's already downstairs with him and the family."

Our car approached the docks before stopping, and the driver popped the locks.

"I got her from here," Renato said.

"Have a good afternoon." The driver stuck his head out of the door.

"Renato, what is this?" I whispered, surprised at our family on the boat.

"Surprise! A boat cruise with the family."

Renato held me close, and I saw hunger in his eyes; his voice was breathless in my ear, and I wanted to take him back to the hotel and show my gratitude. He brushed his hands up my back and helped me up onto the boat. My mom rushed over to us, hugging Renato first, then me. I seemed to be in a twilight zone for that to happen.

"Is that Crystal?' I pointed, glancing at Renato.

"I had everyone come. Before the sun sets, I will have your cake brought out." He snaked his arm around my hip.

"You've topped all my birthdays with this day."

"Happy birthday, Sonya." Crystal and Rena clung to my side as Renato walked off to his brothers.

"When did you get here?" I took a glass of champagne from Crystal.

"Renato flew me in for the party." Crystal gulped her drink.

The music drowned out the conversation, but I took in the sight of family and friends that came to support me.

"That man of yours hasn't taken his eyes off you since you got here. All he did was talk about how much he wants to give you the world," Crystal announced, then picked up a cocktail shrimp.

"Might be a good idea for you to look into going to

school and maybe start dating," I suggested, then motioned at Renato's cousins, who had focused on her.

"Marriage is not in my life plans; you two can have it." Crystal smirked. McKayla approached with a gift bag.

"Happy birthday, sister." McKayla raised the bag, and I took it from her hands.

"Thank you, McKayla. What did you get me?"

"A little gift I thought you'd love," McKayla bragged; I opened the bag and pulled out an art book detailing the late eighteenth century.

"Thank you, McKayla, can't wait to read."

Rena grabbed my hand and pulled me to dance with her as the band played mostly late eighties and nineties rock music. Deborah carried RJ over to me, and I danced with him in my arms, pointing to balloons, then showed him the cake in the corner.

"Mommy's birthday."

"Birthday, Mommy."

"Yes, thank you, baby." I kissed him on the side of his head.

Three hours later, the boat pulled back up to the dock. Renato helped us off, and Savio and the rest of the brothers assisted their wives. A few limos were lined up for us to get back to the hotel; I helped RJ into his car seat.

"This was the best birthday I could ask for." I softly rubbed my fingers through his hair; he nuzzled his face in my neck.

"We still have our own private party later," he replied right before Savio came up to us.

"Sonya, happy birthday again," Savio stated.

"Thank you so much. Get McKayla home before she passes out." I giggled at McKayla hanging on to his arms, half asleep. All of the gifts and some black bags were loaded into the trunk.

"I need to talk to Savio and my cousin. You'll ride with Deborah."

"We can wait."

"I'll follow right behind you." He turned to leave.

"Wait, is something wrong?" I pleaded for an answer; he looked at me, then shook his head and cupped my chin, slowly pushing his tongue into my mouth.

"Nothing is wrong; go and get back to the hotel. RJ is tired." Renato wiped the lipstick off.

He helped me in the car, shut the door behind me, and stayed back as the car drove from the dock. I slipped my shoes off, released a breath of exhaustion, and listened to the peace and quiet in the car as we got on the main road headed back to Manhattan.

Renato: You looked beautiful tonight

Me: You make me feel beautiful.

Renato: Stay awake for me.

Me: Are you delivering my favorite present?

I posted the eggplant emoji, and he sent a tongue emoji.

The first car arrived, coming to a stop a few minutes later, and the door was yanked open.

"Oh, my God!" Crystal shrieked in shock, then covered RJ.

"Where is it?" Gallagher held the flashlight on our car.

"Agent Gallagher!" Crystal shouted, trying to push him away. I stepped out of my limo and rushed to get to RJ's side. We'd already sent Crystal the information on him and his photos to be on the lookout.

"Who the fuck are you?" Gallagher growled at Crystal.

Another limo pulled up next to him, and Renato jumped out with his gun drawn, angled at Gallagher's head.

"No, Renato, not here," I yelled, tugging on his arm. Too many people, out in public, with cameras recording.

"Go ahead, you want to shoot me. Do it and see how

you're hauled off to jail," Gallagher argued and held his hands up in the air.

"Savio!" I shouted for his help.

All of the brothers and cousins approached the scene.

"Get RJ and go inside, Sonya." Renato gritted through his teeth.

"No! I'm not leaving you."

I heard police sirens in the distance.

"Renato, put the gun down, he's no threat." Savio spoke evenly.

"Listen to your brother. I'm an FBI agent, and he's trying to kill me!" Gallagher shouted, and the crowd started to take pictures.

"Crystal get out of the car," I told her, and she carried RJ. Gallagher's eyes ballooned wide as he took in Crystal's identical outfit to mine.

"You've harassed my people for the last time."

"I know this was a setup. Check his trunk!" Gallagher pointed when the cops approached them.

"We got it from here," the police officer said. He took the gun from Renato, turned him around, and placed the handcuffs on him.

"Check the trunk! I followed them the other night, and they're a known mafia family in Chicago. Look up my name, Agent Cade Gallagher."

A police officer moved to the trunk, and Renato popped it open, showing the gift bags and bags of clothes for RJ.

"They probably moved the drugs, I'm telling you."

"We have a restraining order against you, sick bastard!" I screamed and tried to push Renato out of the way to hit Gallagher. The day Renato saw us out shopping at Saks, I sent him the video I'd recorded and he suggested I talk with the police to get a protection order against Gallagher as backup. I'd marched into the police station in New York and spoke with the desk clerk before asking for the captain of police.

"Can I help you?" The clerk stood at the desk.

"I need to speak with whoever is in charge."

"And you are?"

"Sonya Calabresi."

"What can we do for you, ma'am?"

"I suggest you call the director of the FBI or whoever you need to, but I need something done about Agent Cade Gallagher harassing me and my family."

"Let me check if the captain is free."

"Please do, because this is ridiculous."

The clerk picked up the phone, and I waited for her to finish.

"Captain Newark is coming out now."

"Boss is waiting in the car," Dome said, showing me the text message.

"I'm Captain Benedict Newark. How can I help you, Mrs. Calabresi?"

"You know who my family is, so I won't go into detail, but we've been harassed for a few months in Chicago and now here in New York."

"How is he harassing your family?"

"Confronting me in public, following me and my child."

"Do you have proof of this?"

"I do." I pulled out my phone and showed him shots of Gallagher outside our home, in New York at the hotel, and at the restaurant.

"How long has this been going on?"

"It appears he's upset at not being able to charge my husband with a crime a few months back, now he's here in New York."

"All I can do is take your information and look into the situation."

"I hope you do, because I don't want to have to come back up here with the media and a lawsuit."

Captain Newark must have believed me because he was here, talking with Savio and Renato.

"We'll handle it from here, Gallagher. All we have is evidence of your harassment and a restraining order," Captain Newark said.

"That's bullshit! I can call my superior," Gallagher went off.

"We did, and they said they've closed the case on the Calabresi family," Captain Newark informed him; Gallagher put his head down.

"Go inside while I handle this," Renato muttered, and I took his face in my hands to face me.

"Let the police handle him."

He smirked, and I knew that only meant he'd do whatever he wanted. Crystal and Rena helped me take RJ and our things into the hotel. I looked back at Renato and Savio talking with Captain Newark as Gallagher was placed in the back of a police cruiser.

CHAPTER 35
Renato

"HOW MUCH ARE WE TALKING ABOUT?"

"At least five million," Captain Newark stated; I glanced at Savio, and he nodded in agreement.

"Take him." I shook hands with Captain Newark, and Remo held out his phone as I typed in a few numbers from an offshore account and sent Captain Newark a bonus for a new beach house.

"We'll keep him on hold for you," Captain Newark remarked.

"I don't want to see him in Chicago. If I do, our agreement is null and void," I demanded.

"He'll be in safe hands," Captain Newark said, and his driver started the car before the captain hopped in, smiling.

"You played that well. I could tell you wanted to shoot him right then and there." Giosuè removed a cigarette, offering us one.

"My hand was itching to kill him."

"You stood your ground and didn't move the needle, like I thought you would." Savio faced me.

"If he gets out, I can't promise I'll be this calm, Savio. He got too close to my son."

"If that was my son, I would be the same way, but we need to try other avenues," Savio stated. After a moment, I relaxed my shoulders.

My heart sank at how Gallagher had the audacity to just charge at our cars and demand to search them without a warrant. He'd really fallen down a long road of manic and reckless behavior to try and put me behind bars. RJ, thank God, was asleep and didn't understand too much of what was going on, but I was proud that Crystal and Sonya had played their parts so well. It was a last-minute idea, and I'd flown Crystal out here for Sonya's birthday, but also as a way to make it look like Sonya was in on our business after he followed her after the play and Saks store. Crystal dressed up like Sonya and dyed her hair blond and put on the same burnt orange dress. The limos were all the same, and when we got into the cars, I saw him parked across the dock in the corner, with the limos next to each other. Crystal climbed in first and then Sonya, but we had Sonya climb back out and follow in the second limo with me.

"I need to go check on my family."

"I'll check in if we have any problems on the shipment," Giosuè said, leaving me and Savio outside.

"Go be with Sonya and your son. Gallagher isn't going anywhere for the night." Savio shifted around, placed his arm around my shoulder, and rode the elevator with me. He was on another floor with McKayla and Sante. I slid the key in the door, then Sonya jumped up from the couch and ran into my arms.

"I was so scared."

"Shush... I'm fine." I lifted her up and carried her to the couch; she straddled my lap.

"I thought he was going to provoke you to kill him."

I wiped the tears from her eyes.

"He wanted me to, but I wouldn't do anything that takes me away from you and RJ."

"Can we go home? I just want to be in our bed and house." Sonya snuggled on my chest.

I rubbed circles on her back, kissing her forehead.

"If that's what you want."

"Yeah, I have the opening of the gallery and school."

"Fuck Sean."

She slapped my chest lightly, and I chuckled.

"Leave my friend alone."

"He's your friend now?" I pushed her hair behind her ear, raising my right brow.

"You're my best friend and husband. He's just a friend."

I sucked my teeth and squeezed her butt.

"Let's go to bed, and tomorrow we'll be back at home."

"What happened to Gallagher tonight?"

"Captain Newark has him."

"In jail?"

She stopped walking.

"Yeah, for now."

"For now?"

"If he tries anything else, then I'll have no choice but to protect my family."

I opened the bedroom door and removed my jacket and shoes. Sonya climbed on the bed, watching me hang up my coat.

"Besides what took place, it was a great birthday." She pushed the comforter back, and I removed my pants but left my boxers on.

"I'm glad you enjoyed yourself."

"Only you could turn a nice situation into a crime scene." She laughed, and I winked at her, then snuggled her back to my chest.

"Go to sleep."

I turned the light out and listened to her talk about her plans for graduation and our next vacation.

Back in Chicago

I came straight to the Calabresi building from the airport and let Sonya head home with Deborah and RJ to get unpacked. Savio requested we meet with the board about what happened in New York so there was no blowback if Gallagher got out and created a narrative that we set him up.

"Are you ready?" Savio stood at the conference room door.

"Long as no one pisses me off."

Savio opened the door, and I saw my father at the head of the table. Normally, he'd never come to a meeting unless something happened. I checked my phone and didn't see any messages from my cousin.

Me: Captain any changes?

Captain Newark: He's still locked up.

Me: Keep me updated if anything changes, even if he wants to get an extra bag of chips.

I closed out of my messages.

"Thank you for coming back and meeting so swiftly, Savio and Renato," said Gilbert, a long-time board member at Calabresi Holdings.

"What's the point of a meeting today, Gilbert?" Savio quizzed; I sat back and listened.

"We've seen all over the news and social media of Renato holding a gun to an FBI agent's head."

"It doesn't concern you, Gilbert."

"That may be, but we need to make sure it won't come back on the business," Gilbert replied. He pushed papers across the table, and I caught a photo of me and Gallagher in front of the limo.

"He's harassed my family for a few months. I took care of the situation, nothing else to talk about."

"Did you need to point a gun at his head?" Gilbert asked.

"Gilbert," Dad grunted, then stood.

"I'm sorry, but you never hold your boys accountable for anything. I can't be the only one that thinks you've allowed them to drive too much traffic here."

"Our name is on the building, Gilbert. You understand that, right?" I argued, crossing my hands over my chest; he sounded like Tommaso.

"They've made all of you very rich, so let's not put a label or try and downplay our work."

"All I'm saying is that I think you need to be careful with your side business," Gilbert hissed, and Savio clenched his fist. That was a jab at our mafia business, and Gilbert didn't want to make me angry. I couldn't get to Gallagher; Gilbert could be a replacement for my fist.

"Gilbert, you can walk out if you want, and we'll give you proper compensation," Savio expressed.

"Savio, you know I'm loyal to this company. We just need to know Renato won't go around killing cops now." Gilbert took another hit at me, and that was enough. I jumped over the table, gripped him by the collar, and pushed his face down onto the wood.

"I suggest you take the offer my brother gave you, or I'll kill you myself."

"Renato!" Father shouted, and I released Gilbert, holding my hands up in the air.

"Go home," Savio said.

"Fucking animal! Are you going to do something about him?" Gilbert fussed at my brother.

"Fucking show you an animal," I muttered slowly, snatching the door open and stalking to the elevator. I removed my phone, relaxing at a picture of Sonya and RJ together in our bed, taken months ago, when we started to get close after the cabin.

———

I stopped at the store and grabbed flowers and candy for Sonya as a surprise and shut the car door. I climbed up the stairs and heard laughing. I peeked around the corner and saw Sonya on the floor with RJ; I cleared my throat.

"Awww, are those for me?" Sonya jumped up and reached for the flowers.

"For the opening."

"Thank you, Renato."

"You're welcome."

"Thank you. So how was the board meeting?"

"Same fights, like being in the family, nothing is different, but you know, I'm handling it as best as I can."

"With you, I know some people aren't happy."

"Glad it didn't turn your mood bad." She opened the box of candies, passing a piece to RJ.

"I heard laughing when I walked inside."

"RJ and I are painting." She showed me our son's colorful hands.

"What are your plans for today?"

"Suppose to meet McKayla, but I think she's still tired from the flight."

"Be careful, RJ." He tried to put paint on my pants.

"I think your cousin and Crystal would make a cute couple."

"No."

"Why not?"

"I know him."

"So?"

"I know him and because he's my favorite cousin, and that's because he's like me."

"Meaning?"

"We like to start shit, and this is a happy pre-gallery opening occasion."

"Thank you, but don't change the subject."

"Look who brought presents." Courtney came into the room.

"See, he got flowers and candy."

"Nice job, Renato," Sonya's mom said.

"This has been the best birthday slash pre-gallery celebration."

"You're welcome. Are you happy?"

"Extremely happy. Are you?"

"I told you, when you and RJ are happy, that makes me happy."

"Thank you."

"You're welcome. Is lunch ready?"

"Yes, we need to hurry up before it gets cold."

I scooped RJ up, and he scrambled to get down. I rubbed my hand through his hair and placed him in the highchair.

"After lunch, I have a surprise for you."

"Another surprise?"

"You've accomplished a lot, and I want to spoil you the right way."

"Tell me now." Sonya picked up an empty plate and made RJ's food first, then took another plate and fixed one for me.

"Once RJ is settled, we can go and check it out."

"If you love me, then tell me now." Sonya pouted, and I laughed.

"She's spoiled because you got her like this," her mom teased, and Sonya rolled her eyes.

"I agree, but she's cute like that."

Sonya flipped me off. RJ tried to mimic her, and we laughed.

"I have something to celebrate," her mom said.

"What?" Sonya put her fork down.

"I had my last chemo treatment. Nothing to get too excited about, but it's a start," Courtney confirmed.

"Happy to hear that, Courtney."

"Thank you, Renato."

Sonya jumped up and hugged her mom, crying in her arms.

"You did it, Mom," she murmured.

"We did it, Sonya, and I can never thank you enough for helping me. I know Renato and I didn't get along off the first meeting—"

"Let's not go back," I replied.

"No, Sonya explained and told me what Brilynn did. It was hard for me to picture her like that, but you've proven me wrong and taken care of my daughter and grandson."

"She deserves everything."

"Brilynn is in the past," Sonya announced.

"I'm glad, and the situation with the police, if you hadn't been there, Renato, I'd be burying my daughter."

"Gallagher will never get the chance to hurt my wife," I snapped, and Sonya glanced at me.

"He's right, Sonya. You have a husband that will put his life on the line, and all I want is your happiness."

"I promise," Sonya answered.

"Will he be charged with stalking?" Courtney wondered.

"Depends on the law in New York."

"Hopefully he doesn't, because I could kill him myself," she hissed.

"Come on, you two." Sonya sat back down in her chair.

"Daddy!" RJ screamed, and I picked him up to sit in my lap.

Deborah helped to wash the dishes after we ate, and I

grabbed Sonya's hand, led her out of the house to the garage, and unlocked the door.

"Why are we in the garage?" Sonya went quiet at the large red bow on top of a brand-new Audi twenty-two.

"For you."

"Renato, I can't take this."

"You deserve this and more."

"But…"

"You still won't be driving every day, unless my men are with you or following."

"But I do get to drive myself?"

"Yeah, but if something happens, back to being driven." I pointed my finger in her face, sternly.

"Thank you!" She snatched the keys out of my hands and jumped in the car. McKayla and Rena came into view when she opened the garage door and together, they climbed in the back.

"He got me a new car!" Sonya shouted, and Rena laughed.

"Time for a spin," Rena said.

"Buckle up, and let's go driving." Sonya reversed out of the garage.

"Remember what I said, Sonya." I elevated my head at Dome and Ian in the black SUV behind her.

"Yes, sir." She blew a kiss at me, and I watched them slowly drive out of the access gate after the iron beams opened for them to leave.

CHAPTER 36

Sonya

PRISM ART GALLERY OPENING

NEVER IN MY wildest dreams did I see myself doing what I love as a future art buyer at the Prism Gallery. The rush I got in New York on negotiating a deal that would bring millions in profits was exhilarating. Even my confrontation with Cade helped Renato to see I wasn't some helpless woman he'd found in a strip club a year ago. Hopefully today with the grand opening, and as a full-time employee, I could score more contacts for the gallery. I was also close to graduating in a few months and had just finished studying for another exam when we flew back from New York.

"Dome is going to drive us, right?" McKayla asked.

I shoved the empty plate in the sink, picked up the sponge, and turned the water on to wash dishes.

"Yes, Renato is meeting us there."

"Sante left early too, can't speculate, something is going on." Rena sipped on her mimosa.

"What did he say about your confrontation with Gallagher?" McKayla investigated; I remembered our argument hadn't gone in the direction I'd hoped.

"Not good, but he understood it was for our family."

"If he's like Sante and Savio, they don't like men in our faces," McKayla recalled, adding more pancakes to her plate.

"Renato wants to control everything, but I challenge his beliefs."

"Over time, that control will loosen."

"Not fast enough." I laughed.

"Do you have your dress for the opening?"

"I do. It's in the closet upstairs."

"How many people are coming?"

"Rocky sent out fifty invites."

"That sounds good."

"The wealthiest people will be here."

"I'm intrigued." Rena poured more orange and champagne for her drink.

"If you drink too much now, you won't have any room for later," I joked.

"I'll go home and sleep this off and be fine for later."

"I was thinking of inviting Sean and a few other people from school."

McKayla turned in her chair.

"What are you doing?"

"Looking for your husband. I don't want him to accidentally turn into the Hulk and break the table."

I grinned at her statement.

"He's gotten better with my friends."

"A gorgeous friend," Rena teased.

"I don't look at him like that."

"Then you're a fool, because Sean is hot!" Rena and McKayla clinked glasses.

"Who's hot and why are you talking about another man, Rena?" Sante and Renato marched into the kitchen and stared at us.

"Honey, you look so handsome." Rena tried to sweet-talk her way out of the question. Sante came around to her side of the table and kissed her on the forehead.

"Can't change the subject with a compliment." Sante pretended to bite her shoulder, and she laughed.

Renato strolled over to me and lifted his arm around my shoulder.

"I was telling the girls I invited a few friends for the opening tonight."

"What friends?" Renato asked, pulling me in front of his chest.

"Classmates from school."

"Like who?"

"Your best friend Sean," I joked, and he rolled his eyes.

"You let her have a male best friend?" Sante taunted his brother.

"Shut up, Sante," I said.

"I'm her best friend," Renato argued back, lifting my ring finger to his lips.

"We'll leave you two alone. Come along, Rena and Sante. I need to check in with Savio," McKayla said and stood.

"Congrats again, Sonya, proud of you for accomplishing your goal," Rena said, putting her plate and glass in the sink.

"See you in a few hours." My heart rate kicked up a notch.

"Come upstairs." His tongue darted out of his mouth to lick his lips.

"Why?" My eyes lifted to the smirk on his face.

"So I can give you your gift." His words caused the hairs on the back of my neck to rise.

"What did you get me?" I bit my top lip.

"Something that will keep you mellowed for the rest of the night. You seem tense."

"Do I?" I twisted the wedding ring on my finger.

He crushed his lips on mine.

"Very tense."

———

Agnese addressed the crowd holding her champagne glass high in the air and talked about the new season the Prism Gallery was entering and what clients could expect from it as the best place to capture the allure they'd come to admire. I'd arrived an hour early to help set up balloons, signs, drinks, and coordinate the photographers and reporters that wanted to do interviews.

"Mrs. Calabresi, I'd love to do an interview with you for News Nine." Patrick was a co-anchor on the biggest news station in the city.

"Agnese would be the best person to speak to about the history of the gallery." I tried to ease out of being on camera. I knew mafia women didn't talk to the media, even about the smallest thing.

"Sonya, you're modest. You're more than qualified, she's graduating soon and already has some potential clients ready to talk with her," Agnese encouraged.

"All I can say is that I'm excited about what is coming for Prism."

"Anything you can say about the mayor's claim about your family?" Patrick pointed the microphone in my face.

Renato walked up next to me and put his hand on my lower back. I looked up at him and smiled.

"Patrick, I think that what you do is important for the public, but my family and I have nothing to say in regards to the former mayor."

"Do you believe it's helpful to have that type of whispers and gossip running around about your family?" Patrick insisted on bringing up the past.

"I never listen to gossip, and you shouldn't either.

Thank you, Patrick. Please look around, I hope you find something you like."

Renato walked me away from the crowd of reporters and grasped my hand as we went over to my office, and he locked the door behind us.

"You did good, Sonya."

"He's always going to try and get some reaction out of me."

"I agree, but you held your own. Taste this." Renato held a glass of his favorite whiskey to my lips.

"Strong. What are you trying to do to me at work, Mr. Calabresi?"

"Anything I want." He took a sip of the liquor and passed it back to me.

"I haven't been punished in a few days." I dropped to my knees and unbuckled his belt slowly, licking my lips. I should be scared to do this at work, but the visible pleasure in Renato's eyes gave me confidence.

His eyes were framed by a grin.

"Don't ask for something you can't handle, Sonya Calabresi." He bore down hard on me with his gaze.

"Renato, you exist for me." Goose bumps covered my skin.

The piercing look in his eyes told me I existed for him too, and our story was just starting, and anyone that tried to break us apart would bear the consequences.

<h1>Epilogue</h1>

RENATO

Graduation day, and Sonya received her diploma and the entire family had a section reserved to make sure they all attended. Sonya held her diploma up in the air as she bounced over to her mother, passing it over for her to see. The smile on her face made our journey worth every bump we'd crossed. I still kept my guard up and watched who came and went when she had late classes. Agent Gallagher was out and still lurked around, and until I had a full plan on how to make him disappear, I had to play nice. Captain Newark had informed me that he'd been suspended by his superiors, but I should watch my back. It had been a few months since I'd seen him.

The waves hit against the sand, and I lifted my son up into my arms; his eyes marveled at his mom's humorous laugh. At the age of two, everything was new and exciting to explore. Everybody told me I wouldn't be able to deny him as my child when it came to his temper, and they were right. To everyone's surprise, I did the most disciplining, and Sonya allowed him to find out the consequences of his actions. On many occasions, he'd try to take something from another child, and I'd have to put him on time-out or send him to bed.

After Sonya finished with pictures with her classmates —even the Sean guy I'd hated at first, but I'd decided to drop my possessiveness and push my annoyance with him to the side for Sonya's sake—we headed to Sonya's beach party I'd planned with McKayla's and Rena's help. We rented tents and invited a few friends from school and her job. The food choices were all her favorites—burgers, tacos, even my mom's lasagna she loved so much. Balloons displayed her name alongside a banner, and waitstaff brought the cake out. I watched Sonya and McKayla play in the water with Savio Jr., while my parents sat under the canopy with my brothers, laughing and observing. As the next son with a kid, my parents wanted more grandkids, but Sonya and I had agreed to wait while I focused on my business and she worked full time at the gallery.

"You haven't moved from this spot." Savio showed up next to me and stared at our wives in the water.

"I need to keep watch at all times. You know anything could happen when McKayla and Sonya get together." The both of us knew I was right, and he nodded and relaxed.

"Proud of you."

"Thanks, I appreciate that coming from you."

"Always knew you would find someone that made you happy."

"Never thought it was in the cards for me. Women and the work I do never meshed well together."

"Sonya proved you can have it all."

"She makes it easy."

"Then you have no worries. Remember all of us support you two." As we shook hands, Savio and I embraced.

"Any word about New York?"

"Nothing yet. Giosuè is overseeing the deal."

"Keep me in the loop."

"EJ is the contact going forward. I'll step in if I need to if the shipment becomes a problem."

"Make sure that it doesn't." He clapped his hand on my shoulder and then returned to the table with our parents.

Rena ordered Sante onto the dance floor, and he chased her. Then I turned to see Sonya in her wet clothes running up and putting her arms around me.

"Are you having fun?"

"I am. I love the surprise party on the beach."

"Good. All I wanted to do was surprise you."

Sonya lifted her dress and tied it in a knot to keep it from getting dirty in the sand.

"Over the past couple months we grew closer. Probably wouldn't be in this place together, like a real family until we did the work on us. We're a real family now."

"Never doubt that."

"What do you think about my promotion at the gallery?"

"Happy they see your potential and value."

"Probably had something to do with that little deal I helped you out on." She winked, lifted on her tiptoes, and kissed me on the lips.

"No doubt your skills at negotiation helped."

"Thank you again for trusting me with your heart and saving mine. I know when I threaten to run, it hurts you."

"It's understandable. I know that you had to make a hard decision, and it's time to forget it now. You have to forgive yourself."

"I do, I think. I finally realized that I needed to be here with you, and that scared me."

"Going forward, our family." I lifted her bridal style in my arms.

"Only us. Any more secrets I need to know about?"

"You know Gallagher is a ticking time bomb."

"He sounds dangerous."

"Only if I let him get to that point. I love you."

"Your love is dangerous."

"Why do you say that?"

"Your love will set the world on fire." She cackled when I dipped her low, still in my arms.

"You better know it."

Flashes from cameras went off; I placed her on her feet, tucked her small hand in mine, and listened to the music play while I danced slowly with my wife by my side.

Sneak Peek: Elio Jr

Christmas Eve

Knock! Knock!

"I'm in here!" After opening the door and locking it behind me, I stalked over to her at the sink as she washed her hands. It was our annual holiday dinner with family and friends at my parents' house. We'd done this dinner for many years. We'd sleep here and wake up together, have breakfast, and exchange gifts. Now that some of my brothers had kids, they wanted to start their own traditions for their families, but Christmas Eve was still something my mom wanted to have every year.

"Get out!" She tried to push me away.

"You didn't answer my call."

"EJ, leave me alone." When she brushed past me, I extended my arm and grabbed her around the waist, pulling her to my chest.

"I'm sorry," I whispered in her ear.

"You're ten years too late." Cora unlocked the door and trudged out.

"Fuck!" I smacked everything off the counter, and it fell on the floor.

Then I stalked out of the bathroom, glanced around the hallway, and spotted Cora talking with my mother and Rena. A hand on my chest stopped me from moving in their direction.

"Leave her alone."

Cora caught my eyes as Savio extended his arm around my shoulder. She rolled her eyes. For the past few days, I'd called, texted, and even showed up at her house, all to no avail. The avoidance had to stop, and I was ready to take action.

"She's been avoiding me. I'm done playing games."

He chuckled, and I pushed him off me.

"Not funny, Savio."

"Cora's like a sister to the family. If you aren't ready, then leave her alone." He stared at me.

"She saw me at a club with a few women."

"Let me guess, you saw her with a guy and ran him off."

"She's too young to date."

"She's twenty-four, EJ," Savio said.

I ran a hand down my face in frustration.

"We're friends. I was looking out for Marilyn." I proceeded into my father's office and plopped down on the couch, rubbing my temples. Savio trailed behind me and shut the door.

"Friends, my ass. Stop being sensitive. I have other things to discuss."

"Where's Pops?"

"Playing with the kids in the backyard. I need you to go to New York. Giosuè needs some assistance."

"How long?" Cora was heavy on my mind.

"Not sure, probably a few days or weeks. A situation

with Gallagher might need your help. Have Sante connect with you."

The words he spoke caught my attention.

"Remember nothing is set in stone. Any blowback coming back on us, I could get Vaughn and Thompson to have us cleared."

"I'm not stupid, EJ. Something is happening, and the question is are you ready for it? I'm not sure what's going on with you and Cora."

"Leave it alone." Right now wasn't the time to talk about my personal life.

"Marilyn and Cora mean too much to our family. If you hurt her—"

"I'll kill myself before I hurt her." I glared at him, walking off.

"Cora, why are you so dressed up?" I heard Rena ask.

"I have a date," Cora answered. I marched over to her at the dining room table.

"No, the fuck you don't!" I barked.

"Why do you care, EJ?" Rena taunted, and I flipped her off.

Cora's nose flared as all eyes watched us.

"None of your business."

"Whoever he is, you can say goodbye to him. Because we're gonna send him to an early grave and pay for his funeral."

Ding!

Cora jumped up from her seat and ran to the door. I heard a voice.

"Are you ready?"

I stalked behind her and yanked the door wider.

"What the fuck?" I removed my gun and pointed it at his head.

Elio Jr

DARK MAFIA BILLIONAIRE ROMANCE BOOK 4

Elio

I wasn't supposed to take it this far, I was young and thought I knew what love was, but she couldn't be mine forever. She hates me for what I did and reminds me every time that I'll never have her again.

Cora

I've loved him since we were young and have known him since my mother worked for his family. They set the Calabresi lives from the beginning, and our worlds could never collide again after he broke my heart.

Will Elio convince Cora that the love he has never gone away, or will it be too late when her life is hanging in the balance?

A second chance, friends to lovers, hate to love, forbidden, Dark Mafia romance, Book 4 in an interconnecting stand-alone series, and guaranteed to have an HEA.

Upcoming Releases:

Elio Jr.
Vincenzo
Giosuè
Armani
Bosco

About the Author

L.K. Ryan is an author of Romantic Suspense, Dark Romance, and Contemporary Novels. Join my newsletter and sign up for the latest news and updates on my books and releases:

Calabresi Mafia Series

Savio: Book 1
https://books2read.com/u/mlEAW7
Sante: Book 2
https://books2read.com/u/mdd1oW
Renato: Book 3
https://books2read.com/u/4AjAQd
Elio Jr: Book 4
Vincenzo: Book 5

Thank you so much for reading. If you enjoyed the crazy ride and decide to leave a review, we'd appreciate the support.